BORN
BEHIND
THE
VEIL

Doreen Nelson

To
My family

May their journey through life always take them down the path that leads to the light at the end of the tunnel.

Also by Doreen Nelson

Maternal Instinct:
A game of life and death

I'll Always Love You
Even After I Die

When Werewolves Howl

Capone
The American Pit Bull Terrier Ambassador

The Mean Gene

The Journey Home

Introduction

In my forty year career as a labor and delivery nurse, I experienced one Caul (behind the veil) birth. Although I would never lay witness to another such birth, at the time I did not realize how special and rare these births were historically and throughout all of time occurring in *less* than 1 in 80,000 births.

After cutting and clamping the cord, the obstetrician quickly handed the newborn over to me. The baby was not breathing. It was grey in color. There was no movement or rise and fall of the chest. I rushed the infant over to the warmer to begin resuscitation when I noticed a thin translucent piece of the amnion, the inner lining of the amniotic sac more commonly known as the bag of waters, tightly sealed over and fully covering the baby's face. Taking my fingers, I poked two holes at the nose and one at the mouth. The baby began crying immediately. I then carefully peeled away the *veil* in its entirety from the face.

Those born behind the veil are called Caulbearers. They may be either male or female. Their births are predictable. They are said to be in possession of special talents and powers. As a result, they are held throughout the world in high esteem. In addition to having the supernatural abilities of seeing the dead and foretelling the future, they are known as hands on healers as well. They have great leadership abilities. They are high on the list of Buddhist groups when looking to choose the next Dalai Lama. In medieval times, their births were seen as good omens. In the Middle Ages, those born behind the veil were burned at the stakes as witches.

Some well-known Caulbearers include Napoleon, Alexander the Great, Albert Einstein, Liberace, Lord Byron, Queen Christina of Sweden, Sigmund Freud, and Moses. According to the teachings of The Nazarene Way in the Prophecy of Jesus Christ, Jesus was the sixth of the Seven Caulbearer Prophets.

About The Book

Every one hundred years, like clockwork, God bestows a baby born "behind the veil" unto one of four families living high up in the mountains. If that one hundredth year comes and goes without such a birth, the red eyed beast kept prisoner in the deep dark tunnels that lie beneath their cabins will be released and all of life on the planet earth will be annihilated.

Revelation 20:1 - 20:3

Then I saw an angel coming down from heaven, having the key to the bottomless pit and a great chain in his hand. He laid hold of the dragon, that serpent of old, who is the Devil and Satan, and bound him for a thousand years, and he cast him into the bottomless pit, and shut him up, and set a seal on him, so that he should deceive the nations no more till the thousand years were finished. But after these things he must be released for a little while.

Chapter 1

Hebrews 9:22 *Indeed, under the law almost everything is purified with blood, and without the shedding of blood there is no forgiveness of sins.*

It was dark out everywhere, 'cept for a few lone stars in the sky and a half-assed moon makin' a half-assed try at shinin'. *Perfect!* This was the night. Chilly. No rain for days now. The night we been waitin' for. Daddy got all dressed up in his almost clean bib overalls. He even spit combed his hair. Slicked it all back nice and smooth. Said he don't need no shoes tonight. Nobody spoke 'less daddy said so. Not tonight anyways. Banjo in hand, he readied his pickin' fingers to play. I sat on a log layin' on the ground whittlin' a branch with my knife. Mama and Annie was sittin' next to me. Mama had on her only dress. She looked real nice with her hair pulled back. Daddy held up his hand. He put his harmonica 'tween his lips. Havin' no teeth helped him play better he always said. He leaned down to rub his bad leg. It must've been hurtin' him 'gain. He was havin' a hard time walkin' lately. It was daddy who chose this night to be him and mama's special night. Quick as he tapped his right foot to the ground four times, he started pluckin' that ol' banjo like we never heard him pluck 'fore. Mama, Annie, and me jumped up and went to dancin' all 'round. *twang twang twang* Kicked up our heels and laughed and hollered. 'Round and 'round we spun arm in arm. *twang twang twang* Daddy playin' hard and fast.

Fingers strummin'. Lips blowin'. You'd never knowed he had a bad leg the way it was stompin' up and down. He was happier than he'd been in a long, long time. Mama got winded so she went and stood by the ol' man tappin' her foot to the beat and clappin' her hands. Annie and me kept dancin'. Beads of sweat pourin' down all our heads. All worked up, we danced and danced and danced 'til the music.......suddenly stopped. Mama and daddy was holdin' hands with big smiles on their faces and their heads tilted back to heaven. When daddy dropped his banjo and harmonica to the ground, I stepped up, pulled my knife outta my back pocket and sliced both their throats clean through. Gurglin', coughin', spittin', and sputterin' they fell hard to the ground twitchin' right at me and Annie's feet. When they was done doin' all that, facin' up at us holdin' hands, eyes wide open, they was still smilin'.

"Hallelujah! Praise the Lord! Amen!" Annie shouted droppin' to her knees and raisin' her arms in the air.

She was pregnant with our fifth child. The others was sleepin' sound in the cabin. Our first born, Bobby, was in his twelfth year on earth. His sister, Emma, was ten. She laid next to Bobby on the mattress we throwed on the floor. We only had the one mattress so 'nother boy, Samuel, was layin' scrunched up at their feet. He was eight. Layin' huddled next to him was their six year old sister, Mae. God didn't give us no babies between Mae and this one. Now we knowed why. The baby growin' inside Annie was due to come out tomorrow. That's why daddy chose this day. He knowed there was 'lot of work to be done. I couldn't do it 'lone. I needed Annie's help. She'd be down for a day or two after givin' birth. Daddy taught me everythin' I knowed. Don't need no city school learnin' us how to live evil like the rest of the world. Livin' way up in the mountains, we was taught early on how to live off the land. The men taught the boys. The women taught the girls. Our family went back a ways. Daddy said hundreds of years. Maybe more.

"Annie!" I yelled.

She was still down on her knees praisin' the Lord. Grabbed her up by the back of her hair and yanked her 'round to face me.

"Yes sir, Calvin!" she mumbled all sassy-like with the corner of her mouth turned up, "Sorry. Got caught up in the moment."

Still holdin' her by the hair, I pulled her in close and kissed her hard. We both started laughin'. Annie sure was a wild one. She knowed how to get me goin'. We had to hurry. The children gonna be 'wake in a few more hours. Daylight was comin' up on us fast. While she stripped mama and daddy of all their clothes, I got ready a strong solid tree branch shootin' out from an oak tree to hang 'em from. Draggin' 'em naked to the tree, I hoisted 'em up with a rope by their feet upside down so the blood could run out faster. Then, Annie took mama and I took daddy and we pulled their skin clean off. With all the blood drained to the earth, we lowered 'em flat on the ground. Takin' a hatchet, I chopped 'em up into eatin' size pieces. Winter was comin' soon 'nuf. We had to be ready or we'd die. Nothin' was laid to waste. I was careful cuttin' off mama's hands and daddy's legs. Set 'em 'side special. Innards, flesh, eyes, bones, hair, teeth. Everythin' saved. The innards was food. Annie could make some nice winter coats and clothes outta their skin and hair. Bones was made into eatin' utensils or tools. I'd make Annie a real nice necklace or bracelet from their teeth and hair. 'Cept daddy didn't have no teeth so I'd take one of his bones and carve up somethin' nice for her. I don't know. Maybe I'd file 'em down so they looked like teeth and hang 'em side by side with mama's on a thick string or thin rope. That'd make a real pretty necklace or bracelet. I knowed Annie would like that. Somethin' to remember 'em by. This was a day of great jubilation. Mama and daddy went to heaven! Hallelujah! Praise the Lord! Amen!

After we got done strippin' the bones of all the meat, we had to pack it up just right and store it proper for the winter. We ain't totally without modernization. All of us got a root cellar for storin' vegetables and salted meat. Every cabin got a brick hearth for cookin' and stayin' warm. Homemade candles is used for seein' at night. The cabins all got one big room that's the livin' room, kitchen, and bedroom. We got outhouses for doin' our business. The men hunt all spring, summer, and fall to save up for winter. The women take care of the saltin' and storin' of food. We only have what we need to survive. That's all. No more. No less.

Our family was six strong with one on the way. Bobby, Emma, Samuel and Mae sure was gonna miss their mamaw and papaw. They understood though. They said their goodbyes to 'em last night 'long with the rest of the families. The day's comin' soon 'nuf when Bobby's gonna have to do for me what I did for my daddy. Daddy just couldn't pull his weight no more with that bad leg of his. Mama was gettin' up in age, too. She couldn't hardly bend her hands to cook or sew. They just didn't have nothin' left to give to the family no more. It was decided long time ago by those 'fore us and those 'fore them when the day comes the head of a family cain't do his job no more, he was to give himself up to God. His wife is given the privilege of goin' with him if she so chooses. Don't nobody wanna be a burden to his family. In heaven they'd feel young 'gain and be waitin' on the Lord. Mama and daddy wanted to go to heaven together. It's the oldest son who gets the honor of sendin' his mama and daddy off to God. In this case, that was me, Calvin Sanders.

Daddy and mama's cabin sits on higher ground than the rest of us. Me, Annie, and the kids live down and off to the right of 'em bein' I's the oldest son. Then over to the left of us and down the mountain lives my brother Ray and his family. His wife come from the Taylors. Ray's somewhere in the middle of all us kids. Him and his wife got six children, three boys and three girls. Daddy used to say they was like a couple of rabbits. Just down the road from him and a little to the left there's my sister Sarah and her family. Sarah's the oldest of us all. She's married to a real good man from the Nelson family. They got five kids. Two boys and three girls. She sure can be bossy. Sometimes I stuff cotton in my ears when we go to visit and just nod my head yes whenever I see her lips movin'. She's a tough one though. Daddy taught us all, includin' sister, how to shoot a rifle and use a knife. I got two more younger brothers, Karl and Tobias. They's twins. They come to mama and daddy late in life. Mama darned near almost died givin' birth to 'em. They must've tore her up real bad inside cuz after they was born, mama couldn't have no more babies. They got the two cabins to the left of Sarah. The first one's Karl's then Tobias's on 'count of that's how they come outta mama when they was born. The twins they both been eyein' the ladies lately. They just turned fourteen so I reckon it's time. Now that mama and daddy's gone, me, Annie, and our children is gonna move into their cabin bein' I's the oldest son. That'll free up the cabin we's stayin' in now. It'll be filled up fast 'nuf though when Bobby gets to marryin' age in a couple more years.

Just by lookin' at us, no one would know our cabins are set up in an exact pattern to make us stronger together. They goes in a circle. We got an underground tunnel runnin' from daddy's cabin to my cabin to Ray's and then to Sarah's and on to Karl's then Tobias's and back to daddy's. Been that way for as long as any of us remember. Daddy said his daddy said, his daddy said, his daddy said the tunnel was only to be used in emergency or cuz of some kind of catastrophic event in the world. A natural disaster, daddy said, is one thing but somethin' caused by anyone other than God *Himself* that's made to kill humankind ain't right. That's when we fight goin' to God cuz it ain't God callin' us.

We called the tunnel the *dungeon* when we was kids. Daddy said the men who dug it knowed what they was doin'. The land they built the cabins on is our land and ain't no government can ever take it from us. We got squatters rights that goes back hundreds of years. Maybe longer. Just cuz we ain't book learned don't mean we's stupid like the city folks think. Don't never see no city folk up this far in the mountains nohows. Once every five years or so we send someone down there though just to have a look 'round so we know what they's up to. It's better that way for us and them. They cain't be pokin' their noses in our business. It's cuz of us they's still livin' anyways. The tunnels was dug by our ancestors to make sure we can keep livin' the way God wants us to. There's three other families livin' up in these mountains just like us. The Nelsons, the Taylors, and the Andersons. Each family has a tunnel set up like we do. All the tunnels eventually meet up and settle together somewhere in the middle down below.

One time, me and two of my friends snuck down into the *dungeon.* Daddy was out huntin' and mama was out workin' in the garden. I was ten years old then. If daddy would've found out, he'd of whupped my bottom red so I couldn't sit down for a week. When we got to the middle where all the tunnels come together, I swear to Jesus Christ in heaven we seen two bright red shinin' eyes lookin' up at us from way down at the bottom of a deep hole just like was talked 'bout at every monthly meetin'. We up and run outta there so fast you'd think we growed wings. We swore one 'nother to silence that day. Even spit and shook hands on it. The only thing better than a spit handshake up here in the mountains is swearin' on the Bible. Ain't one of us ever mentioned it since. Not even to each other. That was sixteen years ago.

All the children in the families know from the day they's born 'bout the *secret*. Few of 'em gonna ever lay eyes on it though. Just the oldest sons of the heads of each family is all. The heads of each family talk 'bout it at our monthly meetin's at the lodge. The secret's somethin' we's sworn on the Bible to never tell no one. If we do, our tongues'll be cut out. My daddy said there ain't no tryin' to hide it if you tell. He said he has the power to know. Then, he pulled his knife outta his back pocket and sliced real quick like through the air in front of my face....

"Just like that," he said.

For that reason, I ain't never told no one. When my daddy said he'd do somethin', he meant it. I never questioned his word. So when he pulled the Bible out, I put my hand on it and swore to the good Lord in heaven I'd never tell no one. It's mama's job to swear the girls to silence. Same goes for them. They tell, tongues get cut out. I don't know of no girl or boy ever told nobody the secret. 'Least everyone I know still got their tongues. The day daddy had me swear, I never mentioned it 'gain to no one, not even Annie. Both of us knowed the other one knowed but we don't never talk 'bout it.

Now that daddy's gone to heaven, I gotta take over his job. Just like the oldest sons of the heads of the other three families gotta do when their daddies go to heaven. I reckon the only one left of us from this generation to take over his daddy's spot though is Jeremiah Taylor cuz his daddy, Simon, is still with the livin'. All the rest done gone to heaven.

18

Daddy went on his last walk through the tunnel tonight. I could've done it for him but my daddy's an honorable man. He ain't one to leave loose ends for someone else to clean up after him. When he got back, me, mama, and Annie was waitin' for him. That's when he handed over his timepiece and the Sander's Bible to me. I remember daddy's words when he gave me his timepiece....

"Never be late, son! Never! Every night at midnight. Like clockwork."

When a boy turns fourteen, he's expected to take a wife. A girl can marry after she's had her first menstrual cycle. Early on, we's taught that sex is for procreation only. Sexual enjoyment is the devil's work. The families who have sons turned fourteen call a *choosin' a mate meetin'* night to be held at the lodge. The women do the cookin'. The men sit 'round talkin'. The kids run 'round playin'. All the eligible girls from the different families are grouped together on one side of the room. All the eligible boys stand on the opposite side. We don't never go outside the four families to find a wife or husband. It ain't allowed. We got one rule. You cain't never choose no one who was born into this world with your last name. We don't get married like the city folk neither. When the boy makes his choice and the girl agrees, they go off hand in hand, engage in sex and that's that to that. From then on, they set up livin' together. More times than not, a baby comes 'bout from that night. The female has as much say 'bout who she copulates with as the male. Most times though when a girl's chose, she goes off with the boy who chose her whether he's the one she wanted or not cuz she don't wanna take no chances bein' no ol' maid.

We live in peace and with love in our hearts for our families and friends in these here mountains. Everyone knows though, family comes first. Ain't never had no problems up here no ways. We's God lovin' peaceful folk. If any one person in any of these four families wants to leave, he can go. He just has to know, he cain't never come back. Never! No matter what! And that's an absolute! Oh yeah, and his tongue gets cut out so he cain't never tell the secret to no outsiders. Ain't nobody left yet.

Later on that night, we invited the other three families to come up to the lodge to partake in mama and daddy. Annie cooked up their brains, hearts, livers, and lungs in a special concoction of vegetables, herbs, potatoes, and broth. The rest was stored for winter eatin'. 'Cept mama's hands and daddy's legs. They was special. There'd be plenty of mama and daddy to go 'round without 'em though. We all sat 'round tellin' remembrances of 'em. When the broth was gone and every bowl licked clean, we smiled knowin' mama and daddy would always be part of us. Then we all bowed our heads in prayer while sister Sarah belted out *Ave Maria.* She sure was blessed with a beautiful voice. Sang like an angel of God. Reckon it made up for some of that bossiness in her. All I know is, there wasn't a dry eye in the room, includin' my own. We wasn't cryin' over sadness. We was cryin' tears of joy. Hallelujah! Praise the Lord! Amen! Mama and daddy went to heaven! We celebrated mama and daddy's lives as late as we could. Everybody knowed we had to be in our own homes 'fore midnight and the women and children tucked safe in their beds. We had 'lot of rules and have to's but we knowed breakin' even one of 'em meant the total annihilation of all life on the planet earth. So the men played their harmonicas and banjos while the women kicked up their heels and twirled 'round and 'round shufflin' their feet and swooshin' their skirts. Even the children took time outta playin' to stomp their feet. At one hour 'fore midnight, all the music and dancin' stopped just as fast as it started. Not sayin' 'nother word, everyone gathered up their children and left for their homes. None of the families ever locked their front doors. They knowed it wasn't nothin' outside that was gonna hurt 'em.

Ten minutes to midnight, just like I was taught by my dearly departed daddy, I opened the trapdoor in the floor of my cabin that led to the tunnel. This was my first time doin' it without daddy. I climbed down the stairs careful not to make no noise. Didn't wanna wake the children. They was sound 'sleep now. I carried a candle to light my way. Had a plate with mama's hands and daddy's legs on it. When I got to the middle where all the tunnels join, I stood at the edge of a deep hole and throwed my plate down into it. Three more plates was bein' throwed in at the same time by the heads of each of the other three families. There was Joshua Nelson, Simon Taylor, and Daryl Anderson. Simon was the only one left of the patriarchs now. His oldest son, Jeremiah, gonna take his place one day. One plate had a raccoon on it. 'Nother a rabbit. And 'nother a coyote. Nobody said a word. Soon as I heard the plates hit bottom, I turned 'round and run like the wind! So did the others. I felt the ground under my feet rumblin'. I smelled the stench. I heard teeth crunchin' and grindin' the bones up in mama's hands and daddy's legs. When I got back to the trapdoor, I flung it open and closed it even faster. I jumped into bed with Annie and held her real tight. I was shakin' so hard I thought my teeth was gonna pop clean outta my mouth when Annie whispered....

"My water just broke."

Puttin' my mouth next to her ear, with more fear than joviality, I whispered....

"Hallelujah. Praise the Lord. Amen."

Chapter 2

Revelation 20:1 - 20:3 *Then I saw an angel coming down from heaven, having the key to the bottomless pit and a great chain in his hand. He laid hold of the dragon, that serpent of old, who is the Devil and Satan, and bound him for a thousand years, and he cast him into the bottomless pit, and shut him up, and set a seal on him, so that he should deceive the nations no more till the thousand years were finished. But after these things he must be released for a little while.*

We knowed the baby was comin' today. We been ready for it even 'fore Annie knowed she was with child. This was gonna be a special child. One with special powers. A child like this only comes 'round every hundred years. Yes sir, like clockwork, every one hundred years. Annie woke me one night a ways back to tell me the Lord come to her in a dream. *He* told her to be ready. When she heard a baby cry at the end of that dream, she knowed what *He* meant. We was chosen. We got to havin' sex that night and sure 'nuf a baby started growin' inside her. After we was done, we gathered all the families up and Annie told 'em 'bout her dream. Everyone celebrated the news cuz it meant God was givin' us more time at repentin' our sins. Every one hundred years a woman from one of the four families has the same dream Annie had. Hear tell, the last one come from the Nelsons. We knowed one thing for sure, if it's been one hundred years and that year done come and gone without a woman from one of the families havin' that

23

dream, it's time to prepare for Armageddon cuz we done run outta time with the Lord.

I suppose that's 'nother reason why daddy chose the night he chose to be him and mama's goin' to heaven night. That way they was helpin' keep the secret by contributin' the diseased parts of their bodies to feed the evil we got trapped in the tunnels. I reckon he figured that'd keep *It* busy long 'nuf for Annie to do what she had to do in the way of birthin' this special baby without *It* findin' out 'bout it right 'way. The kids all had big smiles on their faces when we woke 'em. It was a little past midnight. I just got back from feedin' the beast. Since this was such a special child, all the families needed to lay witness to the birth, so 'stead of tryin' to squash everyone into our little cabin, we'd go on up the mountain to the lodge.

When we got there, Annie went to gettin' everythin' ready. I rung the bell outside lettin' everyone know it was time. After she took off her underwear she was wearin' under her nightgown, she gathered up some pillows and blankets and laid 'em down on the wood floor. After she got everythin' situated to her likin', she laid a sharp knife next to her where she could grab it real easy. She called it her *freedom knife* cuz she used it to cut the cord to separate the baby from her. I always thought that was a funny thing to call it cuz once Annie had the baby, it was still all the time attached to her at the breast or hip. Anyways, she made sure that knife was nice and clean by boilin' it in water 'fore wrappin' it up in a clean cloth. One by one, the families come to settle 'round Annie who was now squattin' down in the middle of the floor. 'Sides the

Sanders, all the Nelsons, Taylors, and Andersons come runnin' up the mountain just to witness the miracle God was 'bout to give us. Men, women, and children 'like. All the women come bearin' gifts they made special by hand.

The water was pourin' outta Annie so she grabbed a towel and stuffed it 'tween her legs for the time bein'. She went 'bout her business of huffin' and puffin' real fast then slow. My Annie sure was a natural at birthin' babies. Me....I just done what I was told to do. She never once looked out into the crowd that gathered formin' a circle 'round her. This was her fifth time at doin' this so it wasn't long and she was ready to push. She called me over by her so she could squeeze my hand. No matter how hard she squeezed, I never complained. I figured it was the least I could do. All the families was quiet. Squattin' down over the pillows and blankets, she hung onto a wood chair with one hand and me with the other. Two pushes later, she looked over at me and nodded her head real quick like up and down. That meant for me to get ready to catch it next time she pushed. After four kids, I reckon we was pros by now. Her nightgown was soakin' wet. Big drops of sweat was runnin' down her face. I didn't wipe her down none though. I knowed better. My job was to shut up and just do what I was told. Men folk on this mountain learned long time ago not to mess none with a woman gettin' ready to birth a baby. When she dropped the soakin' wet towel between her legs to the floor, I pushed it outta the way with my foot. Gettin' down on my knees, I got into my ready position by leanin' in closer and cuppin' my hands under her. Her face was all red and puffed up from heavy breathin' and pushin'. She sure didn't look like the Annie I took to be my wife twelve years ago. That Annie had long red hair, pale skin, big blue eyes and a face full of freckles. She probably didn't weigh but 110 pounds. She might've been tiny but she sure was mighty.

"Good things come in small packages," she'd always say.

No one gonna ever hear me objectin' to that.

I fell in love with Annie from day one back when we was kids just havin' fun together. She come from the Anderson family. When she turned thirteen and me fourteen, we went to a choosin' a mate meetin'. I remember runnin' over to her side of the room fast as I could so nobody else would get to her first. At the same time I was runnin' to her, she was runnin' to me. I was sorta scrawny and tall for my age back then. My nose took up most of my face. I didn't mind none. My mama told me the years would balance out everythin' that needed to catch up or slow down with the rest of me. 'Sides, none of us is prideful people. I figured as long as all my body parts was where they's supposed to be, I was happy. Nothin' outstandin' 'bout me I reckon. Annie always tells me I growed into myself through the years. Well, I gotta admit workin' the land and climbin' these mountains to hunt for food packed some muscle weight on me sure 'nuf. Annie liked my ordinary dark brown hair and eyes. She said she fell in love with the deep dimple I got on the right side of my face. I fell in love with everythin' 'bout Annie. Inside and out. Through all our time together, I loved her more and more every day. I don't know how that's possible since I loved her so much already, but it was.

I'll never forget us walkin' off hand in hand back to the cabin my daddy built for me to live in with my new wife. Nobody knowed who I was choosin' to be my mate for life but they was sure I was gonna pick out someone. I was more scared than a long tailed cat in a room full of rockin' chairs but I tried real hard not to show it. Annie later told me she could tell. That Annie got a way of tellin' everythin' 'bout me. After layin' down on the mattress special prepared by my mama and daddy for us that night, we went to kissin'. A little ways into it, I opened my eyes to see if her eyes was closed. They wasn't. We both started laughin' so hard we was rollin' all over our weddin' bed. To this day, twelve years later, when I close my eyes, I can see Annie's beautiful blue eyes starin' back at me. When we quieted down, Annie turned to me, took a gulp, and nodded her head up and down. Liftin' up her dress 'bove her waist, she didn't have no underwear on. I reckon you could say she come prepared. With as much confidence as I could muster up, I unzipped my pants, and we went to it. Sex in these parts is for makin' babies only, so after doin' it 'bout five or six times, we felt sure we might've made one....or two....or three.

All at once, Annie groaned and pushed down hard. She looked like she was darn near gonna explode. When I took both my hands and put 'em under her, it plopped out and fell right in 'em.

"It's a girl," I whispered to Annie.

The baby didn't cry like all the others done when they was born. I could hear everyone standin' 'round us take a deep breath in and hold it there. Then, she pushed one more time and the afterbirth dropped to the floor. While I was holdin' the baby, Annie took her freedom knife she laid next to her and cut the cord. Then, she tied the cord on the baby's side nice and tight with a hair braid she cut off mama's head for just this purpose. I plopped the afterbirth in a bowl and handed it off to one of the women. We'd bury it later. Still, the baby didn't cry. I held her up in the air so everyone could get a look at her. So they could all lay witness to this special child sent to us by God. So there'd be no doubt by anyone. Then, I took to walkin' 'round and 'round that circle a few times holdin' that baby up even higher so all could bear testimony to the miracle that was 'bout to happen. She still wasn't breathin'. Her little face, body, arms, legs, feet and hands was blue. She laid all limp in my hands. Her arms and legs was just swingin' back and forth like they was dead. When I was satisfied everyone got a good look, I handed her over to Annie so she could do what she needed to do. All eyes was on Annie and the baby now. With her eyes flooded with tears, Annie poked two holes at the nose and one at the mouth. Then, she nice and gentle like peeled off the bag of water's membrane that formed a clear sealed mask over the baby's face. When she handed the *veil* over to me, I put it real careful like in a jar of water. The baby started cryin' like no tomorrow. So did Annie. So did I. So did all the Sanders, Nelsons, Taylors, and Andersons. We was all cryin' tears of joy. We lay witness to a miracle from God. Everyone shouted loud and clear as they could....

"Hallelujah! Praise the Lord! Amen!"

Just then, from out of nowhere, in the middle of everybody's jubilation, Annie let out 'nother scream. She hollered at me to lay the baby down. So, with hands shakin', I wrapped her up real good in a blanket and laid her next to Annie on the floor. In the meantime, Annie went and ripped her nightgown off and was layin' there buck naked in front of everyone. I just passed it off as her not bein' in her right mind at the time. Annie raised herself up and squatted down holdin' onto the wood chair and me like 'fore. She looked over at me and nodded her head up and down. Then, she pushed. And she pushed. And she pushed. The whole room got quiet 'gain. The women was standing off to the side holdin' their hands over their mouths. Later, I'd be told by some of the men, I looked like I was 'bout near ready to pass out. I was sure this here would come to be one of the favorite dinnertime stories for all the families. I just hoped it wouldn't become a habit of bein' told at the monthly lodge meetin's. One of the women must've been so worried 'bout me, she reached out and wiped my brow with a cold wet rag. The room was spinnin' all 'round me but I knowed if I let Annie down, I'd never forgive myself. For the life of me, I couldn't 'magine what she was up to now. I started into mumblin' the Lord's Prayer to myself. Whatever was goin' on with Annie right now, I asked *Him* to help us through it. So like 'fore when Annie nodded her head up and down at me, I got my hands 'neath her ready to catch whatever fell out. This time, when

Annie pushed down extra hard, somethin' round and smooth plopped right into my hands. When I seen what it was, I went to shiverin' all over.

Leanin' down and peekin' 'neath Annie, I seen I was holdin' a baby's butt. If that wasn't bad 'nuf, the head was still stuck up in there. When I told Annie it was hangin' by its head inside her, she laid on her back and pulled her legs all the ways back so her knees was touchin' her ears. She told me to put my fingers up in there and find it's mouth. So I did like Annie told me to do. When my finger dropped into a hole, I figured that was the mouth. Annie said to pull down on it hard as I can without breakin' the jaw. So, tryin' the best I could to steady my hands, I did like I was told. When I did that, Annie pushed and glory be to God in heaven, a second baby popped clean outta there.

"It's a boy," I said whisperin' to Annie.

Then, nearly chokin' I shouted out to all the others, "IT'S A BOY!"

Everybody just stood 'round near in shock. Couple of women had to sit down cuz they got to feelin' faint. Even I felt myself teeterin' back and forth. Not my Annie though. She went 'bout her business of cuttin' and tyin' the cord. The woman who took the other afterbirth from me held out the same bowl and I plopped the boy's in there on top of the girl's. When I went to hand him over to Annie, I looked at him and he was all blue. Annie said to show the others. So I did. Nice and high I held him up so they could all see him layin' all ragdoll like in my hands not breathin'. When I handed him over to Annie, she done like she done with the other one 'cept this time there wasn't no need to poke a hole where the mouth was cuz I already done that. All eyes was on Annie while she went to pokin' two holes at the nose. When he still didn't breathe, she grabbed him up by his two legs and hung him in the air upside down. When she smacked him on the butt a couple times, he started in kickin' and hollerin' right 'way. Everyone standin' 'round by this time was dropped to their knees. When Annie nice and gentle like peeled the membrane off his face and handed it to me, I put it in the same jar of water with the other one. Reachin' down, I picked the girl up off the floor and handed her over to Annie. She sat there holdin' 'em both, one in each arm. The boy, he was still screamin' and raisin' a fuss. The girl, she was lookin' up at Annie all wide eyed and quiet as a mouse.

Our baby girl and boy was both *born behind the veil.* They was *Caulbearers,* the same as Moses in the Bible. Ain't never heard of two of 'em born at the same time 'fore but this here that happened tonight was livin' proof for sure. All the families lay witness to it. We don't question what God does. We just take everythin' on blind faith. *He* will sure 'nuf let us know why *He* blessed us with two babies born behind the veil when *He's* good and ready. All's we knowed is they was chose by God to save mankind and the world from destruction. 'Least for a hundred more years. We ain't outta the woods with God yet though. We gotta do everythin' right by these children for the next seven years so they can carry out God's mission. If we fail *Him* in anyway, we can kiss what we call livin' and life goodbye. We was chose by God to help *Him* show 'em the way *He* wants 'em to go.

31

Annie leaned back 'gainst that chair and pulled both her breasts out. Then, kinda gentle like, she put one in each of their mouths. They both started sucklin' on Annie right 'way. I'd never seen more beautiful babies. They looked like angels layin' in Annie's arms. I guess in a way that's sure 'nuf what they was. The girl had lots of dark brown curls all over her head, blue eyes, rosy cheeks, and she even turned one side of her mouth up like Annie does all sassy-like from time to time. The boy had poker straight red hair and plain brown eyes. His skin was pale as the winter snow. I reckon if he was gonna have freckles, they'd pop out later on down the road. He was 'lot smaller than the girl. Scrawny, I reckon was what he was. Truth be told, it looked like the girl ate all the boy's food while they was inside Annie and throwed him table scraps.

No one made a move or a sound. Everybody just stood starin' at Annie and those babies. Silence filled the cabin. Annie looked up at everybody gathered 'round and said....

"She will be called *Grace*. He will be called *Jacob*."

That must be what they was waitin' for cuz sister Sarah went to beltin' out the words to *Amazing Grace* while everybody else fell to their knees 'gain cryin', hollerin' and praisin' the Lord Jesus Christ! Then, one by one they filed past Annie, Grace, and Jacob. Men, women, and children 'like. There wasn't a dry eye 'mong 'em. Annie had the biggest smile I ever seen her wear. In my eyes, Annie was never more beautiful than when she was sucklin' her babies after givin' birth.

When sister Sarah finished singin' *Amazing Grace,* she went right into singin' *We Are Climbing Jacob's Ladder.* All the folk joined in singin' loud as they could with her. Even with all that goin' on, sister Sarah's voice could be heard thunderin' 'bove 'em all. Sarah was my older sister by a couple years. She ain't never been one to be outdone. Her eyes and hair was dark brown like mine. She looked 'lot like our mama in the face 'cept she was taller. Hear tell, her husband picked her to be his wife cuz he fell in love with her voice. Everybody laughed when he found out what everybody else knowed already. 'Sides singin', sister Sarah loved to talk....and talk....and talk. When Sarah stopped singin', the women all formed a circle 'round Annie and them babies. One of 'em reached down and draped a real nice quilt she made over all of 'em. I knowed Annie was 'specially thankful for that bein' she was still naked and all. 'Nother one leaned over and wiped her face from all the sweatin' she done. All the others was wipin' down the floor. By the time they was done, that ol' wood floor would be darned near shinin'. Annie kept tellin' 'em thank you all nice and proper like. All the while them babies kept sucklin' on her and she just kept on smilin'. The men folk was all gathered in the back of the room now givin' the women more room to spread out and do what they do best tendin' to a new mama and her babies. God sure 'nuf knowed what *He* was doin' when *He* created woman. Ain't no doubt in my mind, man could've never made it in this world without her.

While Annie was gettin' her hair brushed and pulled back off her face, I gathered up Bobby, Emma, Samuel, and

Mae. Takin' the bowl with the two afterbirths and the jar of water holdin' the two veils outside with us, we chose a maple tree on a hill on our land to bury 'em under. After diggin' a hole in the ground, we laid 'em real careful like side by side. After pattin' down a mound of God's earth on top of 'em, we got down on our knees and praised the Lord for blessin' us with these two precious gifts of life. Hallelujah! Praise the Lord! Amen!

Chapter 3

1 Peter 5:8 *Be sober-minded; be watchful. Your adversary the devil prowls around like a roaring lion, seeking someone to devour.*

'Bout a couple weeks after the twins was born, we was havin' our monthly meetin' at the lodge. Like clockwork, the first Sunday of every month, come hell or high water, the four families gather together. The only way you was excused from goin' was if you died. The lodge was built by our kinfolk way back in time for praisin' God, passin' on the story, celebrations, and the choosin' a mate meetin's. It sits at the top of the mountain we all live on. It looks down on the four families. Ain't nothin' fancy. We's plain simple folk for the most part. What's important to city folk, ain't to us. Our fate was carved out by our great great great great granddaddies hundreds of years ago. Maybe more. Cuz of the birth of the twins and the recent passin' into heaven of my mama and daddy, it was my turn to talk. With me bein' daddy's oldest survivin' son, and since he ain't here no more, it was my duty to take over his spot as head of the Sanders family. 'Long with other obligations, it's the heads of the families who take turns tellin' the story every month. Takin' my place up at the pulpit, I felt I was overflowin' with the love and joy of God. When I was ready, my oldest son, Bobby, would ring the bell outside the lodge. That's when everyone's gonna come listen to what I gotta say. We was all quiet folk. Kept pretty much to ourselves. We never went outside our land, 'cept to check up on the city folk every five years or so. Had no callin' to. Everythin' we needed for livin' was right up here in these mountains.

Early mornin' I had Bobby run on up the mountain to stoke up some heat in the lodge. It was gettin' colder out now. Didn't need no fidgetin' goin' on while I was passin' on the word. When I stepped outside the cabin to fill myself up with a breath of fresh clean mountain air, I stood for a time to take in the silence and peaceful glory of the Lord all 'round me. This was my favorite part of the day….when the grass was covered with a blanket of icy frost and the fog drifted in and outta the trees….but mostly cuz it was the time when God gave all of life who made it through the night 'nother chance at wakin' up and livin' 'nother day.

This was my first time tellin' the story. Used to be my daddy's job for our family. Someday, it'll be Bobby's. I knowed what to say though. The same thing said time and time 'gain, over and over. Most folk up here could say it word for word from the time they was five or six years old. It's the only way we know to keep the world safe. Cain't make no mistakes. Gotta pass it on just right. We figure if you hear somethin' 'nuf, it'll stick in your head and after 'while it'll come to be a part of you. So far it's worked anyways.

All the families got one Bible 'piece. Four Bibles for four families. Each family's Bible stays with the head of their family. 'Fore daddy left this earth, he handed the Sander's Good Book over to me. None of us know how to read though. But we know scripture as good as if we was readin' from it. I don't know how that is. It just is. We was born that way I reckon. Mainly, we use the Bible for swearin' on. Ain't nobody gonna swear on the Book of God and not tell the truth or not keep his word by it. Not up here anyways. If we lie, we done went and condemned ourselves to hell. And nobody knowed better than us that hell is for real. All those city folk procrastinatin' 'bout whether they believe or not need to take a hike up here and we'll show 'em how real *It* is. They'd sure 'nuf drop to their knees and start walkin' a more Godly path.

My family was the first to arrive at the lodge. When Bobby rung the bell, all the families come outta their cabins and started walkin' up the mountain. Bobby, Emma, Samuel, and Mae was sittin' front and center with their mama, baby Grace, and baby Jacob. They all had big smiles on their faces. I stood at the pulpit gettin' ready to pass on the story. I wasn't near as nervous as I was when Annie was goin' 'bout the business of birthin' our babies. I kept a glass of water near 'nuf for me to grab just in case my mouth went to dryin' up. I wanted to make my daddy proud. I knowed he was lookin' down on me. I straightened myself up good and tall when one by one they come filin' in and takin' a seat. The Sanders. The Nelsons. The Taylors. The Andersons. Pretty much in that order, too. Since the Andersons live the farthest down the mountain, they's the last to come marchin' in. I'd start talkin' when the head of the Anderson's, Daryl, closed the lodge door behind him and took a seat.

While all the folk was still walkin' in, I took a minute to look down at my family. Bobby, he's tall and skinny just like I was when I was a boy. He's gonna be thirteen come summer in the new year. When I was ten I snuck into the tunnel. Gotta remember to have a talk with him 'bout that soon. I hope it's not too late bein' he turned ten a few years ago. He sure looks 'lot like me. He's got dark brown hair and eyes. Don't look so ordinary on him like it done me when I was his age. And there sittin' smack dab in the middle of his right cheek was my dimple. Matter of fact, five out of six of our kids got that dimple and dark brown hair and eyes like me. Grace though, she's different. She was born sure 'nuf with my dark brown hair, just like our other four oldest kids. Her hair's real curly like her mama's, just like our other four oldest kids. She got my dimple too, just like the other four. What's different 'bout her is her eyes. The others, they all got dark brown eyes like mine….but Grace's eyes is the same color blue as her mama's. You stare at 'em long 'nuf they'll put you in a trance. I was sure of it.

Jacob's the one who sticks out like a green thumb when we's all together. Nobody pays him no mind though like they do Grace. He's the only one don't got my dimple. 'Long with Annie's red hair and pale skin, he's got my plain ordinary brown eyes and poker straight hair. Poor little guy, he's kinda sickly lookin'. I'd never let Annie hear me but he's not a very pretty baby. He's all the time tryin' to spit out his mama's milk like it don't sit right in his stomach. Annie's always havin' to clean herself and him up after he's done eatin'. He's cryin' 'lot, too. Sometimes all night long. When he goes to cryin', his face turns so red he looks like he's 'bout to pop.

It's only been a couple weeks since Grace and Jacob was born but I can tell Annie's gettin' wore out already. She don't never say nothin' 'bout it. Grace, she just lays in her mama's arms lookin' up at her like a little angel. She don't fuss or spit her food out all over the place. Next to Jacob she looks like she's real healthy. She's smilin' all the time, too. Jacob, he's most the time wearin' a real serious look on his face. His forehead's all the time wrinklin' up and his eyebrows go to pointin' in and down like he's tryin' to touch his nose with 'em. I don't know. He's just lookin' like he's mad all the time. I know better than to say nothin' though cuz Annie loves all her children the same. She's the kindest, most gentle, lovin' woman I know but if someone goes to sayin' somethin' bad 'bout one of her cubs, she'll rip their heads off like a mama bear. Me included.

I don't got 'nuf words in my head to describe my Annie. Beautiful, fiery, gentle, playful, sassy, lovin', opinionated, and a little wild come to mind in a pinch. I loved her the way she was for as long as I could remember. I wouldn't never change her even if I could. Nobody ever gonna be in my heart like she sure 'nuf is. It's like she's livin' in there. Like she's part of me. Like the two of us together make a whole person. One without the other just ain't right. Been that way since we was kids. We was best friends first. We still are. I wouldn't wanna live without her. I'd understand if she didn't choose to go with me though when it's my time if she was still healthy and all. Mostly cuz she loves her children so much and I know she cain't wait to be a gramma. I reckon I'd just have to hang on is all, no matter how much pain I was havin'. Yep, I'd just wait 'til she was ready so we could go to heaven together holdin' hands and smilin', like our mamas and daddies done. Wouldn't seem natural to leave half of us behind nohows. Clearin' my throat real quick and shakin' the thoughts I was havin' outta my mind, I noticed Annie starin' at me from the front row with those big blue eyes. I knowed if I went to starin' back, I'd never come outta the trance in time to tell the story so I took a big breath in, let it out, and stared out at all the folk waitin' for me to talk.

When the last of the Andersons was seated, Daryl closed the door then, nodded his head at me to give me the go ahead. Speakin' loud and clear like my daddy taught me, my voice thundered....

"In the beginnin', way back in time, hundreds of years ago, one man and one woman from each of our four families started out together climbin' this mountain. They was friends in search of a better way. In search of a better life. They was all good people but they wasn't no religious order. As far as any of us know they never even talked religion together. Oh don't get me wrong, they surely all believed in God but He wasn't the reason they was doin' what they was doin'. 'Least not that any of 'em knowed. But God had plans for 'em. Come to find out their climbin' that mountain was His idea and not theirs. They'd find that out sooner than later that's for sure. Alls they knowed was livin' in the city wasn't where they wanted to raise their families. They liked the idea of clean air to breathe and peaceful livin'. The idea of self governin' sounded good to 'em, too. They didn't have in mind no particular place to stop and stake a claim to the land on that mountain. They just knowed somethin' was callin' 'em and they had to go. They was all sure they'd know when it was time to stop."

After pausin' a moment, takin' a gulp of water, and raisin' my arms over my head for special effects, I continued in a much louder, more boomin' voice....

"The higher they climbed, the more they started feelin' God's presence. The higher they got, the quieter they got. When they come to the place where the Anderson family is settled now, the Anderson woman passed out. That's right! She fainted! So that's where the Andersons staked their claim to the land. The other three families kept on goin' up higher and higher. Next a Taylor passed out. Somewhat higher, a Nelson hit the ground. Then, last to feel God's presence was a Sanders, my kinfolk. Hallelujah!"

That's when I knowed I had their full attention cuz everyone sittin' in the audience shouted out....

"Hallelujah! Praise the Lord! Amen!"

With a glory to God bigger than big smile on my face, I moved 'way from the pulpit and hollered....

"Most people would say it was the altitude that got to 'em. But they knowed different. It was the good Lord takin' 'em to where He wanted 'em to be. To where they was needed to be."

Smilin' right 'long with me now, all the Andersons, Taylors, Nelsons, and Sanders was hummin' and shakin' their heads in agreement with me. This is when my daddy would've told me I had 'em under my spell.

Pacin' back and forth center stage, I shouted....

41

"Nobody knowed why they was chose but one thing they did know was somethin' greater than themselves was behind it all. Divine intervention! They was where they was destined to be. None of the families had no idea what was in store for 'em or why God put 'em there. If they did, they might've run off back down that mountain as quick as their legs could carry 'em. Oh, they brought firearms and ammunition with 'em for huntin'. They's the same ones we carry today. They learned how to make bows and arrows and how to catch fish with spears they whittled out of wood. They even learned how to make their own ammunition. They learned how to live off the land by doin' and makin mistakes. The men got to buildin' cabins and the women got to cookin' and makin' clothes. When the babies started comin', they all started workin' faster and harder. Nobody knowed why. Nobody questioned why they was doin' what they was doin'. Whatever they needed, God saw to it they got it. Everythin' they learned was gonna be handed down to the next generation and the next and the next so livin' wouldn't be so hard on their kinfolk to come."

After mannin' the pulpit 'gain, then stoppin' a second to take in 'nother big swallow of water, I lowered my voice to a loud whisper. When I did that everyone craned their necks and heads out tryin' to hear me better.

"Then one mornin', for no reason at all, the man from each family started diggin' a tunnel down below the earth leadin' from his cabin. None of 'em knowed why. They just knowed they had to do it. Matter of fact, they couldn't stop themselves. So they dug and they dug and they dug. Day in and day out they worked tirelessly. A long, long, long time later, 'least a year or two, maybe more, they all met up in the middle underground. When that happened they knowed that's where they was to stop. They knowed cuz right smack dab in the middle where the four tunnels met was a big deep hole. It was so deep they could hear their voices echo when they yelled down into it. They figured if each of 'em laid down from head to foot 'cross it, it'd take all four of 'em and maybe then some to reach the other side."

After stoppin' a minute to give 'em time to take it all in, I jumped out from the pulpit and in a voice that could be heard in the next town, I hollered....

"That's when they saw *IT!* The red eyes way down below at the bottom. Those eyes was starin' up at 'em. And they all knowed It was Satan himself. The smell was so bad they started pukin'. And now they knowed why they was brought there. God hand picked 'em to keep the beast trapped where it was deep down in that hole. It was their responsibility, and all their kinfolk to come, to keep It from gettin' out into the world! It wasn't long after that everythin' started comin' together. What they thought was stupid 'fore, now made sense. What they done mindlessly 'fore was now done with purpose."

With tears runnin' down my face, I dropped to my knees, folded my hands in prayer, looked out into the audience, and softened my voice....

"Shortly afterwards, the first baby was born behind the veil. Hear tell, it was an Anderson. They figured the good Lord was startin' at the bottom of the mountain and workin' His way on up. They knowed she was special but how special they didn't know yet. As the girl got older, she saw things. She knowed things she could've only learned from God Himself. She could see things to come. When she started to talk as early as one year old, she told the families what they had to do. More important though, she told 'em what she had to do. It was her destiny to save mankind from the evil that lay down in that hole where all the tunnels meet in the middle. In seven years, she'd go to takin' on the job of holdin' the devil down in that hole. She told 'em all, every hundred years a baby would be born behind the veil unto one of the four families."

Jumpin' back up to my feet and pumpin' my fist up and down in the air, I warned....

"We all know Grace and Jacob is those babies sent to us by God. It's our duty to raise 'em right and keep 'em safe so they can fulfill their destiny to save all of mankind for 'nother hundred years. They's not ours. They's God's children sent to us as a gift. If we misuse or mistreat 'em in any way, if we don't lead 'em down the path they's destined to walk, God Himself will set the beast free upon us and the earth as we know it will suffer total annihilation. We got just seven years to get Grace and Jacob ready. Nobody in the entire world knows 'bout this but us. All the city folk and their sinnin' ways don't know that it's us simple mountain folk keepin' 'em all 'live. We have a dutiful and perilous path to pave for Grace and Jacob so they can do what they was put on earth by God to do. If we fail Grace and Jacob, we fail God! None of us of this generation ever had to do this 'fore but we been taught and told over and over 'gain how and what to do."

Slowly walkin' back to the pulpit, takin' a small sip of water, then reachin' my arms up 'bove my head towards heaven like I did in the beginnin', I shouted with deep conviction....

"The time has come for us to stand up and be counted! Just like our great great great great granddaddies did 'fore us. Glory be to God! Hallelujah! Praise the Lord! Amen!"

Then, I got real quiet and let everythin' sink in. Everyone sat in their seats starin' at me. Nobody moved. I wondered if they was even breathin'. Then, I watched as one by one the families raised themselves up to their feet hollerin'....

"Hallelujah! Praise the Lord! Amen!"

All at once, sister Sarah stood up and went to singin' louder than I ever heard her sing, *Mine Eyes Have Seen The Glory Of The Coming Of The Lord.* Everybody joined in. Even Annie stood up and started in singin' with little Grace hangin' tight onto one breast and little Jacob onto the other. When I was done talkin', I knowed I done my daddy proud. I 'magined him grinnin' big as you please right now lookin' down at me from up in heaven.

When I was done preachin' and everyone was done singin', pattin' me on the back, and praisin' the Lord, all the women laid out the food they brought. The monthly meetin' was a day of celebration. It was a day all the kids from the families got together and played. All the men got together and discussed huntin', fishin' and whatever else come to mind. All the women got together and talked and laughed 'bout whatever it is women folk talk and laugh 'bout. It was a day of relaxation. It was the one day we took off from workin'. I heard the city folk take one or two days off a week. Glory be! If we done that, none of God's work would get done. Our time off only lasts 'til we leave the lodge to go back home. Not even a full day I reckon.

Later that night at ten minutes 'til midnight, lit candle in hand, I opened the trapdoor leadin' to the tunnels. I was draggin' a young deer by its two back legs behind me. When I reached the middle, I could tell the devil knowed somethin' was different. I wondered if *It* knowed Grace and Jacob was here. *It* never gave no indication up to now anyways. I figured let sleepin' dogs lie. The longer *It* didn't know 'bout 'em, the better. When I got up to the edge of the hole, I seen two red eyes lookin' up at me from way down deep. I don't know what happened but somehow my eyes locked onto *Its* eyes for just a second and I couldn't look 'way. *It* drawed me in. I don't know. Maybe *It* remembered me from when I was ten years old. I reckon I was more tired tonight cuz that sermon earlier wore me out. I should've been payin' more attention. Then, a familiar voice went to callin' out my name....

"Calvin, Calvin," I heard my mama's voice callin' me, *"Please help me, son. It's mama."*

She was beggin' me to save her. Sounded just like her. A man don't never forget his mama's voice no matter how old he gets or how long she's been gone. Just when I was 'bout to take a step forward, one of the men from the other families snatched me up by the back of my shirt and 'nother covered my eyes to break the spell. Shakin' my head, I tossed that deer into the pit, turned 'round, and started walkin' 'way. The others did the same. No one said a word. Walkin' fast, I heard *It* laughin' all mean and evil like....followed by the sound of bones crunchin' and flesh bein' swallowed. Stoppin' a second, I bent over with my hands on my knees. Takin' in a deep breath and lettin' it out, I made the sign of the cross havin' realized that could've been me *It* was gnawin' on now.

Stompin' my way back down through the tunnel, I thought how stupid I was. I was mad at myself for bein' so foolish. Mostly though, I was 'shamed. Either way, I knowed my face was redder than it'd ever been on 'count of it was feelin' real hot. I could've killed everybody with just one little slip up. My daddy told me to never lock eyes with *It*.

"Satan is a master at disguise," I remember him sayin'.

It was a lesson I'd never forget a second time. I'd pass it on at the next meetin'. Tonight, I'd wake Bobby while I was still scared 'nuf to crap my pants over it. No sense in keepin' it from Annie. She'd know somethin' was wrong soon as she looked me in the eyes. Cain't hide nothin' from my Annie. 'Sides, I'd hate to see what she'd do if I even tried.

After beatin' myself up for doin' what I did, I right 'way started thinkin' back to my talk today at the lodge. City folk think we's a bunch of religious nuts runnin' 'round up here in the mountains. We don't claim no special religion or church as bein' ours. Our church and what we believe sits in our heads. We don't need to be called Nazareth, Baptist, Jehovah's Witness, Mormon, Catholic, Christian or nothin' else that's out there when God *Himself* is guidin' us to do what we's doin'. God is just God. *He* ain't got no special religion name. We don't sit 'round quotin' scripture and makin' sure we's livin' like the Bible says. We was all born to know right from wrong. We don't go 'round testin' the waters just to see what God would do to us if we followed Satan's path. The way I see it, you gotta be a darned idiot not to know when you's doin' somethin' 'gainst God. Our noses ain't stuck in the Bible all day and night. Heck, we cain't even read. None of us got no time for school learnin', fancy clothes, or modernization. We only know what we been told handed down from generation to generation. Do they think we's up here in these mountains holdin' revivals, havin' sex, and drinkin' moonshine all day every day? Well, forgive me Lord for sayin' it outloud but....

"Heck no we ain't havin' no whoopin' and hollerin' celebration every day!"

What we's doin' is just plain a big responsibility and wears heavy on a man's mind. But God called on us to do it so we's doin' it. Like tonight. If they think it's fun to look Satan in the eyes and most near get drawed down into that pit with *It*, they's crazier than I ever thought. But this is our destiny. God gave us a job to do 'til the end of time. We don't go bellyachin' 'bout it. We just get up every day and do it with a smile on our faces cuz it's the way it is and it's what the Lord wants us to do. I just hope the good Lord Jesus Christ has mercy on our souls come Armageddon day! Hope *He* don't go bunchin' us all up with all the city sinners. Hallelujah! Praise the Lord! Amen!

Chapter 4

Matthew 13:38 *The field is the world and the good seed stands for the people of the kingdom. The weeds are the people of the evil one.*

After we got everythin' moved into mama and daddy's cabin, we settled in good and permanent. For me and Annie, the only move we'd be makin' after this one was heaven. The head of each family took to livin' in the highest cabin on their family namesakes land. Now that daddy went to heaven, that was me. When I passed, Bobby would be next in line for it. Then, after Bobby, his oldest son and so on and so on and so on. We didn't have a whole lot to take with us other than a change of clothes, some cookin' utensils and a mattress for the kids to sleep on. Mama and daddy left their one mattress so me and Annie would take to sleepin' on that. At the ol' cabin, we slept on a blanket we throwed on the floor. I reckon you could say we was movin' up into luxury.

Winter was comin' so it was up to the men to make sure we had 'nuf food stored up to feed the beast and 'nuf left over to feed our families. Had to chop 'nuf wood to last, too. The growin', pickin', and storin' of vegetables and the like was up to the women. They also got the job of makin' sure we got good 'nuf winter coats, hats, and snow boots made from the skins and hair of animals. This year, we'd be wearin' mama and daddy to keep us warm. Nothin' goes to waste. Don't seem to matter what the season is. Not much time for playin' or foolin' 'round. Our bones and muscles ache just as bad in the winter as they do in the summer, spring, and fall. Maybe even more bein' we don't use 'em as much as we do in the other months. I know that don't make no sense but it's true somehows. The work we do is back breakin' but we don't do no complainin' 'bout it. We don't get no vacations like city folk do.

'Lot of times we get snowed in up here in the mountains so if one of the families got an emergency, they gotta send one of their own down through the tunnels to call on the rest of us for help. Then, it's up to us to use the tunnels to get to 'em. If the snow's too deep, it's how we get to the lodge for our monthly meetin's, too. Passin' by the beast is somethin' we don't enjoy doin' but just cuz we don't like somethin' don't mean we ain't gotta do it. It's more important the story gets passed down nice and regular. That way, there's no room for forgettin' or gettin' it wrong. The children been taught to never look down at *It*. The mamas go to coverin' their little ones eyes when they go passin' by *It* on the way to the lodge in winter. The older ones know to do the same or look the other way. Most of 'em do both. Ain't nobody really wantin' to see *It*. Other than goin' with their mama and daddy to our meetin's at the lodge in the winter, the children all been warned not to never go down in the tunnels for no reason nohow no way….never! Like I did….when I was ten. I feel real bad 'bout that now. I prayed and prayed to God to forgive me. I sure 'nuf hope *He* did. I reckon my daddy knows 'bout it now that he's in heaven. I didn't lie to him. I just didn't tell him. If he'd of asked, I'd of told him. Sure hope he's seein' it that way now.

The beast acts up more in the winter. Maybe it just seems to be that way though cuz we's sittin' 'round in our cabins more. Maybe cuz *It* knows all the families is separated more at that time of year. Sometimes we can hear *It* up in our cabins snortin' and growlin' from way down there. There's been nights I lay 'wake 'bout ready to jump outta my skin the way *It* goes to bangin' and thumpin' itself 'round down in that hole. My firearm's always loaded and kept where I can grab it fast. I don't never let on I's scared though 'count of I's the man of the family. *It* reminds me of a spoiled child not gettin' 'nuf attention the way *It* goes to carryin' on. Just a whole lot more dangerous is all. Sometimes Jacob comes to mind but I real quick get rid of that thought cuz I know God ain't gonna appreciate that kinda thinkin' outta me. We try to make 'nuf noise to drown it out. Sometimes it works. Other times *It* just gets louder. That's when I go to handin' out cotton to Annie and the kids to put in their ears like I do mine when sister Sarah goes to talkin' too much.

Bobby learned how to hunt real good over the past summer. Samuel ain't doin' too bad neither. They know handlin' a firearm is a big responsibility so I spend lots of time practicin' safety with 'em. Next spring, Bobby's gonna be huntin' on his own. Samuel's got 'nother year or two to go. Most likely I'll let 'em pair up and go together come spring. I reckon won't be too long I'll be huntin' on my own 'gain. Don't get me wrong. I want my children to grow up....just not so fast is all. 'Long as I got Annie by my side, I reckon I's okay with it though. Each family only hunts on their own land. That way there's no accidents shootin' one 'nother. There's all kinds of game up here. 'Nuf to go 'round for everybody. We got mountain goats, mountain lions, bear, rabbits, deer, elk, moose, squirrels, and raccoons. That's just to name some of 'em. The mountains got plenty of streams and rivers for fish catchin'.

We ain't gone hungry yet but we know not to practice gluttony neither. The children is taught to eat what their mamas put on their plates. Got no patience for finicky eaters. Ain't no such thing as goin' back for seconds neither. Same with the adults.

"Waste not want not" was what my mama used to say.

The women in each family cook just 'nuf to fill everyone's belly. There never was nothin' left over to scrape into the garbage. 'Sides, that'd be a sin. Babies eat from their mama's breast 'til they get 'nuf teeth to chew. After that, they's on their own far as eatin' goes. None of 'em died from starvation yet.

We don't got 'lot of sickness in our families. We figure if one of us gets sick, it's meant to be. God be callin' us is all. We don't got no doctors or medicine to heal us. The women use herbal concoctions they stir up now and 'gain....say if one of the little ones gets a bad cough and cain't sleep at night. Mostly it's the old ones who break down. The work is hard up here. The bones and muscles start to ache real bad after a time. That's what happened to mama and daddy. They just broke down is all. They raised their children into good men and women. It's an honor to

54

be called to God. Nobody sittin' 'round cryin' over the loss of a loved one. We figure that's a selfish thing to do. 'Sides, it's not like we's never gonna see 'em 'gain. Everybody gotta go to God someday,'less you been a sinner and you's headed to hell. Plenty of sinners down in the city though. If it wasn't for us, lots of 'em would be burnin' in hell right now. Ain't up to none of us to say who goes to hell and who don't though. That's up to God. Mama and daddy knowed they was goin' to heaven.

Up here in the mountains when you get old and cain't do no good by the family no more, you just go to the oldest son and tell him it's time. That's just a privilege handed down to the head of each of the four families whose job it's been to feed the beast every night. His wife can go with him if she wants. Just like my mama did. That's God's way of sayin' thank you for servin' *Him* righteous all those years. We's not murderers. We's just followin' the path God laid out for us. Ain't nobody askin' no questions. We just do what we been called on to do. Like I said, that's only a privilege for the heads of the families. Everybody else gotta die on their own if they up and get sick or diseased. There's an ol' graveyard was started by our great great great great granddaddies way up in the mountains where we can bury our loved ones. 'Lot of folk go to diggin' a hole for 'em on their own land though so they can go visit 'em whenever they take a likin'. Mama and daddy come to me when they was ready. It was my duty as the oldest son to do right by 'em. The diseased parts of their bodies got fed to the beast. The rest of 'em was for the four families to share.

It don't matter none what city folk say 'bout how we live and what we do. Heck, we heard they was runnin' 'round killin' one 'nother just for sport. 'Lot of folk down there makin' the beast mighty happy is all I gotta say. If they knowed what we know, they'd change their ways of livin' sure 'nuf. Every five years or so, we send a man or two down to the city just to see what they's up to. We's not sayin' everythin' they's doin' is wrong or a sin. That's not up to us to say nohows. We know God made some folk extra smart to think up stuff to make livin' easier. It's what they's doin' with it that matters is all. If they's usin' it any other way than how God intended 'em to, they's followin' Satan sure 'nuf. There's lots of Satan's followers out there stirrin' folk up. May the good Lord have mercy on us all when *He* sets the beast loose on the world. When that day comes, and it sure 'nuf will, we know no 'mount of what we's doin' to keep *It* down there in that hole gonna matter none. Hear tell, when a thousand years done passed, Satan's gonna be unleashed on the earth. Only God knows when that's gonna be. All's I gotta say is we better have our houses in order and be ready when it does. Hallelujah! Praise the Lord! Amen!

There's some things we been taught God frowns on and we ain't never to do 'em. We's been taught not to never envy or be jealous of 'nother man or woman. We don't never go paradin' 'round in fancy clothes. Mostly we wear the same clothes every day. The women go to washin' 'em at one of the mountain rivers 'round every month or two, 'cept in the winter cuz the rivers all frozed up. There's a water pump up by the lodge we can use if we need to but the water's so cold everyone just tries to wait for winter to pass. Everyone's got one spare clean set of clothes just in case we need 'em. God don't judge us none by what's on the outside of us nohows. If we got a tool or somethin' that's useful the other families don't got, we either make 'em one or show 'em how to make it so they can benefit from its use, too. When we choose a mate, we don't never lust after 'nother. That's why when a man passin' by 'nother woman that he don't know, he keeps his eyes to the ground. Same goes for a woman passin' by a man she don't know. When we mate up, it's for life. Not one of us is engagin' in sex 'fore we picked a life mate and been accepted. Anger is okay as long as it ain't sinnin' anger. We know we can get mad over the evils in life. That's what God calls *righteous indignation.* None of us is greedy up here in these mountains. We share and share 'like. If one of us starves, we all starve. Ain't nobody guilty of the sin of laziness. We's hard workin' folk and we teach our children early on to do the same. We's not perfect that's for sure. Everyone's a sinner. But we don't have 'lot of time to sit 'round thinkin' of ways to get into trouble with God. From the time I's woke to the time I get done feedin' the beast, I's movin' 'round doin' the best I know how to make sure my family is stayin' fed, clothed, warm, and safe. And no one never heard even one of us complainin' 'bout what we was chose to do cuz we look at it as a blessin' to be a part of savin' the world and servin' the Lord. We's just happy God thought 'nuf of us folk to help *Him* out some. Must've been some reason *He* chose us. Maybe *He* knowed 'head of time how stubborn we was. None of us ever gave anythin' up easy. Ain't no one let *Him* down since we come to this mountain.

Now that Grace and Jacob's been born, the beast's gonna be actin' up more than ever. Just means the last Caulbearer is startin' to get weak and the devil's gettin' stronger. We got seven years to get Grace and Jacob ready to fulfill their destiny to take over holdin' the beast back from the world. If they ain't ready by their seventh year on earth, all the world and all the folk in it is goin' to hell in a handbasket. Bein' born behind the veil means Grace and Jacob is special. They got special powers. 'Sides havin' the power to see into tomorrow, hear tell they can talk to and see the dead. Each Caulbearer is born with their own special powers though. We won't know what powers they got 'til they show 'em to us. We just gotta be patient is all.

All the families is ready for winter way 'fore the first snow. There's more snow comin' down in the mountains than ever hits the cities. Mostly after the second snow of the winter, we's all snowed in already. Cain't even so much as open the front door. We learned from the first time it happened, if we don't wanna stink up the cabin by doin' our business in a bucket all winter, we better take turns shovelin' a path from the front door to the outhouse. Sometimes we gotta shovel all night long to keep up with it. The men of the house take turns. Nobody puts up a fuss 'bout doin' it neither. We'd all be sufferin' a whole lot more if we didn't do it.

Annie's little sister, Eve, is with child and due to give birth a couple of months into the new year. It's a few months 'way but she's nervous. She's twenty-one. Her husband, Jeremiah Taylor, is twenty-two. He acts as jittery 'bout it as her. I reckon cuz this is the first child Eve carried this long. She lost 'bout three or four babies 'fore they was even formed all the way. Annie promised she'd help her through it so we's most likely gonna have to travel through the tunnel to get to where she is when it's time. Annie's mama helped her with our first one. That was Bobby twelve years ago. Annie said Eve's baby and Grace and Jacob will only be five months 'part so they can play together. I had to remind her Grace and Jacob was chose by God. They ain't gonna have no time to be playin' with other children. They'd be hard at work becomin' who they gotta become to save the world for 'nother hundred years. That's when Annie come up to me puttin' her hands on her hips all matter of fact like sayin'....

"Now *Calvin!*"

I always made sure I turned 'round to face her when she went to callin' me *Calvin* cuz that meant she was all serious 'bout what she was 'bout to say. I wanted her to know she had my full attention on the matter. Didn't wanna get in no trouble with my Annie.

"Now *Calvin!*" she'd say, "Grace and Jacob may be God's special children but they's still children and all children need to play."

I ain't one to ever pick a fight with Annie so I'd just stand there not sayin' 'nother word. It was best for everyone concerned for me to just stand still and shake my head up and down in agreement. 'Sides, I loved the way her face scrunched all up when she was makin' a point. If she believed I was sincere in my head shakin', she'd walk up to me with the side of her mouth turned up all sassy-like and go to plantin' a big ol' kiss on my lips. Then, she'd run off to doin' what she was doin' like she wasn't never there. Annie favored her mama in looks. Red hair, pale freckled skin, blue eyes. Itty bitty of a woman. Her mama and daddy went to heaven a short time ago. They was good folk. Her oldest brother, Daryl, and his wife, Rebekah, sent 'em off good and proper. That's when Daryl took over bein' head of the Anderson family. I's sure they's up there with my mama and daddy dancin' and playin' the banjo... 'sides waitin' on the Lord.

I keep doin' my job feedin' the beast. Every night ten minutes to midnight, I make my way through the tunnel to where I meet up with the three heads of the other families, Joshua Nelson, Simon Taylor, and Daryl Anderson. Exactly at midnight, we all drop our plates down into the hole at the same time. Ever since I locked eyes with *It,* I stand back 'ways when I toss my plate down in there to make good and sure I don't never lock eyes with *It* 'gain. So do the others. That was a real stupid mistake. I sure hope Bobby don't make that mistake when it's his turn to take over feedin' the beast. All's I can do is tell him 'bout it and hope he's listenin'. Like my daddy did with me. I had to go and find out on my own though. I sure 'nuf hope and pray Bobby ain't as stupid as I was. That beast's sure 'nuf a smart one but *It's* not smarter than God. That's why *It's* chained up down in that hole and the good Lord's flyin' free. Don't get me wrong. I ain't no sissy by no means but I ain't no dummy neither. I got 'nuf sense to know I ain't got no supernatural powers to take on Satan.

That's a job God gave to Grace and Jacob. I reckon *He* got *His* reasons for givin' us two of 'em born behind the veil this time. I figure the city folk and their sinnin' ways got somethin' to do with it. Maybe the more sinnin' that's goin' on in the world, the stronger Satan's gettin'. Never heard of two Caulbearers bein' born at the same time 'fore. The Caulbearer that's been down there for the past hundred years must be gettin' weak the closer to the end of his time comin' up. Maybe the good Lord needs two of 'em to hold *It* down this time 'round. Maybe not. Ain't nobody up here gonna do no arguin' with God 'bout why *He* did what, myself included. Hallelujah! Praise the Lord! Amen!

Chapter 5

Matthew 7:15 *Beware of the false prophets, who come to you in sheep's clothing, but inwardly are ravenous wolves.*

This winter was provin' to be a hard one. Never saw so much snow. That's sure 'nuf sayin' 'lot, too. One night, when I was up half the night keepin' a path to the outhouse, Annie's sister, Eve, went into labor. She wasn't supposed to have her baby 'til the second month into the new year but it was comin' at the end of this year no matter what anybody else was plannin' on it doin'. I reckon she figured she was blessed to carry it this long bein' that she lost all the others. Her husband, Jeremiah, come runnin' through the tunnel in the middle of the night to fetch Annie. All outta breath and pantin' like a thirsty dog, he said Eve was havin' real bad pains and bleedin' 'lot. Annie jumped up and gathered everythin' together she needed for birthin' a baby. I woke Bobby and told him where we was headed so he could keep an eye on the other kids. They was all still 'sleep. I figured we'd be back by the time they woke anyways. Annie grabbed Jacob up in her arms while I took hold of Grace. She figured they was too young to be watched. Jacob must've been scared at first cuz he didn't take to cryin' and raisin' a fuss right 'way like he usually done when he was woke. I reckon he wanted us to know how mad he was though cuz he went to frownin' 'stead. Grace, she just kept on sleepin'. When Annie was sure she got everythin' she needed, we took off movin' fast as we could through the tunnel. When we come up on the devil's hole, we tiptoed past it real quiet like so *It* wouldn't know we was there. I was just happy Jacob didn't start into fussin' and screamin'. Anyways, *It* must've been sleepin' cuz we didn't hear *It* movin' 'round.

When we got there, Eve was layin' in her nightgown smack dab in the middle of the bare floor cryin' and screamin' loud 'nuf to wake the beast. There was blood everywheres.

"Ain't nobody got no sense to even lay a blanket 'neath her," I heard Annie mumble to herself while she throwed a *look* Jeremiah's way.

Eve grabbed hold of Annie and said it felt like her insides was bein' ripped out.

"Please, Annie," she screamed, "Help me!"

I saw on Annie's face that it broke her heart to hear her baby sister beggin' her for help. She sounded like a trapped animal the way she was howlin' and carryin' on. Jeremiah went to standin' off in the corner with his nose practically pressed into the wall lookin' like he was gonna pass out or puke, maybe both. Annie knowed fast 'nuf, he wasn't gonna be no help. I was surprised he made it through the tunnel to our cabin. The way he was lookin' I could picture him runnin' 'round and 'round in a circle down there not bein' able to think which way to go....like a dog chasin' it's tail. A smile started comin' on my face when I went to picturin' that so I quick wiped it off 'fore Annie seen it. She ain't gonna find nothin' funny 'bout what was happenin' to her little sister. Handin' Jacob over to me, she tried to clean up the blood poolin' all 'round Eve but she couldn't keep up with it. She just finally stopped tryin'. 'Sides, Eve needed tendin' to more than the floor needed cleanin'. After throwin' some pillows and blankets down on the floor, she helped Eve move over onto 'em while flashin' 'nother one of her *looks* Jeremiah's way. I went over to Jeremiah to see if there was anythin' I could do to help him out. If nothin' else, I figured maybe I could block him from gettin' the evil eye.

As the night wore on, Eve kept screamin' and tryin' to push the baby outta her. Annie kept wipin' her forehead and tellin' her to push harder while she had her squattin' down holdin' onto a wood chair, layin' on her back, and even turnin' from one side to the other. She had her in positions I never knowed was possible. I knowed Annie was doin' everythin' she could to get that baby outta her. One thing I knowed sure 'nuf was I needed to give special thanks to the Lord when this was over for not makin' me a woman. There ain't a man 'live who could live through somethin' like this. If it was the men folk who was gave the job of havin' babies, the human race would've died out long time ago.

It was gettin' daylight out. Eve been at it for hours. Annie said she could see the top of the baby's head but it wasn't movin' none. It was just stuck there. Eve's face was all red and swolled up. She wasn't lookin' so good. Her eyes was buggin' outta her head with red lines runnin' all through 'em. She was breathin' so fast, I thought she was gonna pass out a couple times. She was probably hopin' she would. Whenever she throwed up, Annie quick cleaned it up. I don't know why every time Eve did somethin' that'd turn a person's stomach, Annie took to lookin' over at me now and shootin' me the *look* 'stead of Jeremiah. Maybe cuz he wasn't lookin' back at her no more. Got to wheres I'd just turn my face to the wall like Jeremiah was doin' when she done that so I wouldn't have to meet the evil eye I was gettin'. I think Annie was as tired as Eve after 'while.

"Take a deep breath Eve and just lay on your side for a time," Annie finally told her.

She knowed she was askin' 'lot of Eve, but I could tell by the look on Annie's face she was just plain stumped. She had some serious thinkin' to do so she come up to me and grabbed Grace up puttin' her to breast. Jacob was sleepin' for once so I reckon she figured she'd let him be for now. Annie just sat next to me feedin' Grace and starin' at Eve. I figured she was thinkin' real hard 'bout what to do so I stayed quiet.

When Grace was done eatin', Annie told Jeremiah to run and fetch my sister Sarah, his sister Rebekah, and her and Eve's sister Martha. Rebekah and Martha was due to have their babies in the new year same as Eve. I sure hoped all this runnin' didn't stir nothin' up in them, too. I don't know what my Annie would do if she had to bring three babies into the world at the same time. I trusted Annie though. She knowed what she was doin'. When Jeremiah first went to move, his legs buckled under him. Soon as I helped him back up to his feet, I offered to go for him but he refused. He was mumblin' somethin' 'bout it bein' his responsibility. Wasn't too long after that, he opened the trap door and jumped down into the tunnel. What happened to him after that was anybody's guess. I think he was more willin' to risk passin' by the devil than bein' in that room where his wife laid screamin' and hollerin'. I gotta admit, it was more than most men folk could take. I was surprised he was still standin'. The thought run through my mind that if Annie wasn't so good at havin' babies, I would've been layin' on the floor sure 'nuf, 'specially last time when she birthed the twins. While we was waitin' for Jeremiah to come back, Annie kneeled down next to Eve talkin' real soft to her and wipin' her forehead off with a cold rag. I was hopin' Jeremiah wasn't spinnin' 'round in a circle down there. I knowed Annie was scared but she didn't show it none. Me? I took Jeremiah's place with my nose pressed into a corner of the wall with the two babies in my arms. Seemed to be the safest place to be at the moment.

When Jeremiah got back with Sarah, Rebekah, and Martha, Annie jumped up, grabbed her freedom knife, went to wavin' it in the air, and ordered Eve to turn over on her back. I got real light headed when she done that. Jeremiah hit the floor. THUD! Ain't nobody knowed what she was up to with that knife in her hand. We heard rumors 'fore 'bout some city women gettin' their stomachs cut open when they couldn't have the baby the natural way. All eyes was on Annie. Everybody knowed she was the one in charge tonight. She told Sarah to put a rolled up pillow 'neath Eve's back and to sit kneelin' behind her head.

"Be ready to raise her head up some when I tell you to and hold onto her nice and tight," Annie ordered Sarah.

Sarah ain't one to be told what to do under normal circumstances but there wasn't nothin' normal 'bout what was goin' on here so she done what Annie told her, no questions asked. With Rebekah kneelin' by Eve's leg on the right and Martha at the left leg, Annie demanded they be ready to pull 'em back so her knees was touchin' her ears.

Next time Eve got a pain and went to screamin' and howlin' Annie yelled at her....

"Shut up, take a big breath in, hold it, and push down long and hard!"

I think Annie scared the crap outta everybody when she yelled at Eve so everyone done what they was told to do without even one second of hesitation. Rebekah and Martha pulled Eve's knees back to her ears while Sarah forced her head up pushin' her chin into her chest. Annie took her hand and put it up inside Eve and started turnin' the baby's head 'round clockwise. That's when she felt what was stoppin' the baby's head from comin' out. She grabbed hold of it and pulled it out all the way. Glory be to God in heaven, I wouldn't have believed it if I didn't lay witness to it myself. It was a hand that'd been restin' smack dab on the side of it's head coverin' it's ear. Blood was comin' out in big ol' clots now but Annie didn't stop none. When that pain was done, she told Rebekah and Martha to keep holdin' Eve's legs back so the baby's head wouldn't slip farther back up inside her. She told Sarah to lay her head back down so she could breathe better. Then, she told Eve to relax her whole body 'til the next pain hit. I knowed that was gonna take some doin' bein' that her knees was darn near touchin' her ears. The baby's hand was outside of her now and it just kept movin' 'round and openin' and closin' up like it was reachin' out to grab hold of somethin'. Ain't nobody laughed 'bout it though. We all thought Annie might come over and slash us all with her freedom knife if we did. Everybody knowed my Annie could sure 'nuf be a wild one.

When Eve started breathin' hard 'gain, she nodded to Annie. Everyone got to doin' what they done 'fore 'cept Annie. 'Stead of turnin' on the head, she picked up that freedom knife of hers and cut a straight line goin' all the way down south. When she done that, it gave the baby's head more room to pop out. When it did, it's head looked like a big ol' purple grape stickin' out of Eve. Probably was best Jeremiah was still passed out on the floor is what I was thinkin'. The room started into spinnin' 'round in my head and I was gettin' real sick to my stomach so I laid Grace and Jacob down so I could sit for 'while and close my eyes. I figured I done seen 'nuf now. Jacob all of a sudden started cryin' louder and harder than I ever heard him cry 'fore. It was like he was yellin' at Annie....

"Look at me! I's 'wake now! Get 'way from that baby and come take care of me!"

I remember thinkin' he was selfish but I kept that thought to myself. I hoped God didn't hear my thinkin' cuz I knowed *He's* the one who gave him to us. Grace was sleepin'. Since I wasn't feelin' so good, I just let Jacob cry. Annie and the other women stood their ground doin' what they had to do. After 'while, Jacob's screamin' blended in with Eve's howlin'. Couldn't tell one from the other. I knowed I was gonna hear it from Annie when this was all done and over for not tendin' to him. Just when I was thinkin' that, Annie turned her head 'round and shot me the *look*. After that, she took hold of that head with both her hands and started workin' it up and down. She looked like she was pumpin' water. Up and down. Up and down. Then, all at once I heard a pop and the shoulder belongin' to that hand come floppin' out after it. Once that happened, she pulled the rest of the baby out and plopped it on top of Eve.

"It's a boy!" Annie told everyone.

Sweat was drippin' down everyone's faces, even mine and I was sittin' at the time. Jeremiah, still passed out and layin' on the floor, looked cool as a cucumber. Takin' that freedom knife, Annie cut the cord and tied it in a knot on the baby's side. Cuz the afterbirth was still up in Eve, she tied the cord comin' from it, too. She said to give it time and it'd come out on its own. I was thinkin' how could she be so sure that was gonna go so easy when the rest of this birthin' was an inch short of hell.

Everybody was wore out like they was outside workin' hard in the summer heat. But it was the dead of winter, not summer. I started into wonderin' if ol' Jeremiah wasn't smarter than any of us. He might've been fakin' faintin' for all I knowed. When Annie seen Eve was bleedin' clots 'gain, she pulled on the cord attached to the afterbirth real gentle like and it fell out. She put it in a bowl for buryin' later. That was Jeremiah's job. I had to laugh 'bout that. Everybody just up and started rejoicin'. Well, everyone 'cept Jeremiah. Sister Sarah broke into the hymn, *Hallelujah To The Lamb*. Then, right in the middle of the women kickin' up their heels and dosey-doin' 'round, Eve went to screamin' 'gain. All at once, everybody stopped

70

shufflin', dancin', and singin'. The room got quiet. We was all expectin' 'nother baby to come flyin' outta her like what happened with Annie. Rebekah and Martha went 'round handin' out cold wet rags to everyone in the room. Eve was holdin' the baby out to Annie screamin' and cryin' the whole time. When Annie grabbed the baby back up from Eve, she went to lookin' at it hard all over. It was gray, limp, and not breathin'.

"Hallelujah! Praise the Lord! Amen!" Annie busted out hollerin'.

Then, she did what she knowed to do to remove the clear water bag membrane coverin' the baby's face. Soon as she done that, the baby went to fussin' and cryin'. After handin' the baby back to Eve, she run over and put the *veil* in a jar of water. Not none of us was left standin'. We all dropped to our knees. 'Cept Jeremiah. He was still layin' on the floor cool as a cucumber. Annie was shakin'. She was the only one still on her feet though. Nobody said nothin' but we all was thinkin' the same. This was the third baby born behind the veil 'fore the end of this hundredth year. One girl and two boys. Grace, Jacob, and now Eve's baby. We all was wonderin' what the good Lord was up to but it wasn't for us to question God so we all kept on our knees real still and quiet like with our heads raised up to heaven, hands folded in prayer, and our mouths shut. Just 'fore puttin' the baby to breast, Eve announced with a big smile on her face....

"He will be called Esau."

After everyone got over the shock of three babies bein' born behind the veil, the women took to takin' care of

Eve and cleanin' the blood up off the floor. Ain't nobody heard of two Caulbearers bein' born at the same time let 'lone three of 'em. I took it as a sign from God lettin' us know there's a battle comin' up to end all battles. They say strength comes in numbers. Even sister Sarah was at a loss for words. Never finished the song she started singin'. I think she was scared if she did, Eve would go to screamin' 'gain. So she just stayed kneelin' down and hummin' the rest of it real soft. Like the rest of us, I reckon she was waitin' to see what was gonna happen next.

Annie sent me back to our cabin to fetch her bone needle and deer sinew thread so she could sew Eve up down there where she cut. She said she wouldn't heal up right otherwise. So Annie swooped screamin' Jacob up and started into feedin' him and I went runnin' back through the tunnel leadin' to our cabin. Just as I passed the pit, I heard *It* laughin' and callin' out to me.

"*Calvin, Calvin,*" *It* said, "*Where are you going Calvin in such a hurry?*"

I swear *It* sounded just like my mama 'gain. *It* sure 'nuf wasn't gonna fool me to look down at *It* like *It* done last time. Ain't nobody here this time to pull me back from fallin' into the hole. I just kept runnin' on past *It* when in my dear departed daddy's voice, *It* shouted after me....

"*And how's my new grandbabies, Grace and Jacob?*"

I stopped cold in my tracks. I kept facin' forward though. Took a couple deep breaths and took off runnin' 'gain. When I run past *It* on the way back, all's I heard was

Its evil laugh echoin' all 'round me. Didn't say nothin' to Annie 'bout it. Didn't say nothin' to no one. Never.

When I got back with what Annie sent me to get, Jeremiah's sister, Rebekah, was standin' over him pourin' cold water all over his face. He missed the whole birth. I think she was disgusted with him the way she poured that water on him. Soakin' wet, he jumped straight up in the air and started lookin' 'round at us all crazy like. He seen Eve holdin' somethin' all swaddled up in a blanket. She had a great big smile on her face but was paler than any of us ever seen her 'fore. When he wobbled his way over to her, he seen the baby sucklin' on her breast. Eve looked up at Jeremiah and told him....

"We have a son. His name is Esau."

Annie told him the baby was born behind the veil just like Grace and Jacob. Jeremiah had big tears in his eyes but quick wiped 'em 'way cuz he's a man and ain't supposed to cry. I reckon passin' out was okay though. News travels fast in these mountains. All the men folk gotta laugh outta Jeremiah later that day.

When Annie was done sewin' Eve all up and the other women cleaned the blood from the floor so it didn't look like no one was murdered, we all went back to our cabins. The sun was shinin' but 'lot of snow fell durin' the night. It was gonna take a whole lot of shovelin' to dig a path to the outhouse. Bobby, Samuel, and me took turns. The news of three babies bein' born behind the veil got 'round to everyone in the four families quicker than wildfire. This was the most excitement we had in a long time. I only wish that would've been the end of it.

Little did we know there was gonna be a whole lot more comin' our ways. Just when the hundredth year was 'bout to close up on us, two more babies was born behind the veil. They was both born couple months earlier than they was supposed to be. It was like God was tryin' to squeeze 'em in last minute. One from the Nelson family and one from the Anderson family. Joshua and Martha Nelson had a boy. They named him, Matthew. Daryl and Rebekah Anderson had a girl. They named her Hannah. Five babies born behind the veil. All of 'em born within a few months of one 'nother. All of 'em born 'fore the end of the one hundredth year. Five Caulbearers born to keep the devil down. Two from the Sanders, one from the Taylors, one from the Nelsons, and one from the Andersons. Three boys and two girls. Grace and Jacob Sanders. Matthew Nelson. Esau Taylor. Hannah Anderson. All four families was represented. I didn't know 'bout nobody else but I was shakin' inside. I was gonna find out soon 'nuf, there was good reason to be. Hallelujah! Praise the Lord! Amen!

Chapter 6

Matthew 18:10 *Take heed that ye despise not one of these little ones; for I say unto you, That in heaven their angels do always behold the face of my Father which is in heaven.*

Spring weather don't come to the mountains 'til late April. All the *Caulbearers* was between four and seven months old now. The twins was the oldest bein' they's the ones born first. They was born in the fall. The others was birthed in the winter. Too young to be gettin' any visions or powers I reckon. I cain't speak for the others but Grace and Jacob wasn't showin' no signs yet. When we have our monthly meetin's, we all tell everyone what's goin' on with 'em. Nobody havin' nothin' to talk 'bout yet.

Annie, she been keepin' busy with the twins. Grace's always been a good eater. She's all the time laughin' and smilin'. She's sleepin' through the night without eatin' none off of Annie. Jacob's cryin' 'lot still. He's gettin' up durin' the night to eat or fuss or both. Sometimes, when Annie's in the middle of feedin' him, he goes to chokin' and gaggin'. He ends up spittin' everythin' she put in him out all over her and him. No wonder he's havin' a hard time puttin' on weight. He just don't look good is all. Like he ain't healthy. I cain't help but wonder if the good Lord sent Grace to do *His* work and Jacob just tagged 'long for the ride. When I started into thinkin' maybe Satan slipped him inside Annie when God put Grace in there, I had to shake my head back and forth real quick like to get rid of that thought. I just hope I didn't think it long 'nuf for God to grab hold of it. All's I knowed is my Annie's walkin' 'round with dark circles under her eyes. She's gettin' real skinny and weak. It's like the life's bein' sucked right outta her. Like somebody went and throwed a curse on her. Maybe she's lookin' that way cuz there's two of 'em to take care of. I don't know. I'd help feed 'em if I could but I wasn't made to give 'em what they need. 'Nother reason I's thankful I wasn't born a woman. Emma picked up 'lot of the chores so Annie can rest more. Every time she goes to try to catch up on some sleep though, one or the other starts in fussin' to eat 'gain....mostly the boy.

Jacob's skin is just as pale as the day he was born. His hair's more orange than red. You know, like the color of a blazin' fire. The poker straight hair he was born with turned to frizz and kinda sticks out all over like he's been scared to death. He's a real skinny baby. No rolls of fat on his legs and arms like most babies got at that age. Looks unhealthy. Like a skeleton. I don't like to say it, and I'd never let Annie or anyone else hear me, but he's lookin' like he's been hit with the ugly stick. He ain't nothin' like his sister, Grace. She eats 'nuf for both of 'em....just like when they was inside Annie I reckon. She's just happy as can be. Got a real pretty smile. Her cheeks is all rosy and her hair's real soft with dark brown curls all over her head. She's all the time kickin' and wavin' her chubby little legs and hands 'round. I feel bad for the little guy but when I go to pick him up and walk with him, he cries even harder. 'Sides, I's 'fraid I might break the bones inside him if I hold him too tight or the wrong way. He's a real hard baby to love but God gave him to us so I do the best I can with him. I know Annie cain't wait 'til the day comes when they's both eatin' regular food. Mamas love their babies the same no matter what but Annie's more protective of Jacob cuz he don't get the attention Grace gets. Way I look at it, ain't no one to blame but himself.

Now that spring's here, the food stored up for the winter is gone so Samuel's been goin' out huntin' with Bobby. He knows he's gotta listen to his big brother and never go off by himself. Both of 'em is responsible with a firearm. Bobby's turnin' thirteen this summer. Hard to believe he's gonna be matin' age in 'nother year. I see how he looks at that twelve year old girl, 'Lizabeth Nelson. She been lookin' back at him when we go to the monthly meetin's. Probably be takin' her for his wife sometime next year after he turns fourteen. Well, when Annie, me, and the kids moved up to mama and daddy's cabin after they went to heaven, all the rest of the family stayed in the cabins they was already livin' in 'stead of moving up one on 'count of Bobby's next in line after me to be head of the Sanders. That way when he takes a wife, he can just move into the one we just gave up. 'Sides, it's his rightful place. Hallelujah! Praise the Lord! Amen!

I gotta laugh at myself 'bout wantin' Bobby to stay younger a while longer but lookin' forward to the day Jacob gets older. I don't know. Maybe cuz there's somethin' special 'bout a man's oldest son. Maybe cuz I's all the time worryin' 'bout Annie not gettin' 'nuf rest with Jacob screamin' all the time like somethin's serious wrong with him. Sure would make a difference if the boy slept all night like his twin sister. None of the other girls or boys give us no troubles....just Jacob is all. Grace's gonna fit in real good with Emma and Mae. Emma's already totin' her 'round on her hip when she's out plantin' the seeds for the vegetable garden. She just lays wherever Emma puts her down. She's always real quiet or kickin' her legs and laughin'. Emma don't never take Jacob with her. I reckon she figures he can scream and fuss in the cabin just as good as he can outside with her. He only wants Annie anyways and he's not always happy 'bout that. Mae tries to play and talk to him but he just looks at her and cries 'til he looks like he's gonna explode. Talkin' 'bout explodin', it ain't no fun changin' his bottom neither. I ain't never in my life smelled anythin' that bad 'cept maybe the stench comin' from the devil's pit. We was *all* lookin' forward to the day when he'd go use the outhouse for doin' his business. 'Specially his own mama I 'magine since she's got the job of changin' him the most. When he goes to stinkin' up the cabin, me and the other kids go runnin'. Bobby and me made a little wood table we set outside the front door so Annie could go out there to change his bottom when the weather's fittin' 'stead of stinkin' up the whole cabin inside. It wasn't a smell that went 'way when the windows was opened neither. It stayed 'while.

Somethin' strange happened the other day. Wasn't sure what to make of it when Annie told me 'bout it. She said Grace and Jacob was sleepin' at the same time for once. Me, Bobby, and Samuel was out huntin'. Emma and Mae was outside tendin' to the garden. She said she remembered layin' Grace and Jacob in the wood rockin' bed I made special for our babies way back when Bobby was first born. 'Fore they was old 'nuf to lay on the mattress without rollin' off. She didn't want 'em layin' side by side cuz one might wake the other that way so she laid 'em feet to feet 'stead. She had 'em both swaddled up in blankets nice and tight so they'd feel like they was bein' held. She thought maybe they'd sleep longer that way so she could take a nap 'long with 'em. Both their bellies was full. She couldn't tell me how long she was sleepin' when she woke to Grace gigglin' and squealin' the way a baby does when they's happy 'bout somethin'. Annie thought maybe she was still sleepin' and in the middle of a dream cuz when she looked over at Jacob, he was floatin' in the air 'bout a foot or two 'bove the bed. He was still wrapped up in his blanket good and tight and sleepin' quiet as can be. She said she shook her head and rubbed her eyes and when she took 'nother look, he wasn't floatin' 'round no more. Grace was still woke and laughin' though. I knowed Annie wasn't gettin' much sleep these days so I promised to take the twins with me an hour or two every day right after they got done eatin' so if they cried I'd know they ain't hungry. That way I figured Annie could lay down and get some sleep. I sure hoped Jacob wasn't gonna have the power to float 'round the cabin whenever he took a likin' to. I never raised no child born behind the veil 'fore so I ain't got no idea what they can do. I just hoped it was a case of Annie needin' sleep makin' her 'magine things that ain't really happenin'.

When we went to the next monthly meetin', neither one of us said nothin' 'bout what Annie seen. Matthew

Nelson, Esau Taylor, and Hannah Anderson was all growin' up lookin' healthy like our Grace was doin'. Annie was the only one of the mothers lookin' like she was sleepwalkin' these days. I didn't wanna say nothin' but she looked more dead than 'live. All the other new mamas had lots of energy and rosy cheeks. Poor Annie was lookin' like she's all the time 'bout to fall out. She was nothin' but skin and bones. I knowed everybody was wonderin' what's wrong with Jacob kickin' up a fuss and screamin' all the time. All the folk on the mountain is too polite to say nothin' 'bout it though. You had to be deaf not to hear his voice echoin' through the mountains when he went to screamin' in the middle of the night. 'Specially when everyone and everythin' else out there was all quiet and tryin' to sleep.

Like now. Jacob was screamin' so loud I couldn't hear what Simon Taylor was sayin' up there at the pulpit. It crossed through my mind maybe Jacob ain't wantin' no one to hear. Good thing everyone in the families got the story memorized down to the last word by now. After the meetin, all the girls and women went 'round wantin' to hold Grace, Matthew, Esau, and Hannah. They didn't mess none with Jacob cuz they knowed if anyone even come close to him, he'd start in hollerin' 'gain or doin' his business to the point where he'd clear the lodge out. It got so bad, Annie's own sister, Eve, stopped comin' over to visit her. Annie took to protectin' Jacob more. She was always holdin' and rockin' him so folk wouldn't go to talkin' 'bout him none. She'd whisper to him not to pay no attention to those folks. She said he was just as good as any of those gossipers runnin' 'round givin' him the evil eye. Annie never complained when he throwed up all over her. She'd just clean her and him up and go to rockin' him and singin' him a lullabye. She got mad at me a couple times when I paid more attention to Grace. I was sure to watch myself after that. I don't know. Jacob sure 'nuf was a hard baby to love but I never said nothin' 'bout it to Annie.

I was gettin' mighty worried 'bout my Annie. She was gettin' more and more sick lookin'. Our faith in the good Lord was keepin' us goin' though. We knowed *He* never took no one 'fore their time. I was sure with two new babies to tend to, it wasn't Annie's time to go to heaven. They was still sucklin' on the breast. They neither one got teeth yet. Annie got a cough now, too. Every now and 'gain she'd go to runnin' a fever. I knowed cuz her face would get all red and when I touched her forehead it'd be feelin' hot. Ain't nobody else in the family got what Annie's got. I just figured she was so run down all the germs out there in the air come swarmin' to her.

When the twins turned eight months, they both popped out a tooth or two. Grace bit down on Annie first. Annie said it didn't hurt none. When Jacob bit down on Annie though, he drawed blood. That's when Annie stopped puttin' 'em to breast and started mashin' and chewin' up their food for 'em. She was still lookin' awful sickly though but I figured she'd start gettin' better now that the twins was eatin' on their own. Since she gave birth, her pretty red hair lost most of its curl and shine. In between the freckles, her skin was more pale than Jacob's now. I could tell she lost a bunch of weight. Her dress fit all

81

baggy on her these days and her face was all drawed in. I was hopin' she'd start feelin' better now and even gain back some of the weight she lost. Me and the boys did some extra huntin' so their mama could have more to put on her plate come supper time. We didn't think God would mind.

Emma and me took over with carin' for the twins when Annie couldn't get up to walk no more. She was so weak and tired all the time. Sometimes durin' the day, she'd ask me to carry her out to the front porch so she could watch the twins playin' outside. Little Mae turned seven in the summer. She took to sittin' right next to Annie the whole time they was out there. She always was a mama's girl. Bobby, Samuel, and me carved out a rockin' chair for her to sit in while she was watchin' the twins runnin' 'round outside. I'd wrap a blanket all 'round her, too, cuz she took to shiverin' even when it was warm out. The twins was just over a year old now. I had to send Bobby and Samuel out to hunt for food. Emma did the cookin' and cleanin'. When Annie couldn't get up off the mattress no more, little Mae went to layin' down next to her. After 'while, Emma took over carin' for Mae, too. Every now and 'gain Mae went to followin' Emma 'round like she used to do her mama. I reckon she just didn't know what to do with herself no more without her mama bein' up and 'bout.

Then, one mornin' when the sun come up, Annie laid in bed next to me still as the night. When I went to nudge her a little, her arm dropped off the mattress and plopped down hard on the wood floor. I jumped up and stood starin' down at her layin' there. I could see she wasn't breathin' no more. When I touched her forehead, she felt cold. 'Cept for her mouth turnin' blue, she was so pale she looked like all the blood runned outta her. I knowed I ain't supposed to mourn the loss of no one I love cuz God would make sure we'd be together 'gain when I go to heaven but I couldn't help it. This was *my* Annie. I loved her from the day I laid eyes on her. I was mad at God for takin' her from me and I was mad at Jacob for suckin' the life outta her. I stopped believin' God sent Jacob to hold Satan back from the world. I believed he was sent by Satan to free Satan so *It* could break loose from the chains holdin' *It* down and destroy all of God's followers. I got down on my knees and prayed for God to send me a sign that Jacob was *His* but I didn't get no sign cuz I knowed I was right. He belonged to the devil.

I woke the children and told 'em their mama went to heaven durin' the night. Told 'em to give her one last kiss 'fore we went to buryin' her. None of 'em cried. They was taught not to. This was supposed to be a joyful time. Their mama went to heaven. Hallelujah. Praise the Lord. Amen. They was all holdin' back tears though. I could tell. I could see it in their faces and the way they was bitin' down on their lower lips. After Emma washed Annie up nice and clean, put her clean dress on her and brushed her hair, I carried her up to where we buried the twins afterbirths and veils under that big maple tree that sat on a hill on our land. It seemed like a perfect place since it stood there lookin' down on our cabin and Annie was all the time lookin' after all of us. Bobby, me, and Samuel went to diggin' a hole in the ground 'neath that tree. When we was done, I laid Annie real gentle like in it. We formed a circle 'round her, all of us holdin' hands. Emma said a prayer. At the end, the kids said....

"Hallelujah. Praise the Lord. Amen."

They said it quiet though. Didn't hear no jubilation in any of their voices. I didn't say it at all. I didn't have it in me to praise a God who took my Annie from me. Each of the children dropped a flower on top of Annie 'fore we went to fillin' the hole up with dirt. When we was done, we started walkin' back to the cabin. I'd mark it with a wood cross with Annie's name on it later. Emma was carryin' Grace on her hip. Jacob was sleepin' back at the cabin so I didn't bother to wake him. I didn't think he deserved to be there.

Later that night, I called an emergency meetin' at the lodge. When Bobby rung the bell, everyone from the four families come runnin' up the mountain. When the last of the Andersons walked through the door, I got up to the pulpit and announced to all of 'em my Annie went to heaven.

"Hallelujah! Praise the Lord! Amen!" they all hollered.

Sister Sarah started singin' *Turn Your Eyes Upon Jesus*. Raisin' herself up from her seat and takin' center stage, she led the entire congregation in song.

As I gathered up the children and walked from the lodge down the mountain, I could hear 'em all singin' in happier than happy and louder than loud voices even after we reached the cabin. I slammed the door hard behind me and covered my ears with my hands. I wasn't in no mood for hearin' folks celebratin' my Annie goin' to heaven. 'Specially knowin' they'd all be wearin' bigger than life smiles on their faces the whole time they was rejoicin'. We always believed it was an honor to be called to heaven by the Lord. But that's not how I was feelin' now. No sir! I didn't have even one rejoicin' bone in my body. I was sure of it! Matter of fact, I was feelin' all dark and mad inside.

Emma had to take care of Mae, Grace, and Jacob that day and night cuz I wasn't in no mood to do it. 'Stead, I stomped my way down to the cellar in the tunnel to fetch some moonshine my daddy and granddaddy made long time ago. After all this time of sittin' down there, I figured it was good and strong by now. Comin' back up through the trapdoor, I plopped myself down at the table. If Annie wouldn't have up and died on me I reckon I never would've touched it. Now, normally I's not a drinkin' man but tonight I was gonna be. Sure 'nuf, tonight I was gonna get stinkin' drunk. Just then, Jacob started in with his screamin'. You'd think he'd be past all that screamin' now that he was over a year old. Grace was. He just all the time was miserable 'bout one thing or 'nother. Maybe if he wasn't all the time screamin' and hollerin' my Annie would be 'live. I grabbed up that jug of moonshine and went outside to drink so I didn't have to listen to him cryin' no more. That's probably how Annie got to feelin' at the end was what I was thinkin'. I walked up the hill to where my Annie laid buried 'neath that maple tree and plopped down on top of the fresh mound of dirt that marked where she was. That's when I opened that jug of moonshine and started into guzzlin' it down. I drank and drank and drank. Then, I just hung my head down and cried like a baby. That's the night I turned my back on God. I didn't take up with Satan none but I was givin' the Lord Jesus Christ the cold shoulder sure 'nuf!

Next thing I knowed, I was wakin' up the next mornin' under the maple tree with an empty jug of moonshine layin' at my side. I had the worse headache I ever remember havin'. I got up real easy like and walked slow back to the cabin. When I was walkin' back, I remembered I didn't go at midnight last night to feed the devil. Now I broke my promise to my daddy.

"Just like clockwork," he said to me 'fore he died, "Don't never forget."

Everybody acted like it was gonna bring the end of the world down on us if even just one of us heads from the four families didn't go. Well, I was still standin' and my cabin looked all in one piece.

"What other lies I been told?" I wondered.

I started doubtin' there even was a God. Didn't have it in me no more to go shoutin' Hallelujah. Praise the Lord. Amen.

Chapter 7

Matthew 18:6-7 *But whoso shall offend one of these little ones which believe in me, it were better for him that a millstone were hanged about his neck, and that he were drowned in the depth of the sea.*

When I stumbled my way down the hill and back to the cabin, all the children was up doin' their chores. Bobby and Samuel was gettin' their firearms ready for huntin'. I didn't feel bad when Bobby looked over at me and said....

"I took your place and fed the devil last night. Got there at the same time Joshua, Simon, and Daryl from the other three families did."

He choked up a little when he told me....

"The devil was quiet last night. Not a word, snort, huff, puff, or grunt."

Then he walked out the door slammin' it real hard behind him. Samuel went stompin' out after him. They was mad. Didn't matter none to me.

"Better get used to it sooner than later," I mumbled after 'em, "Life ain't no bed of roses."

Both Grace and Jacob was handfuls these days now they took to runnin' and crawlin' 'round all over. They was 'lot for Annie to handle let 'lone Emma at the age of eleven. Grace was walkin' and Jacob was crawlin'. I don't know where he's gonna be crawlin' to now though. He used to just crawl after his mama everywhere 'round the house. She was either carryin' him on her hip bouncin' him up and down to quiet him or he was all the time screamin' and crawlin' after her. He don't do none of that with Emma. He's just sittin' off in a corner lookin' all swolled up from cryin' so much.

"Well, 'least he ain't cryin' now or sittin' there with crapped in pants," is what I was thinkin'.

Emma was carryin' Grace 'round on her hip while she was gettin' things ready 'round the cabin. Mae was outside pretendin' to work the garden. I could see her little shoulders goin' up and down like she was cryin' real hard. 'Sides me, I knowed she missed Annie the most. She was all the time by her mama's side even after the twins was born. 'Fore they come 'long, she was Annie's baby.

While I was sittin' 'round feelin' sorry for myself and fumin' inside, outta nowheres Jacob up and said....

"Mama" and pointed at me.

He threw me off guard so I looked all 'round thinkin' Annie was standin' next to me. Maybe all this was a bad dream.

"But it ain't no dream cuz she's dead," I went to thinkin' to myself. *"I remember diggin' her a hole 'neath the maple tree up on the hill on our land. She ain't never gonna be here 'gain. Never!"*

Next thing I knowed, Jacob pulled himself up off the floor and started wobblin' his way towards me all the time pointin' his finger at me sayin'....

"Mama."

My mouth dropped open cuz this was the first time he walked and talked. Annie would've loved hearin' him call her mama but I didn't appreciate it none at all. First of all, his mama's dead in the ground cuz he was all the time drainin' the life outta her. I got up 'fore he reached me and yelled at Emma to come get him and take care of him. Stompin' down the steps leadin' to the cellar 'gain, I quick grabbed up the last jug of moonshine and headed out the door. I caught the dirty look Emma gave me when I walked out but I didn't care.

"Sticks and stones," is what I was thinkin' when I slammed the door behind me.

When nightfall come 'round, I was still sittin' 'neath the maple tree where my Annie was laid to rest. I was so drunk I didn't care 'bout much of nothin'. I gave up askin' God to help me, to bring my Annie back, to take me so I could be with her. I lost my faith. No 'mount of prayin' was gonna bring the dead back. I knowed that now. What's done is done. But no one said I had to like it. Everybody says God don't do nothin' without a reason. Everybody says God don't never give you more than you can handle.

"Well, that's a damned lie!" I screamed, jumpin' up and shakin' my fist in the air at heaven, "There ain't one good reason for takin' my Annie. And it's way more than I can handle! So God's a liar! And I's sure 'nuf livin' proof of that!"

Then, knowin' I lost the battle, I threw myself back down on the ground sorta gruntin' under my breath while takin' 'nother slug of moonshine....

"Ain't no God no ways!"

The next mornin' I woke 'gain just like the last one. My head was hurtin' and I felt like pukin'. By the looks of the ground where I was layin', I'd already done plenty of that durin' the night. I shuffled my way back to the cabin. The kids was all sittin' 'round not sayin' a word.

"What's the matter with you kids?" I hollered full of anger and hate, "No time for sittin' 'round relaxin' none. Who you think you is? City folk? Ain't no vacations 'round here. You got chores to do so get up and do 'em 'fore I take a belt to all of you!"

I ain't never took a belt to none of 'em ever in their lives. The thought never even crossed my mind. Annie would've never allowed me doin' such a thing. But Annie ain't here no more is she? Lord Jesus Christ! Amen! Ain't no God no ways so who's gonna judge me?!

When Bobby stepped up to me, I could tell he was tryin' to stand taller than what he was. When he got done puffin' himself all up, he said....

"Mae went to heaven last night while you was up the hill drinkin'. Reckon she was climbin' up an apple tree and fell outta it. Found her layin' on the ground 'neath the tree with an apple in her hand. She broke her neck I reckon. I tried to bring her back but she wasn't havin' none of it. We's gonna bury her next to mama. We been waitin' for you to mozy on 'round to see if you wanna come with us. You can join us if you want, or not. Don't matter none to us neither way."

Bobby and Samuel each had a shovel in their hands. After speakin' his piece, Bobby handed his shovel over to Samuel. Strugglin' some and tryin' not to show it, he picked up Mae's limp, turned blue little body and carried it up the hill to where their mama laid buried under the maple tree. I reckon Emma was the one who done the washin' and cleanin' of her just like she done her mama. She was carryin' Grace on her hip like she always done. Jacob followed after everyone. He wrestled with walkin' up the hill fallin' down every few steps but I wasn't gonna help him none.

"He don't deserve no special attention," is what I was thinkin'. *"'Specially since it's cuz of him Annie's gone to begin with. It'd be my guess he had somethin' to do with Mae's passin', too."*

Samuel and Bobby went to diggin' 'nother hole right next to their mama's. They was careful not to pick the side where I throwed up. Emma shot me that *look* her mama always gave me when she was mad at me, but I didn't pay her no mind. I just went to starin' back at her 'til she looked 'way. When they was done, Bobby picked Mae up in his arms 'gain and laid her in the grave real gentle. Emma said a prayer. All of 'em throwed a flower on top of their little sister just like they done Annie. Even Grace. Jacob was still strugglin' to get up the hill. I didn't pay him no mind. I reckon the other kids figured they had more important things to do right now than to be tendin' to him, too....like their mama had to do when she was with the livin'....all day....and all night.

Bobby tossed that apple she picked in with her, too. She didn't even get a chance to take a bite outta it. Could barely hear 'em when they said....

"Hallelujah. Praise the Lord. Amen."

I didn't do no prayin' or praisin' to a God who I knowed ain't real. After Bobby and Samuel covered her up with dirt, we all headed back to the cabin. No sooner Jacob made it to the top of the hill, he had to turn 'round and follow us back down. I was thinkin' he deserved it. Emma turned 'round though and hoisted him up on her other hip.

"Gotta make 'nother wood cross with Mae's name on it now," is what I was thinkin'.

I was madder than hell inside.

"Yeah, that's what I sure 'nuf said!" I yelled up at the sky with my hand shakin' and balled up into a fist.

"Madder than HELL!" I hollered loud as I could just makin' sure everybody heard me.

The children all looked at me with frowns on their faces but I didn't care. I didn't care 'bout no one or nothin' no more. When we got back to the cabin, Bobby was quick to tell me he done my job 'gain feedin' the devil last night.

"Daddy," he said, "I don't mean no disrespect but that's your job. Not mine. 'Least not yet. The devil was yellin' mama's name at me. *It* said my daddy ain't no real man cuz no real man would go to sendin' his son to do his job 'fore his time."

When he finished sayin' what he had to say, I stood there lookin' down at him tryin' to make sense outta what he just said. I knowed Annie and me never raised no disrespectin' child. I reckon after two days of drinkin' moonshine, I was a little slow on the thinkin' part of me. When I took a step towards him, he jumped back 'way from me.

"Oh, I see," I yelled at him, "So just cuz you fed the devil a couple of nights you's thinkin' you's the one tellin' me what to do now 'stead of the other way 'round? Well, 'fore you go puffin' yourself up at me 'gain you sure 'nuf better think twice 'fore doin' it cuz like it or not I's the man of this family and what I say goes!"

I reckon I just couldn't take it no more. I had so much grief, hatred, and anger inside me, I just wanted it all to go 'way. That's when I took my belt off, snapped it in front of Bobby's face a couple times, flung it up high 'bove my head, and went to whuppin' on him like no tomorrow. *whoosh pop whoosh pop whoosh pop* One on top of 'nother. All the while, my belt went to flyin' high 'bove my head *whoosh* and then come down hard *pop* on whatever part of his body had the misfortune to offer itself up. *whoosh pop whoosh pop whoosh pop* Over and over 'gain. Cussin' and screamin', I gave him everythin' I got. *whoosh pop whoosh pop whoosh pop whoosh pop whoosh pop* I was in such a state of sadness and despair, I didn't even notice Bobby was layin' huddled in front of me all crumpled up into a ball with his arms over his head tryin' to protect himself. *whoosh pop whoosh pop whoosh pop* Finally huffin' and puffin' with no breath left in me, I spun 'round in a circle crackin' my butt whuppin' belt at the other children.

"Any one of you want some of the same?" I heard myself bark at 'em.

None of 'em said a word but if Emma's *look* could've killed, I would've been layin' dead on the floor. Lookin' 'em all straight on in the eyes, I dared any one of 'em to come get what I was givin' Bobby. My face was red and spit was flyin' outta my mouth. If I could've breathed fire and growed horns, I would've. I cursed Jacob and told him he was the reason my Annie and Mae died. I called him Satan's son and then some. I told him I regretted the day he was born. I went on and on and on and the whole time I was lashin' out at him, all the other kids went to standin' real still with their mouths shut tryin' not to make eye contact with me. 'Cept Emma. She just stood straight as she could glarin' at me with that evil eye. That made me even madder so I turned to start whuppin' on Bobby 'gain. Just as I raised my belt up in the air....*whoosh*....Jacob was all of a sudden standin' in front of Bobby. I don't know where he come from so fast but he ended up gettin' the *pop* part of the *whoosh*. After that, he come runnin' up to me clingin' onto my leg and cryin'.

"Cryin' 'gain!" I hollered to anybody who wanted to listen.

So I pushed him 'way from me, turned my belt on him and went to beatin' him 'til he couldn't move. *whoosh pop whoosh pop whoosh pop* Then, I whupped 'em both up and down the room 'til they ended up huddled together in a corner.

"This is for Annie!" I screamed. *whoosh pop* Then, "This is for Mae!" *whoosh pop*

I was sweatin', cursin', and hollerin' loud as I could. Bobby was howlin' like a trapped animal. Sounded 'lot like Eve when she was birthin' her baby. Jacob didn't make a sound the whole time. While Bobby was tryin' to cover Jacob up with his body, Jacob was doin' the same with Bobby. Jacob bein' quiet made me even madder. Keepin' his mama up all night screamin' and fussin' and now when he's got reason to cry, he don't. I was so mad I knowed if someone didn't stop me I'd sure 'nuf kill 'em both. I didn't care though. I just kept whuppin' on 'em *whoosh pop whoosh pop whoosh pop* over and over 'gain.

Emma must've somehow knowed what I was thinkin' cuz no sooner I thought that I was gonna kill 'em right then and there if someone didn't stop me, she put Grace down and 'long with Samuel went to grabbin' for my arms. She was screamin' so loud I thought she broke my hearin' when my ears went to ringin'. When I flung my arms loose from both of 'em, Samuel run to grab a fire poker stick and went to swingin' it at me. Bobby was cryin', Emma was screamin', Samuel was swingin', and Jacob was quiet. Grace, too. By the time they was all done doin' what they had to do to protect one 'nother, I was all red faced and bendin' over pantin' to breathe. I looked like Satan himself.

Emma picked Jacob up off the ground coddlin' him in her arms while Samuel helped Bobby to the mattress. Emma told Grace to follow her. Grace didn't follow her though. She glanced over at Jacob who was noddin' his head up and down at her, then walked over to me and went to wrappin' her little arms 'round my leg.

"Dada," she said.

First words I knowed of she ever spoke. I didn't know what I did so bad to deserve all this. All's I knowed was without my Annie I didn't wanna live. Half of me was gone. The good half of me. I picked Grace up in my arms and carried her up the hill with me. All the moonshine was gone. When I plopped down under the maple tree where my Annie and little Mae was buried, Grace rested her head down on my chest and laid real quiet like in my arms. I could tell she knowed I was grievin'. I was holdin' onto her real tight cuz somethin' told me if I didn't the devil was gonna come get me and deliver me straight to hell. I cried myself to sleep up there on that hill under the maple tree where the love of my life was buried. Grace closed her little eyes and fell 'sleep with me.

While I was 'sleep, I dreamed Annie come to me to tell me I was wrong to take my grievin' out on the children. Little Mae was standin' next to her. They was holdin' hands. Neither one of 'em was smilin'. Mae looked sad. Annie had a real serious look on her face. The kind of *look* she always got when she was mad at me. The same look Emma shot at me back at the cabin. I knowed better than to stare back at Annie though. I was glad to see she looked healthy like she used to. Heck, she looked thirteen 'gain. She come over to me and whispered somethin' in my ear. She told me to take real good care of little Jacob. I figured it was cuz he was so weak and puny and what I done to him. She didn't say nothin' 'bout Grace. Maybe cuz she was there with me now and she could see she was okay. She told me not to worry 'bout her and Mae cuz they was with God. I knowed I was 'bout to hear it when she put her hand on her hip and went to wavin' her finger up and down at me….

"Now Calvin! You better start workin' on trustin' the Lord Jesus Christ 'gain 'stead of turnin' your back on Him like you been doin' so you can be with me and Mae 'gain some day. The way you been actin' you's headed to spendin' eternity with the devil. Calvin Sanders, make sure you take care of all our children. Jacob, too. Throw all

your belts 'way and never raise a hand or say a mean word to any of 'em 'gain!"

I could tell by the tone in her voice, she wasn't askin' neither. She was orderin' me to do what she was tellin' me to do. Then, her and Mae floated 'way. Poof! They was gone.

When I woke, I was noddin' my head up and down like I always done when Annie went to scoldin' me and callin' me Calvin. After that, I sat under that tree on the hill a good while thinkin' real hard 'bout what she said. I don't know how I knowed but I knowed for sure it wasn't no dream. Grace was still sleepin' with her little curly head on top of my chest. When it got to bein' dark out, I pulled myself up off the ground and went to walkin' back down that hill with Grace cradled tight in my arms. I didn't know what I was gonna say to the children. I was 'shamed of myself for the second time in my life. The first time was when I locked eyes with that red eyed monster chained up down in that hole after my daddy done told me so many times 'fore not to. Lettin' my Annie down though gave me a pain in my heart I couldn't hardly stand.

When I got back to the cabin, Bobby was layin' on the mattress moanin'. I knowed I hurt him real bad. All cuz I was feelin' sorry for myself. All cuz I was mad at God for takin' my Annie. All cuz I throwed God outta me and let the devil take hold of me. Grace was woke now. I still had 'hold of her in my arms. Jacob was keepin' vigil over Bobby by sittin' next to him on the mattress with his eyes all squinted up, his eyebrows touchin' his nose, and a big frown on his face. Like he was ready to take me on if I went to hurtin' Bobby 'gain. Emma was fixin' some sort of concoction her mama taught her how to make for pain. Jacob didn't look beat up like Bobby. I knowed I got 'em both the same. Jacob's so little and skinny, I's sure 'nuf blessed I didn't kill him. I wasn't thinkin' right. I know that now. Satan gets you when you's at your weakest. He sure 'nuf got 'hold of me.

When I put little Grace down on the ground, she went runnin' over to where Jacob was sittin' by Bobby. I went to Bobby and got down on my knees tellin' him and Jacob how sorry I was. I promised 'em it ain't never gonna happen 'gain. I begged 'em to forgive me. I told 'em their mama come to me in a dream and gave it to me real good for doin' what I done to 'em. I wanted Bobby to know he wasn't never gonna have to put up with feedin' *It* no more.

"You was right, Bobby," I said, "That's my job. Not yours."

I turned to Samuel and Emma and told 'em I was sorry, too. They all come runnin' up to me throwin' their little arms 'round my shoulders. They forgave me. Just like that. I never been so proud of my children. They knowed I was missin' their mama. They was, too. I hugged 'em all tight, includin' Jacob. We all got down on our knees and asked God to forgive me. All of us 'cept Bobby cuz he was hurtin' too bad to move. That didn't stop him from prayin' for me though.

When we was all done prayin', Grace kneeled on one side of Bobby and Jacob kneeled on the other side. They both laid their little hands on him and closed their eyes. They went to talkin' in a language I didn't understand but I kept real quiet and let 'em do what they was doin'. 'Sides, I could feel little Mae and Annie watchin' me. Emma, Samuel, and me just stood still starin' at the twins. When they was done babblin', Bobby jumped up from that mattress and hollered out his pain was gone. Didn't see not one bruise or mark on him neither. Them babies healed him with the layin' on of hands. That's when we all dropped to our knees and took to yellin' out loud as we could....

"Hallelujah! Praise the Lord! Amen!"

We just laid witness to a miracle from God.

That night, Emma cooked us all a pot of rabbit stew. We was all sittin' round laughin' and talkin' like we used to when we still had Annie and Mae. I know now God had a plan for doin' what *He* done. I'd find out sure 'nuf what it was in time. In *His* time.

After Annie come to me in that dream, I felt her with me all the time. I knowed her and Mae would always be with me in a special part of my heart. I pictured 'em runnin' through the wildflowers in heaven. Annie's curly red hair flyin' and bouncin' behind her. Didn't have to worry none 'bout Mae. She's with her mama. Annie's sure 'nuf gonna take real good care of her. I know Mae was real happy now, too. I had 'lot of gettin' on my knees and beggin' God to forgive me. I hoped Annie and Mae would put a good word in for me. The way I acted, I wouldn't blame God if *He* didn't forgive me though.

I tucked all the children in bed good and tight 'fore I went to feed the beast that night. Gave 'em all a big hug and a peck on the cheek. Even Jacob. I hoped Annie was watchin' me. I got down on my knees and begged God to forgive me for what I said to *Him* and the way I treated my children. I said I was mighty sorry for turnin' my back on *Him* and for losin' my way. I knowed havin' bad thoughts 'bout little Jacob wasn't right neither. I thanked *Him* for lettin' me see my Annie and Mae 'gain. I had so much sinnin' to be sorry for since Annie went to heaven I hoped sayin' sorry was 'nuf. I promised God I was on the right path now. I drunk all the moonshine and promised I was never gonna do that 'gain. I wrapped it all up by sayin'....

"Hallelujah! Praise the Lord! Amen!" And I said it good and loud.

When I was all done prayin' for God's forgiveness, I opened the trapdoor leadin' to the tunnels and stepped down the ladder carryin' a plate of squirrels and rabbits Bobby and Samuel caught. I got to the middle just when Joshua Nelson, Simon Taylor, and Daryl Anderson walked up with their plates. The devil must've realized it was me and not Bobby this time cuz *It* started talkin' to me in Annie's voice. I knowed my Annie wasn't down there. She was flyin' 'round in heaven with Mae and the other angels of God. *It* didn't make me mad. I swore to God I was sorry for followin' the devil's evil ways after my Annie died. I was headed in the wrong direction for a time but I was back on God's path now. I meant what I said so I walked a little closer to the edge of that pit and looked square down into it. When I saw *Its* red eyes glarin' up at me, I started laughin' at *It*. *It* didn't lock into me this time. Joshua, Simon, and Daryl just stood at the edge of the pit starin' at me like I was crazy. But I wasn't crazy. I was all filled up with the love and power of the Lord Jesus Christ! Then, we all throwed our plates down the hole. 'Fore I went to leave, I hollered down into that hole....

"Get behind me Satan cuz there ain't no greater power in me than the Lord Jesus Christ, Amen!"

After I shouted at *It,* I spit into the pit and hoped I hit *It* between those two evil red eyes. Had to jump back some cuz flames of fire come flyin' up at me. *It* was spittin, sputtin', and cussin' but *It* didn't bother me none. I just turned and walked 'way real slow laughin' loud 'nuf so it echoed all through the tunnels....and down into that hole. Hallelujah! Praise the Lord! Amen!

Chapter 8

Ephesians 4:31-32   *Let all bitterness, and wrath, and anger, and clamour, and evil speaking, be put away from you, with all malice: And be ye kind one to another, tenderhearted, forgiving one another, even as God for Christ's sake hath forgiven you.*

After Bobby turned fourteen in the summer, the twins turned two in the fall. He took 'Lizabeth Nelson to be his wife. Just like I thought he would. Since Bobby was next in line to be head of the Sanders family, him and 'Lizabeth took over me and Annie's ol' cabin. Emma, Samuel, Grace, Jacob, and me was livin' in my mama and daddy's ol' place.

'Lizabeth was expectin' a baby already. Bobby's a man now. I's real proud of him. Heck, I's real proud of all my children. I was gonna miss Bobby bein' 'round all the time. Sure 'nuf glad I made peace with him 'fore he moved into his own cabin. I love all my children but Bobby's special. He ain't just my first born, he's my oldest son. Emma's twelve now. She'll be matin' up in 'nother year or two. She don't got Annie's red hair but she got her spirit. Ain't no one gonna slip a fast one past her none too soon. Samuel's ten years old. He's still young but he's a better hunter than most his age. I reckon cuz his older brother took him under his wing after their mama passed.

I finally had that talk with 'em 'bout never sneakin' down into the tunnel to see the beast like me and my friends done when I was ten and sure 'nuf to never look *It* square on in the eyes. Samuel swore on the Bible he wouldn't so I knowed he was tellin' the truth. Kinda told Bobby too late though since he had to fill in for me when I was goin' through that crazy spell last year. He swore on the Bible, too, just to make me feel better I think.

Not a day goes by I don't think of little Mae and my sweet darlin' Annie. If Mae was still livin' she'd be eight now. I often go to wonderin' what made her want that apple so bad. I reckon God and Annie needed her more than me. I made 'em both a real pretty wood cross to put over where we laid 'em to rest. I go up there every day the weather's fittin' to thank God for forgivin' me for what I done to Bobby and Jacob. I thank *Him* for takin' me back into the fold and forgivin' me for losin' my faith.

Sometimes I just sit up there on that hill under the maple tree hopin' to see my Annie in 'nother dream. It don't matter I reckon. I can always feel her 'round me in spirit. The day's gonna come I'll see her 'gain anyways when I go to heaven. Then we'll be together forever. I's sure 'nuf glad our God is a forgivin' one. I miss so many things 'bout Annie. Always brings a smile to my face when I close my eyes and picture her standin' in front of me with one side of her mouth turned up all sassy-like. She sure 'nuf was a wild one. Ain't no one could get me goin' like she could when she took a mind to. She knowed it, too.

The devil don't scare me like *It* used to. I reckon when *It* crawled up in me when my Annie passed and I gave up on God, I learned a lesson I don't none too soon wanna ever forget. Satan takes over folk when they's at their lowest and weakest. *It* knowed I throwed the Lord outta me and I was wide open for *It* to jump on up in me and take my thinkin' and doin' over. One thing I learned is the devil ain't only livin' in that hole down in the tunnel, *It's* livin' inside 'lot of folk, too. 'Lot of city folk gonna be real sorry one day. Maybe God'll give 'em a second chance like *He* done me 'fore *He* goes to makin' any rash decisions. Maybe not. I's glad Annie come to me 'fore I was too far gone and gave me a talkin' to. When I go to thinkin' 'bout Annie and Mae, I just remind myself what Annie said....they's with God now. God's the one who let Annie come to me in that dream after I done whupped my boys so bad. Maybe *He* knowed I needed to know they was okay. I hope and pray I been raisin' my children up right like Annie told me to so if they gotta ever stand up to *It,* they will. I don't want 'em to learn the hard way like I done. I always tell 'em now, "Long as you got the good Lord Jesus Christ inside you, there's no room for Satan. Oh, *It* can rave and rant, holler and scream, thump and bump 'round, but *It* cain't hurt you none when you believe in God. You just gotta be strong and not give in to *Its* evil ways." I figure the most *It* can do is kill me. That's sure 'nuf not punishment to me. That'll only send me off to be with my Annie quicker. I reckon I gotta wait 'nother five years though. Gotta get the twins to seven so they can do what they was born to do. Maybe that's my purpose. Maybe not. By then, Emma and Samuel's gonna be on their own and I'll be freed up to go....if God takes a likin' to take me.

The twins is growin' up big. Even Jacob's lookin' healthy now. His hair's red and shiny like his mama's was.

It ain't stickin' out all over no more neither. He's gone to half smilin' now and 'gain, too. He's still got that serious look most the time though. Like he's gotta whole lot of thinkin' to do. I don't know. I reckon he does.

Grace and Jacob both got good appetites. Next time I go up the hill to talk to my Annie, I gotta tell her there ain't nothin' special we gotta do to raise babies born behind the veil. They's way smarter than we is. I's lookin' after 'em real good. Sometimes I think they's the ones lookin' after me though. They laugh 'lot and play real good together. They call me dada now. That makes me real proud. I been takin' 'em fishin' with me now and 'gain. Jacob hooked a fish. He made me throw it back in the water though. Samuel got a good laugh outta that.

When I take 'em to the monthly meetin's they sit real nice and quiet. Jacob gave up all the screamin' and cryin' he used to do. I reckon he figured with his mama gone ain't no one gonna pay him no mind like she did when he goes to actin' up. The two of 'em got their own language nobody can understand but them. All the girls and women take to fussin' over Jacob now. When we go to the monthly meetin's, they's both all the time bein' carried 'round by one woman or 'nother. Jacob's growed into his own I reckon. Just like Annie said I did. Grace is still the charmer she always was. Everyone's all the time swarmin' to her. The twins go to protectin' one 'nother I noticed. Grace is 'specially protective of Jacob. She's all the time holdin' his hand leadin' him 'round and talkin' for him. He don't never seem to mind. He just does what she wants him to do pretty much. I reckon she figured she'd take Annie's place with him best she could. Who knows? Maybe it's the other way 'round. Maybe she's doin' what he's wantin' her to do. Never know 'bout those two.

I get lonely for my Annie mostly at night when everyone's sleepin' and the cabin's real quiet and dark. I wrap my arms 'round a pillow now and 'gain and hold it nice and tight like it's her. If I try real hard, I can hear her soft voice whisperin' in my ear right 'fore I go to closin' my eyes....

"I love you, *Cal*."

She called me *Cal* when she wasn't mad at me and she had somethin' sweet to say to me. I miss Mae, too. She was the quietest one out of all our children. After she was born, she all the time acted like she wanted to crawl back up inside her mama. Annie used to shake her finger at me when I went to laughin' 'bout that. Just meant she loved her mama is all. She missed Annie the most I think. Mostly on 'count of she was the baby 'fore the twins come 'long. Every now and 'gain, she'd take to followin' Emma 'round like she done her mama 'fore she passed. Sometimes when Emma stopped real quick, little Mae would run right into the back end of her cuz she was followin' her so close. Emma was 'lot like her mama. She'd just laugh and keep on goin' doin' what she was doin' like it didn't bother her none at all. She's gonna make a great mama one day.

Durin' my bad time, I never once thought 'bout how much the children was missin' their mama and little sister. I was selfish. I know God forgave me but there's some things I have a hard time forgivin' myself for. Every time I think 'bout what I done to Bobby and Jacob, I feel like sittin' down and cryin'. Sometimes, I do. I took all my belts and throwed 'em clean 'way like Annie told me to do. I'd rather my pants dropped down to my knees than ever lay a hand on any of my children 'gain. I ain't even raised my voice to any of 'em since that day. When Annie was livin', she'd of never approved of such a thing. She'd of probably took that belt and turned it on me. None of our children is bad. All the children in these mountains is well behaved. They mind their manners and work hard. All of 'em respect their mamas and daddies. They act the way the good Lord intended 'em to act. What I did to Bobby and Jacob was the devil's doin'. All my kids know to keep themselves filled up with God now so what happened to me don't never happen to any of 'em. We had a long talk 'bout it one night. I told 'em they seen the devil's work first hand. I reckon it was a lesson for all of us. Bobby and Jacob was on the receivin' end of it though. I don't like to think 'bout that day but I make myself cuz I don't want nothin' like that to ever happen 'gain. I know I gotta remind myself every day how easy it is for the devil to take you over when your soul's weak. *Its* gotta way of tellin' things like that.

In five more years, when the twins is in their seventh year on earth, I's gonna be all 'lone. They got God's work to do keepin' Satan locked up from the world. I don't know how they's gonna do it but I sure 'nuf know they know. Emma and Samuel gonna both be married and raisin' their own families by then. I sure hope they'll let me be part of my grandbabies lives if I's still livin' and breathin'. I don't know. Maybe I'll be achin' and painin' 'nuf by then to ask Bobby to send me to heaven. I won't ask 'fore my time cuz that'd be a sin. Don't never wanna get God mad at me 'gain. 'Sides, ain't nobody can trick God. *He* knows what you's thinkin' 'fore you do.

Not too long ago, I got elected to go with Simon Taylor into the city to see what the folks was doin' down there. What a mess! They was drivin' round in automobiles. We was told 'bout 'em 'fore but I ain't never seen it with my own eyes. They ain't the crank up kind neither like our granddaddie's granddaddies talked 'bout. They's all shiny and fancy lookin'. Some of 'em ain't even got tops on 'em. They got special roads for 'em to go on, too. Automobiles was zippin' up and down, back and forth real fast. Darned near run us over a couple times. Everybody's in a hurry to go nowhere fast is what I said. Simon said the same. The women's all walkin' 'round in shoes that raise the back end of their feet up higher than the front part. Our women would tip right over in shoes like that. Their hair's all done up and their cheeks and lips got all kinds of pink and red colors on 'em. They's paradin' 'round in fancy bright colored dresses that go up 'bove their knees. Darn near see their undergarments is what I was thinkin'. Some of 'em was even wearin' pants like the men folk. I noticed whenever a woman passed by a man, he'd turn 'round and watch her walk 'way. The more she'd go to swingin' her bottom back and forth, the longer he'd look. Sometimes he'd even go to whistlin' after her. Me and Simon both just looked down at the ground and went to shakin' our heads back and forth. Men *and* women was smokin' tobacco, too. A woman walked past us with one of those in her mouth and the smoke hit us in the face so bad we both went to coughin'. We had to bend over so we could breathe 'gain. All the folks walkin' 'round carryin' a contraption called a telephone. It's a mouthpiece that let's you talk to someone way on the other side of town. They even got a picture box called a television where folk is movin' 'round in it and talkin'. Me and Simon stood in front of a store window for 'while watchin' it. It was the darndest thing we ever seen. I laughed to myself. If we had one of those up in the mountains, we'd never get the Lord's work done. We stood there starin' at it so long we thought it took hold of us. I wondered if the devil put the idea for such a thing in some city folk's mind. I knowed by how Satan took me over 'while back, it was sure 'nuf possible. Alls I know is Simon and me got all wrapped up in it. We watched a man wearin' a gun on each side of him, a wide brimmed hat and fancy boots, jump off a horse, kick in the door to a cabin, slide 'cross the room on his side, and put a bullet in a man's head. After 'while, I had to grab onto Simon and drag him 'way. If one of us didn't break loose from its spell, we'd still be standin' there starin' at it. We didn't even spend a whole day lookin' 'round. We couldn't wait to get back to our homes and families. The city was a scary place far as we was concerned. I don't know. Maybe none of these inventions come from the devil. I knowed God gave certain folk a really smart brain to come up with modernization to make livin' easier for 'em. It's just sometimes they go to usin' it wrong is all. I reckon it'd been different if we was born and raised in the city. But we wasn't. I sure 'nuf is thankful for that. It's not up to me or Simon, or any of us I reckon, to say what's bad and what's good. That's God's job. And I ain't never steppin' on *His* toes 'gain. Never! Had to walk 'lot of miles to get back up to our cabins in the mountains. I was thinkin' one of them automobiles would've come in handy. Bein' that neither one of us knowed how to drive though, I 'magine it was best for everyone concerned we was walkin'. We left for the city just when the sun was comin' up. Headin' back home, it was dark out.

When I got back home to the children, they was all waitin' up for me. They couldn't wait to hear all 'bout what I saw in the city. The whole time I was talkin', their eyes was big as saucers. When I was done, I gave 'em all a big hug. I learned a lesson when little Mae and my Annie went to heaven. Never take the folks you love for granted. Don't never let a day go by without givin' 'em a big hug and a peck on the cheek. I do that every mornin' they wake up and every night 'fore I tuck 'em in to sleep. Sometimes I even do it 'fore goin' down to feed the beast. I tell 'em I love 'em, too. Even if they's sleepin' and cain't hear me, I still tell 'em. Just like Annie always told me 'fore we went to sleep when she was with the livin'. I ain't never too proud to say I's sorry neither. No one knows when the good Lord Jesus Christ's gonna come knockin' on my door to carry me up to heaven....or send me down to hell.

Satan finally gave up tryin' to pull me in with Annie's voice. Sometimes I stare down into the hole and soon as I see *Its* red eyes lookin' back at me, I spit at *It* for good measure. I put a lock on the trapdoor in the floor of my cabin leadin' to the tunnels. Don't wanna take no chances with the twins. I know they got special powers but

I think they's too young to do battle with the devil yet. I beared witness to their healin' powers. I can tell they see Annie now and 'gain cuz they point a finger my way and say....

"Mama."

Annie's probably standin' next to me when they go to doin' that. Mae, she's with Annie all the time so I's sure they see her, too. I think Mae's playin' with 'em sometimes cuz they take off runnin' and laughin' after someone in the cabin no one else sees. Sometimes they's doin' the chasin'. Other times, they's doin' the runnin' 'way. One thing's for sure though, they's havin' a good time cuz they's all the time laughin'. Even Jacob. Oh yeah, as far as that time Annie thought she saw Jacob floatin' in the air 'bove his crib must've been her needin' sleep cuz he ain't never done that 'gain. Hallelujah! Praise the Lord! Amen!

All the families come to the same mind we's gonna make sure all the Caulbearer children get to know one 'nother when the weather gets nice after they turn four. The twins was born in the fall and the others 'fore their time in the winter so we'll wait for a couple of springs and summers to pass by first. They got a job to do together so they might as well know each other 'fore they take on Satan. Oh, they all go to the monthly meetin's with their mamas and daddies but none of 'em had a formal meetin' yet.

Eve's been feelin' guilty for not comin' to see her sister, Annie, 'fore she up and went to heaven. That's when Jacob was fussin' all the time. Pretty much everybody was stayin' 'way from us then. I told Eve that Annie and me both knowed why she didn't come 'round and there ain't no hard feelin' on neither our parts. Not then. Not now. Annie loved her little sister and nothin' was ever gonna change that. She laughed when I told her sometimes I even had to walk outta the cabin to get a breath of fresh air when Jacob took to screamin' or crappin' his pants. Both of 'em's goin' to the outhouse now. I always make sure Samuel or Emma goes with 'em though so they don't fall in or get ate up by a wild animal on the way.

I ain't missed a night feedin' *It* since Bobby put me in my place. I's glad he said what he said to me. Helped snap me outta my crazy spell. That and seein' my Annie in that dream. For 'while, I'd see those bright red eyes pop out at me from deep down in the pit. Reckon *It* got tired of bein' spit on cuz I ain't seen 'em for 'while now. I think *It* knows there ain't a whole lot can be done to hurt me now 'cept through my children and I make sure that trapdoor stays locked. Even though I knowed if *It* wanted to take hold of someone not filled up with the Lord, *It* sure 'nuf could. Ain't no locked up trapdoor gonna stop *It*. I learned that lesson first hand. Annie, Mae, and God is lookin' after us real good though. I got my faith in God back and no one's gonna ever take that 'way from me. No one! Hallelujah! Praise the Lord! Amen!

Chapter 9

Isaiah 5:20 *Woe unto them that call evil good, and good evil; that put darkness for light, and light for darkness, that put bitter for sweet, and sweet for bitter!*

Well, three years done come and gone. Every day passed pretty much like the day 'fore it. Everyone's glad 'bout that. The families went 'bout their routines without no trouble. The heads of the families went down into the tunnel every night at midnight to feed the beast like they been doin' for hundreds of years. Could always see *Its* red eyes glowin' down at the bottom of the pit lookin' up at us but mostly *It* was quiet. We's all happy 'bout that. On the first Sunday of every month, we still gather at the lodge to listen to the story bein' told by one of the heads of the families. I didn't know it then but I was gonna find out soon 'nuf, these three years was the calm 'fore the storm.

The twins gonna be five years old this fall. Fall's just 'round the corner, a few more months 'way. I's caught between part of me wantin' time to slow down on 'count of the twins and the other part wantin' it to hurry up so I'd be closer to bein' with my Annie 'gain. I reckon wantin' somethin' both ways is bein' selfish but I cain't help how I feel. I pray every night for God to help me through it. Oh, I don't mean to sound ungrateful for what the Lord left me with. We's all healthy and happy. I'd just smile 'lot more if I had Annie by my side is all. I miss her. Ain't a day goes by I don't think 'bout her. I don't expect that to ever change. Don't want it to neither.

Grace's dark brown curls still bouncin' all over her head. Only thing different 'bout it now is it growed longer. She's all the time laughin' or smilin'. Got 'lot of energy that one. Real playful and sassy like her mama. Not in a smart alecky way. Just all the time happy. Well, 'less someone's pickin' on Jacob. She can go from happy to mad in one split second when that happens. 'Cept for her mama, she got the biggest deep blue eyes I ever seen. Jacob's got curly hair now, just like all the other kids….and his mama. I don't know how hair can go from poker straight to frizzy and then to curly, but I ain't one to question God never 'gain. Annie probably had somethin' to do with it. Just cuz she's in heaven don't mean she ain't still the children's mama. I know she ain't givin' that up without a fight. Maybe she decided to spruce the little guy up some so folk'll take a likin' to him more. It's a real nice red color like his mama's. Not that orange it was when he went through that frizzy stage. I gotta remember to tell Annie he's lookin' real good now on 'count of she might wanna go messin' with him 'gain. He's still got pale skin but the freckles finally come out all over. 'Least they add some color to his face.

The twins got their own language only they understand. They talk our talk though when they go to conversin' with us regular folk. They both have visions 'bout the future. Sure 'nuf woke me in the middle of the night once to tell me Bobby and 'Lizabeth was expectin' their third baby and it was a boy. Nobody knowed that to be true. Not even Bobby or 'Lizabeth at the time. A couple of months later, Bobby told us 'Lizabeth was carryin' their third child. When nine months went by, they had their first boy. They already got two girls. This was Bobby's first son. Had to laugh to myself. He went to struttin' 'round like a peacock showin' him off to all the folk at the monthly lodge meetin'. I told him how special he'd be to him. Bobby growed up bein' a real good husband and daddy. I's real proud of him. He turned seventeen this summer.

Emma married one of the Nelson boys couple years back, Steven. She's fifteen now. They got one boy just turned two, Elijah. She's carryin' their second child now. She moved 'way to live on the Nelson property. Didn't really have no choice bein' her husband is next in line, after his daddy Joshua passes, to be head of the Nelson family. After him, it'll be their oldest son, Elijah. I miss Emma *and* her cookin'. She still stops by now and 'gain to see how we's doin'. 'Cept for the color of their eyes, Grace and her look 'lot 'like. They's both tiny like their mama, too. Emma growed up to be a real pretty woman. She sure 'nuf is a good mama, too. Annie had 'lot to do with that.

Samuel went and turned thirteen on me. He'll be leavin' to take a wife in 'nother year I reckon. I 'magine me, my brother Ray, and Bobby, 'long with Sarah's husband and my twin brothers, Karl and Tobias, is gonna build Samuel a cabin come next spring. Should be done by the time he turns matin' age in the summer. Gonna squeeze it between Bobby and Ray's cabins. Got plenty of room there so it should work out real good. It's where Samuel said he wants to be anyways. By his brother, Bobby. Those two growed up close. Got even closer durin' my crazy spell I reckon. Well, I's glad 'least some good come outta it.

Don't wanna never forget Mae. She went to heaven but that don't mean she's not one of my children. She would've been eleven. All our girls is real pretty. I miss Mae. I reckon she's where she oughta be now....with her mama. After Samuel takes a wife and moves into his own cabin, it'll be just me, Grace, and Jacob for however long the good Lord lets me have 'em. Not long I reckon. A couple more years anyways. I's just grateful *He* let me have 'em that long. What happens to me after they's gone I don't worry 'bout none. I leave my livin' and dyin' in God's hands now.

All the Caulbearer children been takin' turns goin' to one or 'nother of the families cabins to play together since the start of this past spring. They had the whole spring and most of the summer to get to know one 'nother. Gonna be fall now in just a few more months. We waited 'til they was almost five. All the heads of the families thought it'd be better if they was a little older 'fore we went to introducin' 'em. Winter ain't no time to be goin' back and forth through the tunnel deliverin' the children from one cabin to 'nother nohows. Didn't wanna be givin' Satan no hints 'bout what we's doin'. They's gonna be meetin' *It* soon 'nuf far as I's concerned.

'Bout once a week, we take turns havin' 'em all over to our cabins. Grace and Jacob Sanders, Matthew Nelson, Esau Taylor, and Hannah Anderson. Five of 'em in all. One from each of the families, 'cept the Sanders on 'count of we got two. I's not so sure lettin' 'em play together's a good idea though. More than a few times, they all got into a scuffle over this or over that. Just bein' kids I reckon. Grace is quick to jump in to protect her brother when she feels the need. She don't let no one mess with him or make fun of him. He don't talk 'lot and more than not he's got a real serious look on his face. I reckon he's got 'lot to think 'bout the older he gets. I's glad Grace goes to protectin' him cuz I don't think he's got it in him to stand up for himself. I know their mama's watchin' over 'em and is real proud of her takin' up for her brother. 'Cept for when they all come to our cabin, Grace was comin' home all dirty with cuts, scratches, and bruises from scrappin' with the others. Jacob, he looked like he was all clean and in one piece. Just like he was when I went to whuppin' on him and Bobby that time the devil took me over. When they come home, I ask 'em what happened but they ain't never got nothin' to say. They go to shruggin' their little shoulders up and down then go to talkin' that language I don't understand so I just step 'way and let 'em talk to one 'nother. I was thinkin' maybe there's some things God don't want me to know 'bout so I never say or do nothin' 'bout it.

There was that one time though when Grace come home with her knee bleedin' and her lip all swolled up after they was playin' at the Andersons. For whatever reason, I reckon I done reached my boilin' point that day. They just shrugged their shoulders when I asked 'em 'bout it so I decided to take matters into my own hands. I went stompin' over to Daryl and Rebekah's cabin demandin' an answer.

'Nuf was 'nuf was what I was thinkin'. When Daryl invited me into the cabin, I seen Hannah layin' on a mattress on the floor with what was gonna turn into a real nasty shiner. She was holdin' a cold rag over her eye and whimperin'. When she pulled it 'way so I could see, my jaw hit the ground. I didn't have no words. Daryl went on to tell me Grace and Jacob was all the time startin' fights with the other ones. Daryl said he was tellin' me cuz he thought 'bout me as kinfolk since I was his sister Annie's husband. He felt like he owed me the truth.

"It's mostly Grace startin' all the trouble and fightin' though," he said.

When I turned to look at Rebekah for verification, she was standin' off to herself not sayin' a word. She kept her head lowered to the ground makin' sure she wasn't lookin' me in the eyes. It was the sorta look folk get when they's scared or hidin' somethin'. I knowed Rebekah all my life. I always knowed her to be outgoin' and friendly. Not today though. Hannah was sittin' on the mattress in a full blown cryin' fit now. Didn't see no tears though. I noticed she didn't take her eyes off Rebekah the whole time I was there neither. Rebekah's hands was shakin' and wringin' on a piece of her dress 'til she had it all twisted up. Daryl was doin' all the talkin'. I thought that was strange cuz I knowed sure 'nuf if someone come to our cabin to offer up a complaint 'bout one of our kids and Annie was still with the livin', I wouldn't get a word in. No one would. Once she got to the truth and it wasn't none of our kids doin', she'd put their accusers in their place good and proper. All mothers got an instinct to protect their children. They's born with it.

When Daryl was done talkin', he told me to go ask the Nelsons and the Taylors. They'd say the same. I figured if he already knowed what the other two families was gonna say 'bout the twins then they must've already had words 'bout 'em. Well, I certainly wasn't wantin' to believe none of what he was sayin' or anythin' the Nelsons or the Taylors had to offer up. Grace and Jacob was born behind the veil. They's God's children. But so was the others. Somethin' was mighty wrong. I could feel it deep down inside. I just didn't know what it was yet. I could see I wasn't gettin' nowheres with Daryl. I figured Rebekah was a lost cause the way she done twisted her dress up in the front almost to her knees now. I left more confused than 'fore I came. More questions than answers was swirlin' 'round in my head. I had 'lot of thinkin' to do so I headed back home.

When I got back to the cabin, I asked the twins 'bout it 'gain. They still didn't have nothin' to say. In my mind I was thinkin' they figured not sayin' nothin' don't mean they's lyin'. It just means you ain't tellin' the whole story. I had to laugh inside myself how that one come back to kick me in the behind. I sure as heck didn't know what I was gonna do. I promised to never raise a hand or belt to any of my children ever 'gain and I's a man of my word. I told 'em real serious like I was gonna sleep on it tonight and give 'em my verdict in the mornin'. They just nodded their heads up and down at me while stayin' put on their mattress. Lookin' over at Samuel, he was already 'sleep but that didn't stop me from givin' him a quick peck on the cheek. He didn't even move when I done it. That boy sure 'nuf can sleep is what I was thinkin' to myself. I reckon he'll get his share of sleepless nights when he goes to havin' his own kids. I gave the twins a big hug and a peck on the cheek 'fore they went to closin' their eyes, too. They always said....

"Goodnight daddy. We love you."

Then, they'd look over to the side of me and say....

"Goodnight mama and Mae. We love you," 'fore closin' their eyes.

I was gonna miss those two little ones when they turned seven and went off to save the world. They sure 'nuf pull at my heartstrings. I guess I was gettin' old. I was growin' soft.

Sittin' in Annie's rockin' chair thinkin' to myself, I decided not to send 'em over to the other families cabins to play with the other Caulbearers for a time. I had some figurin' to do. Somethin' told me they wouldn't care none. More than likely they'd be happy 'bout my verdict. Havin' one 'nother to play with was 'nuf for both of 'em. Just then, the thought come to my mind maybe everythin' that's goin' on these days is happenin' for a reason and part of God's plan, 'specially when it come to the twins. When I turned to look over at 'em, they was sittin' up 'gain with their eyes wide open and bigger than life smiles on their faces. Even Jacob. When I told 'em my verdict, Grace went to lookin' at Jacob with one side of her mouth turned up just like her mama used to do. At the same time, he went to noddin' his head up and down at her. Maybe they knowed 'head of time what I was gonna say. Sure was hopin' they couldn't read minds. Just in case, I decided I better watch what I was thinkin' when I was 'round 'em from now on. I waited 'til they was sleepin' 'fore I got down on my knees and went to prayin' real hard for God to lead me down the right path in raisin' those two.

Later that night when I went to feed *It*, I was deep in thought 'bout the twins. When I got to the hole, I tossed my plate of possum in and turned to walk 'way not givin' a second thought to that demon down there. The three other men from the other families did the same. They always walked 'lot faster than I did bein' I was filled up with the Lord Jesus Christ and got no more room in me for the devil. After takin' just a few steps, I heard *It* callin' out to me.

"Calvin! Calvin!" *It* hollered after me.

I paid *It* no mind and just kept walkin'.

"Grace and Jacob are not from your God, Calvin!" *Its* voice echoed all up and down the tunnel. *"They are my children. And in their seventh year, they will set me free! That's why they are always fighting with the other children. Because the others belong to your God, Calvin. I have sent Grace and Jacob to destroy the others so that I may be freed to rid the world of your God's followers. They must be destroyed and Grace and Jacob are going to help me."*

Then, *Its* laughter filled the tunnel. The men from the other families I knowed for sure wasn't out of hearin' range. Trompin' back up to the edge of the hole I yelled back at *It* loud as I could hopin' the other three men heard me....

"YOU'S A LIAR! THEY'S GOD'S CHILDREN AND HE AIN'T GONNA TAKE TOO KINDLY 'BOUT WHAT YOU'S SAYIN'"

I turned back 'round with balled up fists swingin' at my sides. I was madder than all get out. Kickin' the ground with my foot, I went on to walkin' back to my cabin. I knowed the damage was already done. It didn't matter none to Joshua, Simon, and Daryl that they knowed the devil's a liar. *It* done planted the seed in their heads. Evil don't need to be watered every day to start growin' in a man's mind. I got to wonderin' why *It* all the time gotta be callin' out *my* name? Why don't *It* try one of the other men folk for a change? I thought maybe cuz I was *Its* biggest threat. Maybe not. Maybe cuz I got two Caulbearers 'stead of just one. Maybe not. Maybe cuz *It* figured I was the weakest. I hoped not.

After I put the lock on the trapdoor, I sat for a good while starin' at my two babies layin' sleepin' so innocent. I knowed their souls was good and filled up with God. There's no way they's from the devil. No way! I knowed I'd fight to the death to protect 'em. I owed God and Annie that much and more. I fell 'sleep rockin' back and forth in that ol' rockin' chair Annie used to sit in singin' lullabyes to 'em. 'Specially Jacob cuz he was all the time fussin'. Annie didn't mind. She loved that little guy when nobody else did, includin' me I's 'shamed to say.

I don't know how long I was sittin' there sleepin' when all of a sudden I was bein' carried down into the tunnel. I think I was flyin'. I was dreamin' but I knowed it was for real, too. Annie and Mae was 'head of me wavin'

126

their hands to follow 'em. So I did. I'd follow my Annie to the ends of the earth if she wanted me to. I don't really think I had a choice this time though. They both had real worried looks on their faces so I knowed they wasn't jokin' 'round none. I heard voices when we got closer to the hole. They was gettin' louder and louder the closer I got. Annie put her finger to her lips to shush me. Then, her and Mae disappeared. I wondered why she had to keep disappearin' like that. Couldn't she stay long 'nuf for me to just talk to her 'while? Reckon I knowed the answer to that.

When I looked down, I couldn't believe what I seen. At the edge of the hole where Satan was chained up at the bottom stood Matthew Nelson, Esau Taylor, and Hannah Anderson. They was talkin' in a different language and lookin' real different. I don't know how I knowed who they was but I did. They didn't look nothin' like children. They looked more like child demons. Their faces looked mean and their eyes was glowin' red. They had horns on their heads and long tails. Their hands had long sharp claws stickin' outta the ends of 'em. Their skin was scaled, grey, and peelin'. Satan was tellin' 'em they had to kill Grace and Jacob. All three of 'em was noddin' their heads up and down. When they dropped to their knees, I seen the devil's two evil red eyes come flyin' right up to the edge of that hole. I figured they was either under *Its* spell or they was worshippin' *It*. The answer come to me when they went to foldin' their hands like they was prayin' and called *It* *"Father."* They was agreein' with everythin' *It* was sayin' includin' the part 'bout killin' my two babies. Even in my dream, the smell was so bad I wanted to puke. Probably cuz

127

they's all rotten inside. Fire was shootin' up through the hole and twirlin' 'round 'em from their feet to their heads. It didn't even burn 'em none. They just laughed a laugh that started out low soundin' but got louder and shriller the longer it went on. The thought come to me they ain't really children. Matthew, Esau, and Hannah was Satan's disciples sent to the Nelsons, Taylors, and Andersons to pose as God's children so they could kill Grace and Jacob. *It* knowed when the twins was gone there'd be nothin' or no one left to stop *It* from breakin' loose and wipin' out everyone on earth who followed God. The Caulbearer that's been holdin' it down for the last hundred years was growin' weaker and the devil was gettin' stronger with the help of *Its* disciples.

I don't know if that scared me 'wake or what but the next thing I knowed I was back up in the cabin sittin' frozed up in that ol' rockin' chair with sweat drippin' down my face and eyes wide open big as saucers. When I looked over at little Grace and Jacob, they was sittin' up on their mattress starin' at me like they knowed what I just seen. Both of 'em come over to me and crawled up on my lap. None of us said nothin'. We all knowed we had a fight to end all fights comin' up on us. That's when a cup come floatin' through the air and stopped midair in front of us. The twins both started gigglin'. I don't know which one did it but if I was a bettin' man I'd sure 'nuf put everythin' I owned on Jacob.

That night I slept in the middle of the twins holdin' onto 'em tighter than I ever done 'fore. Made sure my firearm was in arm's reach, too. Ain't nobody gonna hurt my babies is what I was thinkin'. God put 'em in my care when *He* took my Annie and I ain't gonna never let *Him* down 'gain....or her. Then, takin' a big swallow I mumbled real quiet like....

"The devil be damned."

The twins fell right back to sleep like they ain't gotta care or worry in the world. Me? I didn't sleep none after that cuz I knowed I got 'lot of thinkin' to do. It was up to me to keep Grace and Jacob safe no matter what the cost. I was thinkin' more and more that's my purpose. Even if I had to give my own life so they could live long 'nuf to do their job, I was sure 'nuf ready to make whatever sacrifice God had planned for me. I'd already lost my Annie and little Mae. Anythin' else I figured would be hard but I'd already been through it once so I could do it 'gain....if I had to. Bobby and Emma was both married with families of their own now. Samuel, Grace, and Jacob's the only ones left to me. I knowed the day was comin' when Grace and Jacob's gonna be doin' what they was born to do. No doubt in my mind Bobby would take his brother Samuel in 'til he was of marryin' age if I ain't 'round no more. Once I was gone, Bobby and his family's gonna be movin' into my cabin at the top of the Sander's land. That'd mean when Samuel took a wife, he could move into Bobby's ol' cabin. Ain't nobody gonna have to worry 'bout buildin' him a cabin next spring then. Seemed to me everythin' was worked out. I knowed better than to think like that though cuz just as soon as I did, somethin's gonna sure 'nuf happen to prove me wrong.

The twins was still sleepin' when mornin' come up on us. I was woke by a loud bangin' at the front door. Samuel was already out huntin'. I got up real quiet so I wouldn't wake Grace and Jacob. When I looked out the window, Joshua Nelson, Simon Taylor, and Daryl Anderson was standin' outside. They was carryin' firearms and lookin' madder than hornets in a bee's nest. I went tip toein' over to the twins and woke 'em. I told 'em to get up 'gainst the wall behind the door and don't move or say nothin'. After I tucked my firearm into the back of my pants, I opened the door just a peek and real slow like. I was mindful to keep a hand readied to grab my firearm if I needed to. Simon Taylor stepped up and jammed his firearm through the crack in the door 'fore I had a mind to slam it shut. With his firearm aimed right at my head, he shouted at me....

"Hand over Grace and Jacob and we'll let you and Samuel be!"

"What's the nature of your business?" I asked slippin' my right hand behind my back and grabbin' hold of my loaded firearm.

"We heard the devil tellin' you last night while we was walkin' 'way from feedin' *It*, Grace and Jacob belong to *It* so we come to throw 'em in the hole with their master."

Then, Joshua's voice spoke up....

"Matthew, Esau, and Hannah all three said Grace and Jacob's all the time pickin' fights with 'em. They's tryin' to kill our children for the devil!"

I knowed there ain't no reasonin' with 'em and no tellin' 'em the opposite of what they's sayin' is the truth. Just as I was 'bout to pull my gun on 'em and come out shootin', I heard a man's voice behind the three of 'em say....

"Joshua, Simon, Daryl kindly drop your firearms *NOW!* Then back 'way nice and slow! Me and my brother is standin' behind you with firearms aimed at your heads and we ain't 'fraid to use 'em. We'd drop the three of you 'fore you even gotta chance to turn 'round so if you don't want your children growin' up without no daddy, you better do as we say!"

It was Bobby and Samuel. I ain't never been so glad to see anyone in my whole life. Joshua, Simon, and Daryl done what they was told. They didn't have no choice really 'less they wanted to die. Samuel run up and picked their firearms off the ground and emptied 'em. When that was done, Bobby walked 'round to face 'em. With his firearm still aimed at their heads, he told 'em....

"Take off runnin' to your cabins and don't never come back on the Sanders land 'gain or more of the same's gonna be waitin' for you."

Samuel puffed his chest out and threatened....

"If you do come back, we'll be draggin' your bodies back to your wives and children to bury."

All three of 'em turned tail and run off fast as their feet could carry 'em. I was proud of my boys. I gave 'em both a big hug and a slap on the back. That's when it come to me....they ain't boys no more. They's growed men.

Bobby and Samuel come in the cabin. I told 'em 'bout how Grace was all the time comin' home with cuts and bruises when her and Jacob come back from playin' with the other Caulbearers from the other families. I told 'em how their mama and Mae come to me in a dream last night and showed me what's really goin' on.

"Those other kids ain't no Caulbearers," I said, "They's false prophets sent from the devil to kill Grace and Jacob!"

That's when Bobby reached over the table and grabbed hold of the Sander's Bible. He looked me square in the eyes and told me to swear on God's book that I ain't been drinkin' 'gain. I reckon I deserved that so I sweared to God I ain't touched a drop of liquor since that night I went to beatin' him and Jacob. He asked me to swear what I just told him was the truth 'bout seein' his mama and Mae in a dream. I put my hand down on that Bible and sweared every word I was tellin' him was the truth so help me God! That was good 'nuf for Bobby then. Samuel, too. They knowed no one in their right mind up here in these mountains is gonna go to swearin' on God's book and lie. Bobby said he wanted me, Samuel, and the twins to come stay with him and his family in their cabin 'til we could figure somethin' out. I had to agree. 'Least 'til I got some kind of plan to protect Grace and Jacob. Hallelujah! Praise the Lord! Amen!

Chapter 10

Isaiah 58:7 *Is it not to deal thy bread to the hungry, and that thou bring the poor that are cast out to thy house? When thou seest the naked, that thou cover him; and that thou hide not thyself from thine own flesh?*

Bobby and his wife, 'Lizabeth, 'long with their three children, opened their home to us. I was grateful. Livin' quarters was cramped but I had to do what I had to do to keep the twins protected. They got two girls, Annabelle and Adeline. Annabelle, she's three years old. Adeline, she's two. 'Lizabeth just birthed their third child a few months ago, a son named Abraham. Just like the twins prophesied. Bobby couldn't have picked a better woman to be his wife and mother to his children. She got a real pretty smile and a big heart. I seen how her and Bobby was all the time lookin' at each other and talkin' 'bout just 'bout everythin' there was to talk 'bout, like me and Annie used to do. Every now and 'gain he'd come up behind her and wrap his arms 'round her to give her a big kiss on the back of her neck, just like I used to do with Annie. Watchin' 'em made me miss my Annie even more but I knowed there ain't nothin' I could do 'bout that so I turned my thinkin' to keepin' the twins safe. Since the devil knowed 'bout 'em bein' here, that was becomin' a full time job anyways.

'Lizabeth welcomed us with open arms. She cooked up a big pot of squirrel stew our first night with 'em. 'Fore we went to eatin', Bobby said a prayer over everyone sittin' at the dinner table and thanked God for puttin' food on our plates.

"Hallelujah! Praise the Lord! Amen!" we all shouted loud and clear at the end.

'Lizabeth sure 'nuf was a good cook. She said I was too skinny so she gave me a little more than everyone else. I reckon since Annie left, my appetite went with her. I appreciated the kindness but I hoped we wasn't makin' God mad. I said a prayer to *Him* that night explainin' it was just kindness and not gluttony. I ate it all. Wasn't nothin' left over to scrape into the garbage. I reckon I forgot how much I missed Annie's cookin'....Emma's, too. The women folk up in these mountains learn from their mamas early on how to cook and make just 'nuf food to go 'round to feed their family without havin' to throw none out.

After we was all done eatin', me, Bobby, and Samuel went outside to talk over what we was gonna do 'bout the other three families wantin' to throw Grace and Jacob down into the hole with the devil. It was the man of each household got the job of makin' sure his wife and children was fed and safe. But it was the head of each family who gotta protect all the households bearin' his family name. Everybody with the last name Sanders was my responsibility. After me, it'll be Bobby's job. Joshua's headin' up all the Nelsons now but his son, Steven, will follow in his footsteps. Simon's still takin' care of the Taylors. His oldest son, Jeremiah, is gonna be next in line when Simon goes to heaven. After that, since Esau's outta the runnin' bein' he belongs to Satan, I reckon Simon's next oldest son Carl and his oldest male offspring is gonna have to take over. Last come Annie's brother, Daryl, makin' sure everythin's right with the Andersons. Pickin' up after him is his son, Zachary. Only problem with that is he's only thirteen. Our great great great great granddaddies passed the law the head of a family had to be 'least sixteen. I reckon if it comes down to it and Daryl passes 'fore Zachary turns sixteen, his brother, Thomas, is gonna have to take over 'til he comes of age. It's always been the four heads of the families makin' the decisions together for the entire community. I reckon that's what our ancestors called self governin'. That's how it was 'fore now anyways. Now, cuz of Satan, we been split 'part. I wondered what our daddies already went to heaven was sayin' up there 'bout us. Probably shakin' their heads back and forth not knowin' what to make of us. Me, Joshua, Simon, and Daryl all live in the top cabin on our family name's land. That's just a favor God gave us for all the responsibility that goes 'long with takin' over after *He* done took our daddies to heaven. Since the Sanders was standin' 'lone now, I thought Bobby and Samuel was growed 'nuf to take up with me in decidin' what to do. Samuel's the youngest of us men but he sure 'nuf stood by his brother's side and aimed his firearm at those men's heads when they come to take the twins. They didn't stand a chance 'gainst my two boys. They made me proud. I just hope those three men got good 'nuf sense not to come back. I don't like fightin' and I sure 'nuf ain't a killin' man but when it comes to my family, I'll do what I gotta do to protect 'em. If that means killin', then so be it. I knowed huntin' ain't murder. 'Long as we's doin' it to put food on the table. Sendin' mama and daddy to heaven ain't murder. It's what's been handed down to us from generation to generation by God. Ain't never heard it was a sin 'gainst God to kill someone who was out to murder you or your family neither. That's just plain survival.

The three of us decided one of us had to stay 'wake all night. We went to splittin' the day into three shifts. Mornin', evenin', and night. Bein' that Bobby's a family man, he took the mornin' shift. That way he could get up in the mornin' with his wife and kids and go to bed at the same time, too. Bein' I's an ol' man, I took the evenin' shift. Samuel, bein' the youngest and more than likely got the most energy, took the night shift. We figured he'd be better at stayin' 'wake all night more than us. He agreed. We got 'nuf firearms and ammunition to fight if we's forced into a battle. I sure 'nuf hope it don't come to that. Never had to use firearms for nothin' but huntin'....'til now.

Next we got to talkin' 'bout feedin' the beast.

"That's my job," I spoke up, "I'll keep on doin' it. They's not wantin' to kill me nohows. They's out to kill my babies. 'Sides, I cain't let *It* think I's weak."

So we all agreed to that. Then the question come up whether we's still goin' to the monthly meetin's. Bobby said him and his family would go to find out what the other families is up to. He said they'd be safe. Just in case though, he'd carry a firearm in the back of his pants so nobody could see it. He'd wear a jacket over his shirt to cover it up. We all figured none of 'em was gonna be so stupid to start shootin' in the lodge where all the women and babies was at one time. Spit shakin' hands on it, we all agreed. Spit shakin' hands up here in the mountains was one step 'way from bein' as good as swearin' on the Bible. A man's handshake was as good as his word and we ain't never been lyin' folk.   Grace and Jacob sure 'nuf liked playin' with Annabelle and Adeline. They got 'long real good with 'em. Ain't never no fightin', punchin', hollerin', or beatin' on one 'nother. Alls I heard was 'lot of laughin'. 'Lizabeth had an old wash tub she throwed 'em all in together 'fore bed once a week. On those nights, Bobby, Samuel, and me walked up the mountain to the lodge water pump to fill six big buckets with water to throw in the wash tub for 'em. It was cold but they liked it anyways. When the kids was all done splashin 'round in the water and playin', I couldn't have been prouder of Bobby gettin' down on his knees, rollin' up his sleeves and helpin' 'Lizabeth scrub 'em all down. Samuel went to pullin' his weight 'round the cabin, too. He went to choppin' wood for cookin' and stayin' warm. He even took a broom and started into sweepin' the floor with it. I knowed Annie was lookin' down on 'em just as proud as can be.

"They done growed into men on us," I'd always tell her when I sat under the maple tree talkin' to her now and 'gain.

I'd fill her in on everythin' happenin' with us since she left. I knowed she liked that a whole lot. After the baths and right 'fore bedtime, everyone gathered 'round me so I could tell 'em a story 'bout little Mae and Annie. Annabelle and Adeline never got to know their gramma but I know they would've loved her. Grace and Jacob ain't never gonna forget her. Bobby, Emma, and Samuel neither. I knowed that sure 'nuf. Not in a million years. No sir! Me neither.

After everyone was sleepin' and settled' down for the night, I liked to sit outside on the front porch all 'lone and think 'bout Annie and Mae 'fore it was time to go down into the tunnel to feed the beast. Sometimes, when I closed my eyes, I could smell my Annie's skin and hair. She always smelled real nice. When she was with the livin', more than one time, I'd wake up in the mornin' with my nose buried deep in her hair. Funny the things that make up memories. I'd of never knowed when she was 'live that'd be one of my favorite remembrances 'bout her. So many little things that I didn't pay no mind to back then that'd bring a tear or two to my eyes now. I never told no one I kept hid in my pant's pocket a handkerchief Annie used to carry 'round tucked into the sleeve of her dress. 'Fore we put her in the grave, I sneaked it outta her sleeve and put it in my pocket. I was glad Emma put it back in there when she was done bathin' and dressin' her. I carry it everywheres with me. Even when I's sleepin' so I can smell on it now and 'gain when no ones lookin'. Sure 'nuf got her smell on it. Sometimes I dream she's layin' next to me and when I wake up I catch myself rubbin' my nose into that handkerchief like I used to do her hair 'fore she passed into heaven.

That night, when it was time to feed the beast, I grabbed up a couple squirrels and a rabbit the boys caught earlier that day and made my way through the tunnel with a firearm tucked into the back of my pants. Never thought the day would come when I'd have cause to be more 'fraid of my neighbors than the devil. When I got to the hole, I stood there facin' the other three men. They nodded their heads at me and I nodded back. We all throwed our plates into the devil's pit at the same time. This time when we walked 'way, no one turned 'round. We all went to backin' out nice and slow so we was all facin' each other 'til we couldn't see one 'nother no more. Satan took to laughin' louder than I ever heard *It* laugh. *It* knowed what *It* done. This hatin' and fightin' goin' on between neighbors and friends was *Its* fault. *It* was growin' stronger with every passin' day. I could feel it in my bones soon 'nuf the Caulbearer that's been holdin' *It* down for the last hundred years ain't gonna be able to hold *It* down no more. That's when Grace and Jacob gotta be ready to take over. I reckon that's why the good Lord Jesus Christ had two babies born behind the veil this time 'round. The other ones born after 'em is false Caulbearers. They belong to the devil. Not God. I done laid witness to what they was with my own eyes. Imposters!

When I got back up top, I seen 'Lizabeth went and laid two mattresses down for us. She must've sent Bobby and Samuel to my cabin to fetch 'em. One was for the twins and me. The other one was for Samuel. I felt better sleepin' between Grace and Jacob. That way no one could hurt 'em on 'count of I was holdin' onto 'em real tight. The twins both must've woke and was sittin' up waitin' for me when I got back. I laid down with 'em and they curled up next to me. Grace looked up at me with her deep blue eyes and said....

"Do not worry, daddy. I will protect you and Jacob."

141

I gave 'em both a hug and a peck on the cheek.

"That makes me feel a whole lot better, honey," I whispered with my eyes filled up with tears, "I love you, Grace. I love you, Jacob."

"We love you too, daddy," they said together.

Then, lookin' up 'bove us they whispered….

"Goodnight mama. Goodnight Mae. We love you."

I looked over at Samuel. He was lookin' out the front window with his firearm in hand. He growed up on me, I thought. Time goes by real fast. I remember teachin' him and Bobby how to hunt. I was real proud of 'em both. They was always good boys and they's even better men. Both of 'em was tall as me already. Maybe taller. Tall and skinny they was. Dark brown curly hair with the same color eyes I got. A deep dimple on the right side of both their cheeks. They was both handsome men if I say so myself. After prayin' to the Lord, I tucked my babies one under each arm nice and tight. It made me sad to think I ain't gonna be doin' that much longer. Wasn't long we was all sleepin'.

After Joshua, Simon, and Daryl come to my cabin to take the twins and we moved in with Bobby and 'Lizabeth for 'while, everythin' went on pretty much the same every day. Every mornin', Bobby jumped up and told Samuel to get some sleep. Samuel would lay down on his mattress on the floor and he'd be sleepin' 'fore his head hit the pillow. 'Lizabeth always cooked everyone a good breakfast. After all the children got done eatin', she'd take 'em outside to play 'round the cabin so none of 'em would go to wakin' Samuel. She was real considerate that way. I'd pick up my firearm from the floor layin' at my head where the twins and me was sleepin' and walk outside to go huntin' for that night's dinner. 'Fore walkin' off into the trees, I'd wave back at Bobby who went to sittin' on the front porch outside on a wood chair with his firearm readied to shoot if he had to. I knowed whatever he aimed at he'd hit. Samuel, too.

When it was time for my evenin' watch, I'd eat my dinner out on the porch so I could spot anyone who was comin' our way. Just like Bobby done on his shift in the mornin'. Couldn't see much outside at night so Samuel always took a seat inside at the front window. Just like the sun rised up every mornin', set every evenin', and gave way for the moon and stars every night, there we'd be sittin' to protect our families and lay witness to all of God's glory all 'round us.

The sun shined bright in the summertime and the grass was a real pretty dark green. Fall was comin' 'round in a few more months. That's when it'd get chilly and the grass would go to turnin' a yellow brown. When the kids was younger they all loved fall cuz the tree leaves turned all different pretty colors. When they started droppin' to the ground, Annie taught 'em how to sweep 'em up into a real big pile. They had 'lot of fun jumpin' over and over 'gain into that pile of leaves. I can still hear 'em squealin' and laughin'. Annie, too.

Bobby was eighteen now. Emma turned sixteen. Samuel celebrated his fourteenth year on this earth. Mae would've been twelve. The twins was turnin' six in a few more months. I went to rememberin' back to the day when

143

Bobby and Samuel was boys. They loved the summer even more than the fall cuz it was warm and the sun was out. After their chores was done, they'd go off by themselves to a lake they come 'cross one day high up in the mountains. They'd strip down to their underwears and go swimmin' and splashin' round in it without a care in the world. It was like life should be for boys and girls 'fore they growed into men and women. Annie always made sure her children stayed young for as long as it took 'em to grow up. She never rushed 'em none. If it was up to her, they'd of stayed young longer than any other kid in these mountains. Oh, they had their chores like all the other children but they had a mama who liked to play, dance, and sing with 'em no matter what the weather was like or how ol' they was gettin' to be.

Grace's skin always got darker in the summer. Poor little Jacob was so pale skinned, he'd just burn. God made 'em different in looks but they both got good hearts. Grace, she's the louder, more playful one. Jacob, he's the quiet, more serious one. The older he got, the quieter he got. Sometimes I'd forget he was even 'round. He don't seem to care none if he got no friends. He only needs his sister, Grace. She's the same way. When we was forcin' 'em to go play with those devil children, they'd go to pickin' on Jacob and she'd fight 'em like a mama bear. I could tell she didn't mind none though. She was 'lot like her mama in that way. She loved her brother and he loved his sister. Two peas in a pod is what I was thinkin'. I's glad they's close. I figured they got no choice bein' they was in such

144

close quarters together all that time they was growin' inside their mama's belly waitin' to be born.

Every day when I got back with dinner, Bobby would still be sittin' on that chair outside the cabin firearm in hand. The boys and me come up with a holler we'd yell out when we was comin' up to the house from outta the trees so none of us was shot by mistake. I'd give the holler and Bobby hollered it back to let me know it was okay to come on out. When I'd ask him how the day went, he said the same thing everytime....

"'Sides the kids playin' and havin' a good time, it's been a quiet day."

When dinner was ready, I'd take over watch from Bobby. In the meantime, I'd go to playin' with the twins and Bobby's children. They all got 'long fine. Nobody picked on Jacob. Grace never fightin' with not one of 'em. 'Fore dinner, Grace would come to crawlin' up on my lap.

"Daddy," she'd ask me, "Can we go see mama and Mae up on the hill?"

"We sure 'nuf can, darlin'," I'd say back, "For just a little bit though cuz dinner's gonna be ready soon and 'Lizabeth's gonna be ringin' the dinner bell. Don't wanna be disrespectful."

I'd stoop down to Jacob's level and ask him if he wanted to go with us. He'd go to noddin' his head up and down so I'd grab 'hold of both their little hands and we'd all walk to where Annie and Mae was buried. Each of 'em went to pickin' two pretty wildflowers on the way. When we reached the maple tree where they was laid to rest, they'd put the flowers next to the wood crosses I made for 'em. I'd say a nice prayer and when I was done, we'd all holler loud as we could,

"Hallelujah! Praise the Lord! Amen!"

One time, not so long ago, after we got done puttin' flowers on Annie and Mae's graves and sayin' a prayer, all of a sudden Jacob took to runnin' off into the trees. Grace and me went runnin' after him. When he got to where he was goin' deep into the trees, he stopped real quick and held his hand out to stop us from comin' any closer. Lookin' back at us over his shoulder, he took his finger and put it to his lips to shush us like Annie done to me that time I was flyin' in the tunnels. I didn't know what the little guy was up to. He never talked much. Grace usually done the talkin' for him. He most of the time did 'lot of noddin' of the head and pointin' of the fingers. Grace pulled me next to her while holdin' on tight to my hand. I think it was her job to hold me back. Jacob took three more steps forward then got down on his knees. He was kneelin' over somethin' that I couldn't quite make out. When Jacob looked back at Grace, she said to me....

"Daddy, stay here. Do not worry. We are okay."

I nodded my head okay but I had my firearm aimed and ready to shoot if I had to. When Grace reached Jacob, she kneeled down next to him. Layin' their hands on somethin' in front of 'em on the ground, neither one said a word. Then I seen it's eyes. They was ice blue. It must've got hurt runnin' or bein' chased by 'nother animal or man. It was a wolf. Without no warnin' whatsoever, it jumped up from layin' on the ground and took off runnin' into the trees. The twins healed it.

146

"As I live and breathe," is what I was thinkin' to myself.

When they come back over by me, each of 'em took hold of one of my hands. Without sayin' a word, we walked back to the cabin. I could hear 'Lizabeth ringin' the dinner bell in the distance. Under my breath, I was sayin'....

"Hallelujah. Praise the Lord. Amen."

Chapter 11

Isaiah 11:6 *The wolf shall dwell with the lamb, and the leopard shall lie down with the young goat, and the calf and the lion and the fattened calf together; and a little child shall lead them.*

We'd been stayin' at Bobby's cabin for 'while now. Winter was here and the twins turned six a few months back in the fall. I feel real sad when I think 'bout havin' just one more year with 'em. Samuel's fourteen now. I hope he ain't shunned at the choosin' a mate meetin's cuz of him bein' my son and the twins brother. He said he don't care. He says his daddy and little brother and sister mean more to him than marryin' anytime soon. I don't know how I got so lucky when it come to children. I's sure their mama had more to do with the way they turned out than me. Annie sure 'nuf loved 'em all. I think Annie growed up still hangin' onto some of the child in her the way she played games with 'em inside and outside the cabin even when the weather wasn't fittin'. She all the time told me I should get outside with 'em and run in the rain, have a snowball fight, jump in a pile of leaves, or go swimmin'. I could hear her soft, sweet voice now whisperin' in my ear in the middle of the night when it was dark outside and all the kids was sleepin'....

"*I love you, Cal. Now Calvin, you need to stop bein' so serious all the time. Live while you still got livin' in you. Play with the children now while they's still with us.*

Someday they'll have their own families and be gone from us."

Then she'd snuggle up closer to me and whisper,

"C'mon Cal. Let's try to make 'nother baby."

I gotta laugh cuz I never turned that offer down. Sex in the mountains was for makin' babies only and that's exactly what we'd set out to do. I got lots of good remembrances of Annie but that's one of my favorites. Always brings a smile to my face.

Craziest thing happened after Grace and Jacob healed that wild wolf last summer. He come back. We all the time seen him hangin' 'round at the edge of the woods. I know how crazy this sounds but Grace told me God sent him to protect us. I believed her. I've seen stranger things happen since my Annie and Mae went to heaven. Jacob's all the time goin' outside to lay some meat from his dinner plate down for him when there's not too much snow on the ground. He just leaves it out there and by mornin' it's gone. I told Jacob he might be feedin' other wild animals since we don't never see him come up and eat the food. When I said that, Jacob whispered somethin' in Grace's ear.

She said, "Jacob is sure the wolf is the one eating the food. We named him Caleb, daddy."

All the while she was talkin', Jacob was noddin' his head up and down all serious like. Anyways, sometimes we spot him, 'specially at night, cuz his ice blue eyes shine in the dark. The rest of him is like a silver gray. He's a real handsome lookin' animal. Lot bigger than most wolves. Don't never see other wolves with him so I figure he's a loner. Maybe he got into a fight with the head wolf the day the twins went to healin' him and he was kicked outta the pack. Don't see much of nothin' when the snow is piled up high though. It'll sure 'nuf blind you if you look at it too long in the daylight. I 'magine he finds a warm place to stay at night.

I been keepin' a clear path to the outhouse for everyone. I figure it's the least I can do for Bobby and 'Lizabeth's hospitality. We don't have to stand watch in the winter like we did in the summer. I figure anyone crazy 'nuf to come try to kill us in this snow's gonna die 'fore they get to the front door. I locked Bobby's trapdoor up good and tight like I did mine so no one can get to us that way neither. Well, 'least no human can anyways. Winters are usually quiet up here in the mountains. Like I said, we use the tunnels more for the lodge meetin's or if anybody got some kind of emergency. Nobody knowed 'bout the twins healin' powers so I doubt we get an invite to emergencies. They'd just say it was the devil's work anyways.

Emma come to visit us every now and 'gain. She brought over some hot soup she made just for us the other day. She knows how much I love that soup. Her mama taught her how to make it special. She stayed 'while and played with the twins. She told me she don't believe a word of what the others are sayin' 'bout 'em. Emma's got two sons. Elijah's the oldest. Her baby boy, Gabriel, is still hangin' onto the breast so she was holdin' him the whole time they was here. Nice lookin' boys.

"My grandsons," is what I was thinkin' to myself.

Just like Bobby's children Annabelle, Adeline, and Abraham. When this feudin' gets over maybe I can go visit 'em on occasion. Emma told me I's welcome to come visit whenever I take a likin'. But I knowed better. She was tryin' to make me feel good is all. Since her husband, Steven, is a Nelson, she is too now....and their children. Steven is Joshua's son. His only son. Joshua's the head of the Nelson family. Steven's next in line. Him bein' the oldest son means whatever side his daddy's on is the side he's on. Wouldn't expect anythin' less from him. He's just respectin' his daddy and mountain law is all. Cain't argue none with that. Same with my boys.

One night on my way to feed the devil, I got to thinkin' how little time I got left with Grace and Jacob. They was turnin' seven next fall. Not even a year 'way. Time was closin' up on us fast. I don't know for sure what they's gonna do to keep the devil chained up for a hundred more years. They never shared that information with me. I don't reckon they feel I can take knowin'. They's most likely right 'bout that.

When I got to the hole, the beast was yellin' all kinds of swear words at us. Joshua, Simon, and Daryl was standin' there shufflin' their feet with looks on their faces actin' like I was holdin' 'em up. I wasn't late. I ain't never late. I got my daddy's pocket watch remindin' me of the time. After they threw their plates down into the hole, I pulled my daddy's timepiece outta my pocket, stretched my arms up real high and yawned real big, then went to tappin' my foot to the ground showin' 'em we still had a couple minutes to go. At the same second in time the big hand come 'round and joined the little hand on the top number, I throwed mine in just like my daddy taught me. I wanted the devil and the other family heads to know I was doin' what I had to do on my time….not theirs. I wasn't standin' 'lone nohows. I was filled up with the Lord. Ain't got no room in me for nothin' evil….beast or man. When they went to backin' out 'way from me, they moved real slow and careful keepin' their eyes on me the whole time. For a special touch, I spit down into the hole where Satan was eatin' and laughed 'fore I started backin' 'way, too. All the time, I kept my eyes fixed on the three of 'em. When the devil went to spewing out words 'bout my Grace and Jacob belongin' to *It* 'gain, I got so mad I stomped back up to the edge of that hole and started singin' down into it as loud as I could….

"Mine eyes have seen the glory of the comin' of the Lord; He is tramplin' out the vintage where the grapes of wrath are stored; He hath loosed the fateful lightnin' of his terrible swift sword; His truth is marchin' on. Glory, glory Hallelujah! Glory, glory Hallelujah! Glory, glory Hallelujah! His truth is marchin' on."

I knowed Joshua, Simon, and Daryl could hear my voice echoin' through the tunnel but I didn't care none at all. No sir! Not none at all! Truth was, I wanted 'em to hear it. So they knowed I ain't one bit scared of the devil and Grace and Jacob don't belong to *It*. When I got done singin', I bent over that demon hole and spit the biggest spit I could muster up. Then, I shook my fist at that red eyed demon and told *It*....

153

"I's faithful only to the Lord Jesus Christ, Amen! Grace and Jacob ain't belongin' to you," I yelled down at *It,* "They's God's children and they's comin' to get you real soon! Hallelujah! Praise the Lord! Amen!"

When I said that, Satan got real quiet. Didn't hear *It* say nothin' after that so I walked on back to the cabin real cocky and slow like. Didn't even go to backin' out this time. Matter of fact, I mustered up some whistlin' on the way. I might've been shakin' on the inside but I didn't show no fear on the outside. Truth be told, I was 'bout near ready to crap my pants.

When I got back to the cabin, I decided I was gonna tell Bobby come mornin' me and the twins was goin' back to our cabin to stay. If Samuel wanted to keep livin' with Bobby that'd be alright by me. He already gave 'lot of himself. I figure if he separates from me and the twins, one of the girls might take him for a husband. I'll leave it up to Samuel though. He's sittin' at the window with his firearm layin' 'cross his lap now. I told him to go 'head and lay down to sleep. I knowed by what went on down in the tunnel tonight, Joshua, Simon, and Daryl ain't gonna be messin' with us 'gain no time soon. Too much snow out for anyone to be crazy 'nuf to come our way tonight anyways. So Samuel laid his firearm down next to his head so he could grab it real quick if he had to and laid down on his mattress. Everyone slept good but me. I took to sleepin' with one eye open these days. 'Sides, I had 'lot of thinkin' to do cuz there's lots of things to talk 'bout come mornin'. Gave all my children a hug and a peck on the cheek. Even Bobby, 'Lizabeth, and Samuel. God don't put no age limit on love far as I know. After makin' sure my firearm was where it needed to be, I squeezed myself between the twins and held 'em in my arms real close. Grace and Jacob was both 'wake. They took to waitin' for me every now and then to come back from feedin' the beast. Grace, she smiled up at me. Jacob, he had what looked like somethin' could turn into a smile if he wanted it to. I hugged 'em both extra hard 'fore closin' my eyes.

The next mornin', 'Lizabeth was up early as usual. She was a good woman. Always tryin' to be quiet so's not to wake any of us. When we was all sittin' 'round the table eatin' breakfast, I told Bobby me and the twins was movin' back to our cabin. I brought it up to Samuel 'bout givin' him a choice of where he goes. Samuel spoke right up and said he's comin' with me and the twins. I was glad he chose us but I wanted him to have a choice since what we do reflects back on him and might ruin any chance he's got of takin' a wife. When I thanked Bobby and 'Lizabeth for their hospitality and protection, Bobby tried to talk me into stayin' longer. I told him if we ever needed to come back, we would.

"Sides," I teased, "if I stay much longer, 'Lizabeth's gonna have me rollin' 'round 'stead of walkin' the way she took to fattenin' me up."

She laughed when I said that. She knowed I was jokin'. Turnin' to Bobby, I said....

"Keep that trapdoor locked son. 'Least 'til we get all this mess settled once and for all. Shouldn't be too much longer I's guessin'. The twins is gonna be seven years old in under a year. 'Least that's when we been told everythin's goin' down."

Everybody gave everybody kisses and hugs. You'd of thought we was never gonna see each other 'gain. When I thought that, I went 'round and passed out extra hugs and kisses to Bobby and his family. I don't care 'bout him bein' eighteen and a full growed man. He's still my son....my oldest son....and ain't nobody or nothin' gonna ever change that! I knowed the twins was gonna miss playin' with Annabelle, Adeline, and Abraham. Annie sure 'nuf was right. They got a job to do for God but they's children, too.

It didn't take us much time to get situated 'gain in our own cabin. Bobby and Samuel carried our mattresses back for me. Had to go through the tunnel on 'count of all the snow outside. I tried to help 'em but they'd have none of it. I's sure Bobby, 'Lizabeth, and the kids was gonna get used to havin' all that room to move 'round 'gain real fast. I'd miss 'Lizabeth's cookin', just like I missed Emma's when she mated up with Steven. I missed Annie's the most though. I reckon cuz I was just plain missin' my Annie all the time. Missed hearin' Mae laughin', too. I ain't seen 'em in a dream since they took me flyin' 'round in the tunnel to the hole where I laid witness to what the false Caulbearers was up to. In the springtime, when the snow's all melted 'way, I's gonna go sit up under that ol' maple tree where they's buried. The twins was all the time askin' to go up there anyways. It was too hard to go trudgin' through the snow in the wintertime but soon as it melted and the

156

weather warmed up some we'd sure 'nuf be goin' on up there.

That night, after leavin' to feed the beast from my own cabin 'stead of Bobby's, when I come walkin' up to the hole I seen how the other three heads wasn't makin' eye contact with me. Probably scared 'em all half to death last time. When we was boys, Joshua, Daryl, and me used to play together. If the truth be told, or even talked 'bout, I'd say they was the two friends who sneaked down into the tunnel with me when we was ten. I remember we'd go explorin', fishin', swimmin', and skippin' stones 'cross the lakes. This was beautiful country we lived in. God's country. We knowed our way 'round the mountain real good from when we was just younguns. We was blessed our ancestors was chose by God to serve *Him*. We all knowed that. Maybe everythin' does happen for a reason. I just pray at the end of all this, we can all be friends 'gain and live in peace like we used to 'fore the beast started actin' up and separatin' all of us. I had faith in the good Lord Jesus Christ. *He'd* sure 'nuf end up winnin' this battle. I figured the only reason *He* wouldn't is if that's the way *He* planned it. I ain't got no supernatural powers so I reckon I just have to wait like everybody else to see what God's got planned for the future of mankind. With the way we been actin' up here lately and the way the city folk been doin' more and more sinnin', maybe God's ready to wipe us all out and start all over. Maybe not. Anyways, 'fore backin' out to head back to my cabin, I throwed my plate of rabbit down into the hole. The other three did the same.

When I got back from feedin' the beast, I laid down on the mattress between Grace and Jacob. I was thankful the devil was quiet tonight. That didn't happen too much no more. Lookin' over at Samuel, he was all spread out on his mattress lookin' like he was havin' a real nice dream cuz he had a bigger than life smile on his face. I was glad he still had somethin' to smile 'bout. When I first got back, I leaned over and gave him a real soft peck on the cheek without him knowin' it. After squeezin' myself in good and tight between Grace and Jacob, I gave 'em both their hugs and pecks on the cheeks. I must've falled 'sleep fast.

Don't really know how long I was sleepin' when Annie come to me in a dream. Her and Mae was yellin' at me to wake up. They both got 'hold of me shakin' me. I was so happy to see 'em both 'gain, I fought wakin' up. I don't think I would've woke up if Annie didn't say she ain't never comin' back to see me if I don't wake up. I popped right up and opened my eyes real wide when she yelled at me....

"CALVIN! WAKE UP RIGHT NOW!"

Turnin' my head to the right and then the left, I seen the twins was gone. The cabin was cold. The fire was still burnin' in the hearth but when I looked at the front door, I could see it was open a crack. Maybe more. I thought maybe the twins went to the outhouse together but they knowed not to never go out there without a grownup with 'em. Samuel was sound 'sleep still smilin'. My heart started racin'. I didn't know what I was gonna do if I lost 'em somehow. God and Annie neither one gonna ever forgive me for that one. Heck, I'd never forgive myself.

They's God's children but Annie's their mama and far as I knowed the last time they called anybody daddy, they was sure 'nuf lookin' at me.

Pushin' myself up to a standin' position, then trippin' over my own feet, I runned to the front door throwin' it wide open. Just 'fore I went to runnin' 'round outside like a crazy person screamin' their names, I looked down. That's when I seen 'em right there in front of me in plain sight kneelin' down on the ground. They was tryin' to cover up that wild wolf they saved 'while back with a blanket. I was so happy they was 'live, I dropped to my knees right then and there and hollered out....

"Hallelujah! Praise the Lord! Amen!"

They both looked up at me soon as I started in shoutin' and jumpin' 'round like a crazy person. My face must've been all red from bein' all worked up cuz Grace said....

"Do not be mad, daddy. The wolf is cold. We heard him scratching at the front door. He is our friend. We have to let him inside so he can be warm."

I looked down at those big blue eyes of hers and whispered....

"Wolves don't live in cabins with folk. What if he tries to eat us when we's sleepin'?"

They both started laughin'. Even Jacob. Grace took me by the hand and led me back into the cabin. When Jacob come walkin' in, the wolf followed him. He led him over to the fire and motioned to him with his hand to lay down. That wolf did everythin' he wanted him to do. I ain't never in my life seen anythin' like it. I thought I better

159

wake Samuel and tell him we got a wolf livin' with us now so he don't get up and shoot him in the middle of the night. When I done that, Samuel darned near crapped his pants. Sure 'nuf wiped that smile off his face real quick. He got used to it though. We all did. I gotta say, I slept 'lot better havin' that wolf 'round. He took to layin' himself on the floor by the front door.

"Ain't no one gettin' in this cabin without him knowin' it," is what I was thinkin'.

That night, 'fore I fell back 'sleep, I gave the twins 'nother hug and peck on the cheek. Samuel, too. With one tucked tight 'neath each arm, I told 'em I loved 'em 'lot. I gave Jacob a little bit extra tight hug that night. He might not have much to say but when he does, he makes sure Grace tells me 'bout it. I had to laugh 'bout that. I love 'em both the same. I know Jacob and me had a rough start but I don't in no way love one more than the other. I just feel blessed to have 'em is all. Hallelujah! Praise the Lord! Amen!

Chapter 12

Mark 16:17-18 *These signs will accompany those who have believed: in My name they will cast out demons, they will speak with new tongues; they will pick up serpents, and if they drink any deadly poison, it will not hurt them; they will lay hands on the sick, and they will recover.*

That wolf, Caleb, stayed inside the cabin with us the rest of the winter. We all went to givin' him some of the food we put on our plates each night. I thought he'd take off come springtime when the snow was all melted. But he didn't. He followed the twins wherever they went. He didn't act like no wild animal neither. I caught him eyein' Samuel and me a couple times over the winter when we was all snowed in. I don't know if he was watchin' us to protect us or eat us. We all woke in one piece every mornin' so I figured he was protectin' us. I knowed sure 'nuf though if it come down between Samuel and me or the twins, the twins was gonna win heads up. And that was okay with me and Samuel. We knowed they had an important job to do. I reckon the twins was right when they said he was sent to protect us. None of the other families know we got Caleb.

"The less they know the better," is what I was thinkin'.

The Sanders ain't in much good standin' with the others these days nohows. Best to think twice 'fore addin' fuel to an already burnin' fire.

When springtime come 'round and all the snow melted, all of us Sanders men started buildin' Samuel a cabin next to Bobby. He'd be turnin' fifteen in the summer. Summer was just a few months 'way now. There's me, Samuel, Bobby, Karl, Tobias, and Ray workin' on it so it ain't gonna take us too long to get it done. We planned on havin' it ready by his fourteenth birthday but it didn't work out that way. Usually Sarah's husband pitched in and helped but he's a Nelson. I thought better of even askin' him. Didn't wanna stir up trouble between him and my sister or his family. 'Sides, we was all happy we'd have somethin' other than the devil occupyin' our minds for 'while. Should be ready by summer anyways. Samuel ain't said if he's gonna move in it right 'ways. I reckon he ain't in no hurry to leave the twins and me. He's welcome to stay with us long as he wants. I told him so, too. Ain't said nothin' 'bout goin' to any of the choosin' a mate meetin's neither. It'd probably take a mighty strong woman to take up marryin' Samuel right now anyways. She'd most likely have to do battle with her own family since his choosin' is limited to the Nelsons, Taylors, or Andersons, and they's on the opposite side of the fence from us these days. We knowed we ain't too high up on their lists. Anyways, if he puts his mind to goin' to one of them meetin's, I told him I'd back him up. Bobby offered himself up, too. He knows if he goes to choosin' a mate, she's got the right to refuse. It goes both ways. Most women chose don't refuse cuz they don't wanna end up an ol' maid down the road. But these times is different from all the times 'fore. I reckon Samuel went to turnin' matin' age at a bad time up here in the mountains. The families was always real close 'fore but the Caulbearer holdin' Satan down in the pit's gettin' weaker and *It's* growin' stronger. 'Lot of things goin' on between folk now ain't never gone on 'fore. Makes me feel real bad when I think of Grace and Jacob leavin' me soon. I's not stupid. It's somethin' they gotta do. If they don't, everybody in the world's gonna be wiped out. 'Least all the good ones I reckon.

Always like it when springtime rolls 'round wipin' out all the harshness of winter. Now that the weather's turned for the better, the twins, me, and Caleb been goin' up the hill to sit under the maple tree where Annie and Mae's buried. Grace and Jacob pick a couple wildflowers every day we go up there and lay 'em next to the wood crosses I made for both of 'em. They's startin' to pile up bein' we been goin' 'most every day. It's a peaceful place. I feel closer to my Annie when I's sittin' under that tree more than anywheres else. 'Sides Annie's rockin' chair, I do some of my best thinkin' up there. When I close my eyes, I picture Annie and Mae runnin' 'round laughin' and holdin' hands. Funniest thing, when I get to feelin' sorry for myself, Caleb comes right up next to me, plops down, and nudges himself up 'neath my arm. They say animals gotta sixth sense. I believe it's the truth. Grace and Jacob run 'round in front of us laughin' and playin. After 'while, I tell Caleb to go on and play with 'em. I can tell he wants to the way he goes to waggin' his tail and pantin' the whole time he's sittin' next to me. When I tell him that, he jumps up so fast my arm goes to flyin' in the air. 'Sides, ain't nothin' prettier than to sit 'neath a tree lookin' out at mountain country. We's so high up sometimes I think all I gotta do to touch a cloud is stretch my hand up 'bove my head and grab onto one.

The other day while we was up there, I fell 'sleep. Didn't mean to. I reckon I was just plain wore out from gettin' up early workin' on Samuel's cabin and then watchin' these two high spirited children all day. I ain't complainin' none. Just sayin', these ol' bones ain't what they used to be is all. Takes somethin' outta you when you lose someone you love, too. I's thankful to have the twins to fill up my time and mind these days. If I didn't, I'd be all the time layin' 'round mopin' 'bout Annie and Mae.

It was the time of day when the air was warm and a breeze kept makin' it's way 'cross my face so fallin' 'sleep come easy. I knowed God ain't wantin' me to be feelin' sad 'bout somethin' I should be understandin' by now so I made sure I stayed busier than I used to so I wouldn't do much thinkin' 'bout it. I reckon I just fell into sleepin' without even knowin' it. I could hear the children's voices and Caleb's barkin' comin' in and out while I was sittin' on the ground with my eyes closed leanin' up 'gainst the maple tree with one hand restin' on top of Annie's mound of earth on one side of me and the other hand on top of Mae's on the other side.

When I woke, I was 'fraid to open my eyes cuz I didn't hear the twins and Caleb carryin' on in the background no more. When I got 'nuf nerve, I opened 'em one at a time. That's when I seen they was gone....all three of 'em. I jumped to my feet and 'bout near fell back down. With one hand leanin' on the maple tree and the other blockin' the sun from shinin' in my eyes, I took a few minutes to steady myself. I had to have a clear mind to find my babies. When everythin' stopped spinnin' 'nuf so I could stand and see straight 'gain, I went to callin' out their names, all three of 'em....

"GRACE! JACOB! CALEB!"

Over and over 'gain I hollered runnin' up, 'round', and down that hill. Samuel must've heard me from way back at the cabin cuz he come runnin' up the hill fast as his feet could carry him firearm in hand. Without askin' no questions, he went to hollerin' out their names with me. We must've been yellin' real loud and soundin' real scared cuz ain't long Bobby come runnin' with his firearm at the ready. I stopped long 'nuf to tell 'em....

"Grace, Jacob, and Caleb is gone! I fell 'sleep and when I woke, they was gone. I hope they ain't went to wanderin' off onto the Nelson, Taylor, or Anderson's land. They's sure 'nuf gonna snatch 'em up and feed 'em to the devil. One thing's for sure though, Caleb ain't gonna let nobody put a hand on neither one of 'em without a fight to the death."

Bobby stood still a second with his hand on his chin like he was thinkin' real hard. 'Bout turned my hair white when he up and went to sayin' real loud....

"Not seein' no blood or tore up clothes nowheres on the ground is a good sign then, right? Maybe they wandered off on their own and Caleb went with 'em for protection!"

He was tryin' to make me feel better and he did....a little. Since what he said made sense, after chewin' it up 'fore spittin' it out, Samuel and me both nodded our heads up and down. I was askin' myself though....

"What if the heads from the other families got together and dragged 'em off to throw 'em in the pit with the devil?"

Still, ain't no way on God's green earth Caleb's gonna let anyone touch so much as even one hair on either one of the twin's heads. Not willingly. Not without a fight. I was sure I'd of heard somethin'. My heart was poundin' so hard in my chest I was havin' a hard time breathin'. Bobby and Samuel tried to get me to sit down but I wasn't havin' none of it. Grace and Jacob was the one responsibility the good Lord gave to me and I wasn't gonna mess it up just cuz I couldn't breathe. Annie didn't sacrifice her livin' so I could mess everythin' up that her and God got planned. Strummin' up all my energy by takin' in one big gulp of God, I stood up straight, took a deep breath in, then let it out, and started into leadin' my boys through the woods in search of the twins. When the day come I cain't lead my boys no more is the day I need to ask Bobby to send me off to heaven. That time ain't today! Still got work to do. The one thought that kept me goin' was what Grace told me 'while back, everythin' happens for a reason. I couldn't for the life of me figure out what the reason for this was though.

After a short 'while of callin' out their names, the three of us decided to go lookin' for 'em past our land in case they been grabbed up by one of the other families. I felt like we was lookin' for a needle in a haystack. Never took to mind how big and how many of these trees there was up here in these mountains. We all knowed this land we called home like the back of our own hands though. That had to count for somethin'. Now I knowed why no one never seen no city folk up here. If any of 'em got a mind to blaze these mountain trails, we'd of run 'cross their bones at some point in time when we was out huntin'. They'd of sure 'nuf got lost and either starved to death or been killed by the weather. Excuse my language but ain't nothin' done half-assed up here. We get more rain, sunshine, and snow than city folk ever laid eyes on. Ain't no doubt if anyone even got close to where our families all been livin' for hundreds of years, they'd of died from the elements 'fore reachin' us. Worse yet a wild animal might've ate 'em, bones and all, not leavin' so much as a trace of 'em behind. Not 'nuf luxury up here for city folk nohows. God picked out a perfect place for us to do *His* work and keep the secret safe from the rest of the folk in the world. I had to keep my head up and trudge on no matter how scared inside I was feelin'. 'Sides, I figured with Annie, Mae, and God on our side, the devil ain't gotta chance 'gainst Grace and Jacob....and Caleb. One thing's for sure. We wasn't givin' up. No matter how many miles we walked or how many trees we went through, we wasn't stoppin' 'til we found 'em....'live and breathin'. Samuel and Bobby followin' my lead spread out on each side of me lookin' for any sign of 'em passin' through where we was lookin'. Footprints, torn clothes, blood, broken branches. Was a time not long off we'd just go up to the lodge at the top of the mountain, ring the bell, and all the families would come runnin' to help. That sure 'nuf ain't how it is no more though. The next family down the mountain from us was the Nelsons so that's where we headed first.

Bobby's married to 'Lizabeth Nelson. My Emma mated up with 'Lizabeth's brother, Steven, next in line to bein' head of the Nelson family. Their daddy, Joshua, is headin' up the family now. He not too long ago sent his mama and daddy to heaven 'bout the same time I sent mine off. He's married to Martha Anderson. She's Eve and Annie's middle sister. The only one of our daddies still headin' up his family is Simon Taylor. He's married to Ruth Nelson. Simon growed up with my daddy, Joshua's daddy, and Daryl's daddy. Simon's oldest son, Jeremiah, was next in line to head up the Taylor family. Jeremiah was mated up with Annie's sister, Eve. Last down the mountain was the Andersons, Annie's kinfolk. Daryl was headin' up the Andersons now. He's my age. He's Eve, Martha, and Annie's brother. When I go to thinkin' bout who's mated up with who, my head goes to spinnin' 'round. Our families been close for so long, it's hard to 'magine we could be tore 'part by anythin' so evil. This was a time we should be standin' together. Me, Joshua, and Daryl used to go fishin' and swimmin' together up in the mountains when we was growin' up. We was real good friends. Jeremiah come 'long 'bout four years after us. I reckon Simon and Ruth kept tryin' to have a son 'til they finally got one. A couple years after Jeremiah was born, they had another son, Carl.

Joshua, Simon, and Daryl believed the twins was from the devil. They wouldn't be actin' the ways they's actin' if they didn't. It was Matthew, Esau, and Hannah makin' 'em believe such a lie. If the shoe was on the other foot, I'd most likely be doin' the same. A man's blood means everythin' to him. I understand. They been made to believe a lie spit out at 'em by Satan. I can only keep prayin' for 'em to see the truth. But now they's out to sacrifice the twins to the devil. I ain't one to underestimate Satan's power but I know God's stronger. This here was God's battle 'gainst Satan. I was just *His* instrument to do what *He* wants me to do. I's sure *He* will lead me the way *He* wants me to go. I just pray *He* shows me 'fore anyone gets hurt.

Well, my prayers was answered when just as we was comin' up to the Nelson family land, Caleb come runnin' outta the woods. He was 'lone. He come right up to me and grabbed me by my trouser leg and started pullin' me in the direction he wanted me to go. Bobby, Samuel, and me went to followin' him firearms at the ready.

Just as we come up on the line that separates the Sander's land from the Nelson's, I seen a man layin' still as can be in a clearin' on the ground on the Nelson side of the land. Grace and Jacob was standin' off to the side of him. I started breathin' easier when I seen they was with the livin'. When I got up close 'nuf , I could see it was Joshua Nelson's son, Steven.

"That's Emma's husband!" I hollered out to Bobby and Samuel.

Kneelin' down on the ground holdin' Steven's head on his lap was his daddy, Joshua. He was rockin' back and forth sobbin' harder than I ever in my life seen a man cry.

"Steven ain't just his oldest son, he's his only son," is what I was thinkin'.

All the rest of his children was girls. A man's first boy means everythin' to him. I ain't sayin' the girls don't matter none. A man loves all his children but a man's first born son is special to him up here in the mountains. 'Specially if his daddy's one of the heads of the families. I reckon cuz we know he's gonna take over his daddy's duties some day. That means down the road when his daddy passes, he's gonna be head of all the folk bearin' his last name. It also means he's gonna be feedin' the devil every night.

Joshua was cryin' and tryin' to talk to his boy but he wasn't answerin' him. When we got up to 'em all, Grace come over to me and said in a real tiny soft voice....

"Daddy, Steven's daddy shot him by accident. They were hunting. He is going to die unless Jacob and I heal him. He keeps yelling at us to get away from him."

Then, she hung her head down and with tears in her beautiful blue eyes she looked up at me and whispered....

"He called us the devil's children, daddy. Please talk to him so we can heal Steven. He is Emma's husband. She is our sister."

Jacob was standin' over by himself right on the line separatin' the Nelsons from the Sanders. He went to noddin' his head up and down real quick like. I wasn't sure, and later thought better of it, but I could've swore I seen more than the usual scowl on Jacob's face....the one he all the time got since he was a baby when he'd wrinkle his face all up and his eyebrows went to almost touchin' his nose. No sir, this look was different and 'lot more serious than any look I ever seen him wearin'. I don't know if he was mad or disappointed or just plain tired of Joshua's nonsense but somethin' told me it was a good thing me, Samuel, and Bobby come 'long when we did cuz I don't think Jacob had it in him to wait much longer. He was more of a doer than a talker.

That's when I walked straight up to Joshua and yanked him up by the arm. He was covered in Steven's blood. Bobby and Samuel run up real fast and snatched the two firearms off the ground so he couldn't use 'em on us. I pulled him up off his knees and told him to let the twins do what they gotta do.

"This ain't no time for bein' a prideful man, Joshua! 'Sides, this here's my daughter Emma's husband and my grandbabies' daddy," I shouted at him, "She got more right to make the call than you do and I know she'd say to let the twins at him."

Joshua just stood next to me with his head down cryin'. Satan sure does make a man weak is what I was thinkin' to myself. I gotta say, Steven was lookin' close to bein' dead. There was blood gushin' outta a hole in his stomach. With the ground 'round him turned red, the only reason I figured he was 'live was cuz his chest was heavin' up and down. Turnin' to Grace and Jacob, I told 'em to go on and do what they gotta do. When they kneeled down by Steven, each took a side. Caleb positioned himself at Steven's head snarlin' at all of us. He was warnin' us not to take one step towards the twins or he'd eat us for dinner. I knowed he meant it, too. I respected that. They was God's children but they was my babies, too. *He* must've trusted me to put 'em in my care. I was sure 'nuf not gonna let God down. No, sir! No way! Not 'gain! I reckon Caleb was just makin' double sure.

Grace and Jacob was quiet as can be. They laid their little hands right on top of Steven where he was bleedin'. First Jacob's hands, then Grace's. Steven's face looked like all the blood been drained outta him. Judgin' by how red the ground 'round him was, I reckon that ain't no lie neither. When Jacob looked up into the sky, Grace did too. They started into talkin' that talk only the two of 'em understand all soft like. Joshua must've been gettin' more and more nervous cuz he kept tryin' to wrestle himself outta my hold. I just held onto him tighter so he knowed there ain't no way he was movin' 'way from me. There's no time limit plain folk can put on a miracle from God. So we waited....and waited....and waited. Then, all of a sudden the bleedin' stopped. Since there still was a big hole in the middle of him though, the twins kept their hands on top of him with their heads lookin' up to heaven. The longer they kneeled next to Steven, the more healin' took place. Then, his breathin' stopped heavin' and his eyes popped open. All of us, includin' Joshua, dropped to our knees and went to wavin' our hands and arms in the air when Steven jumped up to his feet whole 'gain. We all went to shoutin' louder than loud....

"Hallelujah! Praise the Lord! Amen!"

Steven might've got all his color back but we all lost ours. There he was standin' tall and lookin' at us all confused. He was probably wonderin' what all us crazy folks was doin'. Joshua was so excited and breathin' so fast, he raised himself up off his knees to take a step towards Steven and 'stead fell face down hard to the ground. *THUD!* When Jacob nodded to Grace, they walked over to him and without any vengeance in their hearts went to layin' their hands on him, too. That's when we laid witness to 'nother miracle cuz just as quick as Joshua fell down, he sprung back up. When he saw Steven standin' in front of him healed, he run over to him and throwed his arms 'round him cryin' like a baby. All the blood that fell to the ground must've jumped right back up into Steven cuz soon as he got his color back, the earth was virgin 'gain. Without sayin' 'nother word and actin' like nothin' happened, Grace and Jacob took hold of one 'nother's hand and started walkin' back to the cabin. Me, Bobby, and Samuel, still dazed and in shock, followed after 'em....and of course, bringin' up the rear waggin' his tail and pantin' was Caleb. I swear that wolf had a big ol' smile on his face.

That night, midnight come quicker than usual with all the ruckus that went on durin' the day. I gave all my children a hug and a peck on the cheek. Grace stopped me short of goin' down the steps leadin' from the trapdoor to the tunnel.

"Be strong, daddy," she said to me quietly, "Jacob and I are not the devil's children but we know who is. Your friends will need your strength and faith one day. Do not look into the devil's eyes ever again. Remember, everything happens for a reason. Leave it in God's hands. *He* will show you the way."

Jacob was sittin' over on the mattress noddin' his head up and down. His red curls was floppin' 'round all over his little head. I was just happy he wasn't scowlin' no more....or whatever that was he was doin' 'fore. Jacob could do more to folk with a look than most could do with words. Caleb took his place layin' right next to Jacob on the floor by the mattress. Jacob had his arm slung over him. Samuel was sound 'sleep. Grace was on her knees prayin' at the trap door.

After I closed the trapdoor behind me, I started walkin' through the tunnel headed to Satan's pit. I was feelin' different tonight. I don't know. Maybe it was what Grace said 'bout bein' strong and not lookin' into the eyes of the devil. When I come up to the hole, the other three men, Joshua, Simon, and Daryl was already there. I stopped short of bein' able to see the devil's eyes. When Grace or Jacob told me to do somethin', I knowed better than not to listen to 'em. The other three men was starin' at me. Joshua spoke up....

"Calvin, I'd like to thank you for what went on today. I want you to know I got no argument with you or your children no more."

I tipped my head at him but kept my eyes on the other two. I could tell by the frowns on their faces, Joshua must've not told 'em what happened. I wasn't gonna neither. That was up to Joshua. Not me. That'd be braggin' and we ain't never been no braggin' folk.

We all looked at one 'nother and tossed our plates into the hole. When we went to leave, we all backed out keepin' our eyes on each other while we left. 'Cept Joshua. He turned 'round and walked out with his back to me. He was sayin' he trusted me 'gain. The ol' devil sure didn't like that none at all. *It* started yellin' for me to look *It* in the

174

eyes and *It* would show the others just how evil me and the twins was. But I didn't pay *It* no mind cuz that's what my little Grace and Jacob told me to do and I ain't one to mess with God or *His* children.

I walked slow back to the cabin with my hands in my pockets and hummin' a song I heard my sister Sarah sing 'fore praisin' the Lord at one of the monthly meetin's. I didn't know all the words so I hummed it 'stead. Blocked out all the foul words the beast was spewin' out at me. I was so filled up with the Lord I's surprised my feet was even touchin' the ground.

When I got back to the cabin, the twins was sound 'sleep. Caleb wasn't layin' next to Jacob no more though. When I looked 'round the room, I seen him layin' in front of the cabin door growlin' in my direction.

"Glory be," I gulped real quiet inside myself while tryin' hard not to move.

Then, under my breath standin' still as can be, I said....

"Hallelujah. Praise the Lord. Amen."

Chapter 13

John 4:1-4:3 *Beloved, believe not every spirit, but try the spirits whether they are of God: because many false prophets are gone out into the world. Hereby know ye the Spirit of God: Every spirit that confesseth that Jesus Christ is come in the flesh is of God: And every spirit that confesseth not that Jesus Christ is come in the flesh is not of God: and this is that (spirit) of antichrist, whereof ye have heard that it should come; and even now already is it in the world.*

Whatever Caleb was growlin' at, it wasn't nothin' outside. He was starin' right past me and at the trapdoor inside the cabin. After I locked it up good and tight, he settled down some but I could tell somethin' was botherin' him. I went 'round the room checkin' on the children. They was all sleepin'. I decided to sit in Annie's rockin' chair for 'while tonight. 'Sides under the maple tree, it's where I done my best thinkin'. If Caleb sensed somethin' wrong then there was somethin' brewin'. No other reason for him to be growlin' like he was. Just for good measure, I had my firearm at the ready and sittin' on my lap as I went to rockin' back and forth. When I sat down, Caleb got up. I watched him walk 'cross the room real slow like with his head down and his nose sniffin' at the air. After glancin' over at the twins, he laid down smack dab on top of that trapdoor. His head was up and his ears was movin' 'round on top of his head like he was tryin' to hear somethin'.

We waited like that for 'while. The twins and Samuel sleepin', Caleb sittin' on top of the trapdoor ears up and sniffin', and me rockin'. The more Caleb sniffed, the faster I rocked. Every muscle in my body was knotted up. I had a gut feelin' somethin' real bad was 'bout to happen. Ain't never had a sixth sense 'fore but here tonight I did. Wasn't long, Caleb quit sniffin' so I quit rockin'. I was sittin' still as can be. Even poked my head out a little and brought my eyebrows in so they was almost touchin' my nose like Jacob does from time to time. At the same time I was doin' all that, I went to squintin' my eyes and turnin' my head real slow from side to side. I was holdin' onto my firearm so tight my knuckles turned white. Me and Caleb was on full alert. When I thought I felt the floor tremblin' 'neath my feet, I quick looked over at Caleb. He jumped up and went to sniffin' all 'round the trapdoor. I frozed to the seat of my chair. When he stopped sniffin', he laid back down and pushed all his weight down into the trap door. Like he was readyin' himself for somethin' 'bout to happen. Somethin' told me I ain't got no time to get up and warn Samuel or the twins so when I let out the loudest holler I could muster up, Caleb joined in barkin' and howlin'. We was so loud I swear we could've woke the dead so I wasn't surprised when Samuel, Grace and Jacob all three of 'em popped their heads up. When they done that, I yelled at 'em....

"Don't no one move! Stay where you's at and hang on!"

While I was hollerin', I grabbed onto both arms of the chair. That's when my firearm dropped to the floor and started firin' shots 'round the cabin. Had a bad habit these days of leavin' the safety off with all that's been goin' on. The whole cabin was shakin' and rumblin' from the ceilin' to the walls to the floor. We was bein' tossed all 'round. At first, I wondered if maybe it was one of those earthquakes you hear folk talk 'bout. Don't recall no earthquake ever happenin' in these here parts though. No sir! I was sure this was no earthquake. This was Satan's doin'. After comin' to that conclusion, I just held on tight as I could and went for the ride of my life. Samuel got rolled clean off his mattress but he managed to somehow crawl back on. I reckon bein' young has its advantages. I tipped over chair and all onto my side on the floor. Grace and Jacob both held out their hands for me and Samuel to stay put where we was.

I was thinkin', *"We really don't got no choice in the matter,"* so we done the best we could consiiderin' the circumstances.

I was thankful it wasn't too long of a time my firearm runned out of ammunition.

When Jacob raised his arms up in the air and looked straight up to heaven, he was lifted 'bout a foot off the mattress and floated over to Caleb who was bouncin' 'round on top of the trapdoor. Just when I thought I got used to strange things goin' on with the twins somethin' like this had to up and happen. I had to remind myself with God all things is possible. Next time I go to sittin' neath the maple tree where Annie and Mae's buried, I gotta remember to tell Annie she wasn't crazy that time she said she seen Jacob floatin' in the air when he was a baby. Jacob motioned with both his hands for Caleb to get up. Then, he pointed his finger to the other side of the room where Grace was sittin' on the mattress. When he seen Caleb needed help gettin' to where he wanted him to go, he put his arms and hands out like he was liftin' him up and floated him 'cross the room. When he reached Grace, he set him down all gentle like next to her. Caleb laid his head on her lap. Grace wrapped her arms 'round him. When Jacob made an upward sweep with his hands, the mattress they was sittin' on raised up off the floor a few feet. After makin' sure Grace and Caleb was safe, he went back to savin' the rest of us. He closed his eyes like he was concentratin' real hard. Then, he went to foldin' his hands together and started prayin'. All the time, he was floatin' in the air 'bove the trap door leadin' to the tunnel. The rumblin' was so loud I couldn't make out what he was sayin' but I knowed it ain't a language I'd understand even if I did hear it. Everybody and everythin' in the cabin was bouncin' all 'round….'cept Grace, Caleb, and Jacob. Samuel was doin' the best he could hangin' onto his mattress but just as he was 'bout to fall off 'gain, I seen Jacob point his way and Samuel's mattress went to floatin' in the air, too. Me, I just pushed my bottom down into that rockin' chair hard as I could and hung onto its arms while I was flyin' 'round the room. When Jacob looked over at me, I hollered….

"Don't worry 'bout me, son. Do what you gotta do to stop it."

Jacob nodded his head up and down at me, raised his arms high up in the air, tilted his little head back to heaven, and then, just as quick as it all started, it stopped. Couldn't have gone on for more than a few minutes but when you's floppin' 'round like we was it sure 'nuf felt like 'lot longer.

When all the shakin' and rumblin' stopped, Jacob, Grace and Caleb come over to check on me. I reckon to make sure I wasn't hurt none. Still layin' on my side in that rockin' chair, it took 'em some doin' to get me to let go of the death grip I had on that chair. Samuel was already up off his mattress and walkin' 'round the room.

It was Grace who said....

"That was the devil, daddy. He is getting stronger. The one who went before us is losing strength. There is so much sin and evil in the world, Satan is gaining power. Be strong, daddy. He will try to trick you but you have to resist him. Mama and Mae will help us when it is time. That is why God took them. Be ready daddy. The time is coming sooner than we thought."

If the twins told me to be ready that's what I sure 'nuf was gonna do. I just wasn't too sure how to go 'bout doin' it and was too 'fraid to ask.

After we got done puttin' everythin' back in its place, the twins fell 'sleep soon as their little heads hit the mattress. I figured they was so full of God nothin' scared 'em. When I wedged myself between 'em, they didn't even move. I laughed to myself 'bout thinkin' I was the one doin' the protectin' when the truth be told, they was the ones takin' care of me. Samuel went back to sleepin' on his mattress. Caleb went back to layin' on top of the trapdoor. 'Least he wasn't growlin' no more. My mind was put more at ease knowin' Annie and Mae was took for a reason. 'Least that's what Grace said. I got no reason to doubt her word. Annie and Mae is gonna help Grace and Jacob take on the devil. I laughed to myself thinkin' the devil sure 'nuf don't know what *It's* goin' up 'gainst with my Annie.

When I finally fell 'sleep, I dreamed 'bout Annie and Mae. They was floatin' 'round the room with big smiles on their faces blowin' kisses at me. When I woke, my arms was stretched out in the air like I was tryin' to grab onto 'em and my lips was all puckered up. I's sure glad nobody seen me cuz I looked like I went crazy 'gain. I know my Annie and Mae is gone. Sometimes I ain't so sad when I's 'wake and watchin' Grace and Jacob laughin' and playin' together. They 'least remind me why I's still with the livin'. I gotta purpose I reckon. Not a day goes by I don't miss my Annie though. I wanna hold her tight in my arms 'gain and don't never wanna let her go. But she's gone to be with God. I know that. I know her and Mae's in heaven but my heart goes to hurtin' real bad inside whenever I remember when our family was all together. Her long curly red hair, freckled pale skin, and bluer than blue eyes. The way the side of her mouth turned up when she was bein' all sassy-like. The sound of her sweet voice when she said....

"I love you, Cal."

Even the way she called me *Calvin* and her face got all scrunched up when she was mad at me or tryin' to get her point 'cross. How at peace she looked when she took to sucklin' our babies. She never complained 'bout gettin' up in the middle of the night to feed 'em. As wore down and tired she got, she never said nothin' bad 'bout her babies. Not my Annie. No sir. I wish I'd of told her I loved her more. When I go to heaven, I's gonna make it a point to tell her I love her every day. Maybe more. Cuz I sure 'nuf do. No one never gonna take my Annie's place in my heart.

News travels fast in these parts even when folk ain't talkin' to one 'nother. 'Sides, Bobby and his family was still goin' to the monthly lodge meetin's. Word was Simon and Ruth Taylor went to heaven last night. When Simon come back from feedin' the beast and all that rumblin' and shakin' started in, he dropped to the ground and never got back up. Even when it all stopped, he just laid on the floor jerkin' and twitchin' all 'round. Their grandson, Esau, was spendin' the night with 'em. Esau's one of Satan's disciples. Hear tell, he went runnin' over to get his daddy, Jeremiah, to help. Jeremiah is Simon's oldest son and is livin' in the next cabin down from his so he come runnin'. Esau must've took his sweet time fetchin' him though cuz by the time he got there, Simon was dead. Hear tell, he had red foam runnin' outta his mouth from bitin' his tongue off and his eyes was rolled back in his head. Simon was the last of the patriarchs. Jeremiah's next in line to be head of the Taylor families now.   Jeremiah called a lodge meetin' today and made the announcement that his daddy and mama went to heaven last night after Simon got back from feedin' the beast. He said when he went runnin' through the door to the cabin, his mama, Ruth, dropped to her knees next to Simon, throwed herself on top of him and went to beggin' Jeremiah to send her off to heaven with him. All the time she was beggin' him, her eyes was dartin' back and forth from Jeremiah to Esau. Like she was 'fraid of her own grandson. Maybe by now she figured out who

Esau really was. Maybe she seen what he done to his grandpa. Maybe he showed himself to her. Everybody knowed she had a real good memory but she started hollerin' to Jeremiah how she'd been havin' trouble rememberin' things these days. 'Cordin' to God's law, she didn't need no reason to go with Simon but I reckon she was just makin' sure she wasn't left behind to be at Esau's mercy.

They was servin' up both Simon and Ruth's brains to the devil. Jeremiah invited all the families to partake in his mama and daddy tonight. His wife, Eve, was doin' the cookin' up of 'em. Like Annie helped me send my mama and daddy off to heaven, her sister, Eve, helped Jeremiah with his.

Word got 'round 'bout the twins healin' Steven when his daddy shot him by accident. After hearin' 'bout it, Bobby said Jeremiah come up to him to offer a special invite to all of us. I figured it might be worth goin' just to see what everyone was sayin'. The twins could hold their own. I was sure of that. Just in case though I'd carry my firearm in the waist of my trousers. We'd be careful and sit way in the back of the lodge. I'd leave it up to Samuel whether he went or not. I told him maybe he'd fix his eyes on a girl he'd wanna share his new cabin with sometime down the road. Even though he's of matin' age now, he says he's happy where he is with me and the twins. That's okay with me. 'Sides the twins, he's the last of mine to go. After that, it'll be just me. Maybe when all this is done, God'll have mercy on me and let me join my Annie in heaven. I don't know. Maybe not.

I gathered up Grace and Jacob and told 'em we was gonna partake in Simon and Ruth's celebration dinner cuz they went to heaven last night. Told 'em we got a special invite from Jeremiah Taylor himself. Bobby and Samuel, too. Caleb was gonna have to stay back at the cabin though. Ain't nobody, 'cept Joshua, knowed we got him yet. I's sure he ain't said nothin' to nobody cuz if he would've all the folk would be at our front door carryin' fire torches. They'd sure 'nuf be thinkin' we was witches or somethin' bein' we was livin' with a wolf. After I said Caleb couldn't come, Jacob whispered in Grace's ear. Grace went over to Caleb and told him to sit and wait for us to come back. Caleb sat down but he growled a little when he did. He wasn't happy 'bout the twins goin' somewhere without him. Jacob went up and whispered in Caleb's ear and all of a sudden Caleb started waggin' his tail all happy like and lickin' Jacob's face all over. Samuel decided to join us for extra protection so we all took to walkin' to the lodge. It was a nice night. The moon and stars was shinin' bright. Cool breeze. Could hear the frogs croakin' and the cricket's singin'. Peaceful....'least for now. Ain't takin' nothin' for granted these days though.

Grace and Jacob brought themselves in closer to me when we passed through the front door to the lodge. They ain't trustin' no one. I was thinkin' maybe they's a little shy. Maybe not. The first one to greet us was Joshua Nelson. Jeremiah Taylor was the next one to come up and welcome us to his mama and daddy's partakin'. Everybody was bein' real friendly to us. I didn't know what to make of it. Neither did Samuel. One of Joshua Nelson's daughters,

185

Rose, come up to him and took him by the hand to show him where he could get a tastin' of Simon and Ruth. I think Rose was 'bout thirteen now. Matthew Nelson was her brother. Matthew was one of the three false Caulbearers I seen that night standin' 'round the devil's hole. I didn't see him at the lodge tonight. Matter of fact, I didn't see Esau Taylor or Hannah Anderson neither. The twins noticed they wasn't there, too. Esau's mama, Eve, who was Annie's sister, was lookin' real bad. She had dark circles under her eyes like she ain't been sleepin' good. Just like my Annie was lookin' towards the end of her life. Her dress was hangin' on her like she lost 'lot of weight, too. A bag of bones is what come to my mind. When I seen Matthew and Hannah's mamas, Martha Nelson and Rebekah Anderson. they both looked like Eve. They was all wore out lookin' like they wasn't gettin' no sleep. Big ol' dark bags was hangin' 'neath their eyes. When I asked Eve where Esau was, she mumbled somethin' sounded like he was sick so he had to stay home. Just as fast as she said what she had to say, she run off with her eyes down like she was scared to say anythin' more. Martha and Rebekah said the same thing when I asked 'em where Matthew and Hannah was. I got to thinkin' somethin' ain't right with 'em. Their voices was quiverin' and their hands was shakin'. None of 'em stopped to talk to no one….not even to each other. All the mamas and daddies of the three false prophets was there. Joshua and Martha Nelson. Jeremiah and Eve Taylor. Daryl and Rebekah Anderson. Made me start to wonderin' where Matthew, Esau, and Hannah really was. Had no doubt though wherever they was, they was up to no good. By the way their mamas was lookin', I knowed time was closin' in on 'em fast.

Eve might've not been lookin' real healthy these days but she sure did Simon and Ruth justice by cookin' 'em up into a real tasty stew. I was just gettin' ready to take a second swallow when Grace come up next to me and pulled on my trousers like she all the time does when she's tryin' to get my attention 'bout somethin' important. When I leaned over to hear what she had to say, she whispered in my ear....

"Daddy, we have to leave now. Something very bad is about to happen. You have to get as many people out of here as you can right *now*."

Jacob standin' on the other side of me was noddin' his head up and down real fast. I learned the faster he took to noddin' his head, the more serious the problem was. This here must've been real serious. I went over and grabbed up Samuel tellin' him to quick go tell Bobby to round up his family lickity split and meet me at the front door of the lodge....

"NOW!"

Samuel knowed when I said *"NOW"*, I mean *"NOW"*, not tomorrow or the day after that! *"NOW"* means *"RIGHT NOW!"*

Wasn't but a minute and the Sanders was all gathered together at the front door. I looked Bobby and Samuel square in the eyes and told 'em I'd be back to help 'em soon as I led our families outside to safety. In the meantime, I told 'em real serious like so they didn't think I was foolin' 'round....

"Bobby, Samuel, the twins just told me somethin' real bad's 'bout to happen and to clear everybody outta the lodge fast as we can. I ain't got no idea what we's savin' 'em from but if those two said somethin' bad's 'bout to happen, it sure 'nuf is! So let's get to movin' *NOW!*"

Bobby and Samuel was used to the twins bein' able to see into the future so they took off runnin' to clear folk outta the lodge lickety split.

Soon as our family was safe outside, I went to joinin' Bobby and Samuel. I recruited Joshua and Jeremiah to help us. I told 'em....

"I know I's askin' 'lot of you to trust me on my word but I just know if you don't, everyone you love is gonna die real soon."

I don't know why they started helpin' us but I was glad they did. Maybe they seen the fear in my eyes. Maybe not. All five of us was runnin' 'round the lodge tryin' to talk everyone into filin' out the only door to the lodge in single file. A few of 'em refused to go sayin' me and my twins was doin' the devil's work. Those folks just kept on eatin' Simon and Ruth and laughin' at all the folks who was leavin'. Just as we was standin' outside and the last one of us willin' to walk out the front door filed out, the air was filled with the sound of a bunch of big explosions....

BOOM! BOOM! BOOM! BOOM!

One right after 'nother. It was so loud we all went to coverin' our ears. Soon as we done that, the lodge filled up with fire. That's when the sky and the whole area 'round the lodge lit up like it was daylight out. Bright orange and red flames reached up so high I thought they was tryin' to burn up heaven. The kids was all oooin' and ahhhin'. Never seen nothin' like it 'fore. Sure 'nuf hope I don't never 'gain neither. If there'd been snow on the ground, it would've all melted. As far back 'way from the lodge I was standin', I could still feel the heat from the fire on my arms and face. I knowed the others felt the same. Those who refused to follow us outside, died. All the men formed a line from the water pump to the burnin' lodge and went to passin' buckets filled with water from one man's hands to 'nother quick as they could to try to put the fire out 'fore it spread to the trees and all our cabins. We all knowed it ain't gonna do no good but we had to try anyways. While the men was busy doin' that, the women rounded up the children tryin' to keep 'em close and safe. Sister Sarah broke into song, *Be Still For The Presence of the Lord.* Couldn't recall ever hearin' a quiver in her voice 'fore. Didn't stop her from singin' loud as she always did though. Maybe even louder.

Fire blazin', Sarah singin', folk droppin' to their knees prayin', the high-pitched cries of doubters left inside the burnin' lodge screamin'. There was two forces in our presence that night. God and Satan. The lines was drawed. The battle was waged. Sides was chose.

When I turned 'round to check on the twins, I seen Jacob whisper somethin' to Grace. She went runnin' fast as her little feet could carry her towards our cabin. I knowed she was gonna set Caleb free in case the fire got that far. Jacob come up to me and whispered in my ear....

"I am going to put the fire out. Please do not follow me. This is the work of Satan. Matthew, Esau, and Hannah are helping the devil tonight."

189

The little guy never talked to me much 'fore. He all the time had Grace doin' his talkin' for him but since she went runnin' to save Caleb, I reckon he was stuck with me. I must be gettin' soft cuz I had great big tears fillin' up in my eyes. I nodded my head *yes* to Jacob. The tables sure 'nuf turned tonight is what I was thinkin'. Jacob was doin' the talkin' and I was doin' the noddin'. After that, Jacob disappeared. I knowed God, Annie, and Mae was watchin' over both of 'em. Nothin' for me to worry 'bout. But I couldn't help it. I loved those two little ones. I didn't want neither one of 'em to be leavin' me any sooner than they was supposed to.

A few minutes after Jacob left, the fire stopped burnin' as fast as it started. Everyone's mouths went to droppin' wide open like they was in shock. Like they done witnessed a miracle. I didn't say nothin' to any of 'em but they sure 'nuf was right. Bobby, Samuel, and me knowed Jacob put the fire out but it ain't gonna do us no good to say nothin' cuz nobody'd believe us no ways.

Shortly after the fire stopped burnin', Jacob come back to me. He took hold of my hand. Grace come up on the other side with Caleb standin' next to her. Nobody was payin' no mind to us. They was all gathered together with their jaws dropped to the ground starin' at the lodge. I had to laugh, even sister Sarah stopped singin' and was at a loss for words. Now that there sure 'nuf was a miracle. 'Lot of things goin' on these days though ain't never been seen 'fore.

Bobby, Samuel, Joshua, and Jeremiah went 'round tellin' all the folks to go on home now. Ain't nothin' any of us could do tonight. In the mornin', we'd all take to cleanin' up the mess left by the fire. We was gonna have to find a few bodies for their families to bury when daylight come, too. Soon 'nuf we'd be knowin' who they was.

Me and the twins walked back to our cabin. I had lots on my mind tonight. 'While later, Samuel come walkin' in, too. Hear tell, he walked Rose Nelson home. I sat 'em all down and told 'em there's somethin' I gotta do. It wasn't midnight yet but I had to go down into the tunnel to check on somethin'. I could tell by the way Grace and Jacob was lookin' at me, they knowed what I was thinkin'. I asked Samuel to keep an eye on the twins for me. He sorta laughed to himself and nodded his head. When I unlocked the trapdoor all quiet like and took to goin' down the ladder leadin' to the tunnel that led to the hole where the devil was chained up, I seen Samuel take his post at the window firearm at the ready. Ain't no doubt what I was doin' was dangerous. But I think I knowed who was responsible for the lodge blowin' up tonight 'sides the devil. If I's right, I knowed where the devil was gettin' *Its* extra power. With the flickerin' light of a candle, I sneaked through the darkness of the tunnel careful not to make no noise. When I got close 'nuf to the hole where I could see what was goin' on without me bein' seen, I found out I was right.

The three false prophets, Matthew Nelson, Esau Taylor, and Hannah Anderson was all standin' 'round the devil's pit chantin' words in 'nother language I didn't understand. Their eyes was glowin' red as the devil's eyes. The fire in the hole was flamin' up so high, it was burnin' way 'bove the ground where the three of 'em was standin'. Satan was yellin' at 'em....

"The day is coming when we will be together and YOU will be standing at my side when I take over the world and destroy all of God's followers! Death must come to Grace and Jacob first so the chains holding me down can be broken and I can be freed at last. I am your Father and the ones who call themselves your mothers and fathers are your enemies. The children who say they are your brothers and sisters are your enemies! They are liars! All of them! You must kill them all!"

That's when Matthew, Esau, and Hannah went to pumpin' their clawed fists up and down in the air and chantin' real loud....

"THEY MUST ALL DIE! THEY MUST ALL DIE! THEY MUST ALL DIE!"

Scared the crap outta me is what it done so I turned 'round and walked back fast as I could without makin' no noise. Just when I come up to the steps leadin' to the trapdoor to my cabin, I heard 'em all laughin' and yellin'....

"DEATH TO THEM ALL!"

When I got top side 'gain, Jacob and Caleb was gone. My heart went to beatin' real hard and fast 'gain but Grace run over to me and told me not to worry. They'd be back soon. Samuel just shrugged his shoulders like he ain't got no power over those two. I knowed exactly what he meant. A few minutes later, Jacob and Caleb come back. I knowed better than to even ask what they was doin'. I'd find out in good time. I couldn't stop worryin' 'bout what I just heard Satan tellin' Matthew, Esau, and Hannah....to kill their mamas, daddies, brothers, and sisters. I got to wonderin' if they was just under the devil's power. Did *It* put a spell on 'em to make 'em do what *It* wants 'em to do? Or is they the devil's children like the twins is God's children? I had to make sure they was born devil worshippers and not just under *Its* spell 'fore I went to killin' 'em. That'd be murder. Then what would God think of me? So far, everythin' was pointin' at 'em belongin' to the beast. I prayed for God to show me the way.

Midnight was comin' up on me fast. I'd be goin' to feed the beast in a short time. This time, it would be me, Joshua, Jeremiah, and Daryl since Simon ain't with us no more. Jeremiah took over his daddy Simon's place. Daryl took over his daddy's place and Joshua sure 'nuf did, too. And as I live and breathe, I took over my daddy's place. I don't know if any of the others thought 'bout it yet but each of us was daddy to a Caulbearer. Three of us was daddy to a false Caulbearer. I knowed I ain't one of the three. I was so deep in thought when there was a knock at my door, I near jumped outta my skin.

Me and Samuel went to the door, firearms at the ready. Grace, Jacob, and Caleb was all three sittin' on the mattress. Caleb got up, stood in front of the twins, and went to barin' his fangs.

"Who's knockin' and what's the nature of your business?" I hollered out.

"It's Joshua, Jeremiah, and Daryl. We's not armed. We wanna talk. It's important," a man's voice soundin' like Daryl's yelled back.

I couldn't think of no good reason why these three men would come knockin' at my door this close to midnight. They should've been gettin' ready to go feed the beast 'stead of comin' here tryin' to ambush us 'gain. Just as I was 'bout to tell 'em to go 'way or I'd shoot 'em all down, Grace was at my side pullin' on my trousers. Bendin' down to hear what she had to say, she whispered....

"Daddy, you can let them inside. They do not have any weapons on them. Their intentions are good. They have not come to harm us."

Lookin' back at the mattress, Caleb was layin' down next to Jacob 'gain.

"Okay, sweetheart," I told Grace, "but first you go over there and sit on the other side of Caleb with Jacob just in case you's wrong."

We both knowed there ain't a snowball's chance in hell her or Jacob was wrong but it made me feel better. She nodded her head *yes* with a little turned up smile on her face and went to sit next to Caleb. I took a deep breath in, then let it out slow, put one hand on my firearm in the waist of my pants and the other on the doorknob. Slowly, I opened the door all the while mumblin'....

"Hallelujah. Praise the Lord. Amen."

Chapter 14

Proverbs 27:10 *Thine own friend, and thy father's friend, forsake not; neither go into thy brother's house in the day of thy calamity: for better is a neighbour that is near than a brother far off.*

I opened the door a crack or two slow and easy. Lookin' back at Grace and Jacob, they was noddin' their heads up and down so I opened it all the way. Keepin' my eyes on the three men, I made a quick jerk of my head to let 'em know it was okay to come inside. Kept a frown on my face so they'd know I was serious. Samuel patted 'em down first just to make sure they wasn't carryin' no firearms or knives. Had to laugh inside myself when Caleb come over to each of 'em for a sniff and a growl. I told 'em....

"Don't worry. He's just warnin' you is all. If he was gonna bite you, he wouldn't give no warnin'. Just one minute you'd be breathin' and the next you wouldn't. Long as you all keep both hands on the table and stay sittin', he won't bother you none."

For special effects, I added....

"'Sides, 'least it'd be painless cuz he'd just rip your throats out faster than you could even blink an eye."

When I was sure they wasn't carryin' anythin' to kill us, I motioned for 'em to sit down at the table. Caleb walked back over to the twins and layed down on the mattress between 'em. Both of 'em rested a hand on top of him. The men looked over at the three of 'em. Most the time, they kept their eyes fixed on Caleb. I told 'em Caleb's a friend and won't hurt no one 'less they went to hurtin' us. When I said that, Caleb showed 'em his fangs and snarled at 'em.

"Glory be!" Daryl said, "I ain't never seen nothin' like it!"

"And you most likely won't never 'gain," I said back, "Now, what's the nature of your business?"

Samuel stayed standin' behind 'em leanin' 'gainst the wall with his firearm at the ready. He could shoot all three of 'em 'fore they even had a chance of doin' any harm to the twins or me. Heck, I knowed full well they ain't gotta prayer 'gainst Caleb neither. Not to mention how Jacob goes to floatin' 'round the cabin when he takes a mind to. Our army might be small but we was mighty….just like Annie used to say to me….

"Dynamite comes in small packages, Calvin."

I knowed she was talkin' 'bout herself but I reckon it could be used to fit our situation right here and now, too. Annie sure 'nuf was a wild one. Had to laugh inside myself 'bout that.

Since the Nelsons was the next family down the mountain from us, Joshua must've been the one chose to talk. He started out sayin'....

"Calvin, we knowed each other all our lives. The Sanders, Nelsons, Taylors, and Andersons never had no feud 'fore now. All of a sudden everyone's goin' to fightin' and arguin'. Well, me, Jeremiah, and Daryl took notice all that's left of us at the heads of our families now is the oldest sons. All our daddies went to heaven one right after 'nother. Somethin's goin' on 'round here is all we's sayin' and whatever it is, it ain't right."

"You sure 'nuf is tellin' the truth, Joshua," I said back to him, "I was noticin' that, too. What you three thinkin' is goin' on?"

I didn't wanna jump in tellin' 'em I seen their children in cahoots with Satan. If they was thinkin' they was gonna tell me it's my babies fault though, we was gonna have a scuffle right here and now cuz I knowed better. I laid witness to the truth with my own eyes. Daryl was the next one to talk.

"Calvin," he said, "me and you go way back cuz you married my sister, Annie. For that reason I feel we's related and I can trust you like family."

I nodded my head *yes* at him but I was thinkin' he sure didn't let our bein' kinfolk matter none lately. Truth be told, he would've shot me dead when the three of 'em come stompin' up to my front door firearms in hand and pointed at my head. If it wasn't for my two boys, Bobby and Samuel, they'd of come home from huntin' to find me layin' on the ground in front of my own cabin with three bullet holes 'tween my eyes. If they'd done that, Grace and Jacob would've been fed to the devil by now.

"When Annie went to heaven," Daryl interrupted my thinkin', "We was thinkin' it sure 'nuf was those twins that put her in the ground. You gotta say, Calvin, she wasn't lookin' so good at the end. Big ol' black circles under her...."

197

"Go on and spit out what you's tryin' to say, Daryl," I said cuttin' him off in the middle of what he was sayin'.

I didn't wanna sit there rememberin' how bad my Annie looked 'fore she went to heaven and I didn't need him remindin' me 'bout it neither. I done 'nuf of that on my own. Caleb, still sittin' between the twins, growled at him.

"Okay," Daryl swallowed real hard, then said as fast as he could talk, "After the fire burned the lodge to the ground, the three of us got to talkin'. All our wives is startin' to look just like Annie 'fore she went to heaven. They's near death, Calvin. And we think it's cuz of Matthew, Esau, and Hannah. We just wanna know if you think Grace and Jacob had anythin' to do with Annie goin' to heaven. There! Now, I said it! We's not accusin' 'em of anythin'. We been honest with you and now we want you to be honest with us."

'Fore he continued his say, he shot a look Caleb's way. Caleb lowered his head and squinted his eyes at him and went to snarlin' real low and deep. Daryl's hands started shakin' and his eyes was dartin' back and forth from Caleb to me when he went to spittin' out real quick the rest of what he had to say....

"We was thinkin' though, it's Matthew, Esau, and Hannah who don't belong to God."

Then, after takin' a big gulp, he said....

"We believe Grace and Jacob do belong to *Him* on 'count of they was the first ones born behind the veil. They didn't come early like the others. Our wives didn't have no dream like your Annie had neither. I knowed we wasn't supposed to see Jacob puttin' the lodge fire out last night, but we did. We followed him. All three of us laid witness to it. Not one of us spoke a word 'bout it to no one else. Not even our wives. Joshua told us how they saved his boy Steven, too. We's askin' you to join forces with us to help us. If you know anythin', we's beggin' you to tell us 'fore our wives go to joinin' your Annie in heaven. The three of us been doin' 'lot of talkin'. All of us know now our wives is scared of their own children. Not the ones that come 'fore Matthew, Esau, and Hannah. That ain't right. It ain't natural is all. My Rebekah won't even look Hannah straight on in the eyes no more."

When he said that, Joshua and Jeremiah both was noddin' their heads in agreement. The way it was put to me left me no choice but to help 'em. They was askin' for our help. Don't know of no one in these here mountains who's ever turned anyone down needin' their help, 'specially if they's askin' for it. We ain't been raised that way.

I could tell by lookin' at 'em, they was wantin' to cry. But they's men and men ain't supposed to so they was tryin' real hard not to. Grace come over to my side and whispered to me....

"Daddy, they are telling the truth. We have to help them."

Lookin' over at Jacob, he was busy workin' on keepin' two stubborn red curls on top of his head from droppin' down into his eyes. I didn't know how safe it was where we was with the tunnel leadin' to the hole holdin' the beast bein' so close and all so I told 'em I'd meet 'em under the maple tree where my Annie and Mae's buried after we go feed the devil shortly since it was near midnight now. I don't know why. I just felt better if we done our talkin' outside. Got more of God 'round us that way. They agreed.

After Joshua, Jeremiah, and Daryl left, I piled up a plate full of racoon and rabbit. Had 'lot of thinkin' to do. Maybe that'd keep my mind busy 'nuf to pay no mind to the beast tonight. 'Least it'd make my walk to the pit seem shorter. Unlockin' the trapdoor, I headed down the tunnel to the hole. While I was walkin', I heard my Annie's voice echoin' all 'round me....

"Be careful, Cal. You cain't believe everythin' you hear. 'Specially outta the mouths of liars. Those men is plantin' a trap for our babies."

I kept walkin' wonderin' if that was my Annie talkin' or one of the devil's tricks 'gain. It was gettin' hard to figure out what was God's doin' and what was Satan's. Grace and Jacob would've knowed but they ain't here with me. 'Fore I reached the hole, it come to me. It had to be the devil pretendin' to be my Annie. Nobody knowed but me, Annie only called me *"Cal"* when she was tellin' me she loved me or when we was tryin' to make a baby real quiet like in the night when the kids was sound 'sleep. She called me *Calvin* when she was tryin' to get her point 'cross 'bout somethin' important or she was mad at me. I figured ain't nothin' more important to Annie than her babies. Sure 'nuf the devil ain't wantin' me to believe what Joshua, Jeremiah, and Daryl was sayin' bout Matthew, Esau, and Hannah belongin' to *It. It* didn't know I already knowed who they belong to. I seen all three of 'em chantin' and worshippin' *It* at the hole two times now and not one of 'em looked like no human child I ever seen. *It* didn't want their daddies joinin' forces with me and the twins. It'd be easier for *It* to pick us off one by one if we's separated and at odds. I took a big gulp when it come to me....we was forcin' the devil's hand now.

Soon as we all met up at the edge of the hole, we dumped our plates in. None of us even looked up at each other. All of us turned 'round and hightailed it back to our cabins. Fast as we could, we went runnin'. Then, I heard Annie's voice comin' outta the hole followin' me all the way back to the trapdoor....

"Don't listen to those men, Cal. They belong to the devil. You cain't trust 'em. They'll kill our babies. You have to protect 'em. You have to, Cal."

When I was almost at the trapdoor, I turned 'round and yelled,

"You's not my Annie! She's in heaven with God. And she knows as much as I do that Grace and Jacob's Father is God!"

The ground went to shakin' and rumblin' 'gain but I didn't pay it no mind. I dropped my candle to the ground durin' the commotion and plopped myself down while I went to bouncin' 'round in the dark waitin' for *It* to stop throwin' a fit. When the devil was good and done, I lifted myself up off the ground, brushed off my pants and continued on my way. I don't know. Maybe this was the first time the devil met up with stubborn. Maybe not.

When my head popped up through the trapdoor, Grace, Jacob, Samuel, and Caleb all four was standin' 'round it waitin' for me to come through. The twins throwed their arms 'round my legs and went to huggin' me real tight. Grace spoke up first....

"When the cabin started shaking, I was about to come down there to save you, daddy, but Jacob stopped me because he said you have so much of God inside you, there is no room for the devil."

I leaned down and gave 'em both a big hug and a peck on the cheek. Then, I ruffled the hair on top of Caleb's head. I went to shake Samuel's hand since he's a full grown man now and he might not want none of that huggin' sissy stuff no more. But 'fore I could get my hand out there, he throwed his arms 'round my shoulders pullin' me into him and patted me hard on the back. He might've been a man, but he was still my son. I never noticed 'til now that Samuel went and growed up taller than me. I was thinkin' to myself, no wonder Rose Nelson was all the time lookin' at him. He growed up into a tall, mighty good lookin' young man. I noticed a couple more of the girls was lookin' his way at the lodge. He ain't one to do 'lot of talkin' these days so I don't know if his mind's made up yet. I was the same way when I was his age. I knowed I wanted Annie to be my wife but I didn't go spreadin' it 'round. I was too 'fraid one of the other boys of matin' age might try to get to her 'fore me. I didn't want no competition. Mama and daddy had their suspicions I was gonna pick Annie but I never told 'em what I was plannin' on doin'. Kept 'lot to myself those days. From the day we was best friends, I told Annie everythin' though. I'd hate to seen what she'd of done if I ever kept a secret from her. I swear she'd of knowed. I think she had a sixth sense....like Caleb. I reckon Samuel's waitin' for all this to be over 'fore he goes to choosin' a mate. Ain't got no time for women right now no ways. He's gonna be a fine catch for any woman he picks the way I see it.

After we all got done kissin' and huggin', I told 'em I was headin' out to Annie and Mae's tree to meet with Joshua, Jeremiah, and Daryl. Jacob whispered in Grace's ear. Grace stepped up and said....

"We are going with you, daddy."

Samuel grabbed up his firearm and announced he was taggin' 'long, too. Caleb went runnin' to the front door waggin' his tail and barkin'. Well, I figured none of us got no secrets. Looks like we's a team now. Ain't got no need to discuss nothin' since we all knowed what was goin' on. Together we all walked out the door and started up the hill. We looked like a small army headed up the hill in a line straight 'cross. There was me in the middle with Jacob on my right and Grace on my left. Next to Grace was Samuel. Next to Jacob was Caleb.

When we was almost at the top where the maple tree stood, Annie and Mae showed up. They was holdin' hands but their faces wasn't smilin' none. They didn't say a word. Didn't have to. Out of nowheres, Eve popped up next to 'em. Eve is Annie's sister and Jeremiah Taylor's wife. She's Esau's mama, too. Annie held her hand out real gentle like to Eve. Annie was all the time takin' care of her little sister when they was with the livin'. She helped her birth Esau. Somethin' they both was sorry for now I reckon. I started wonderin' if Esau had anythin' to do with

203

his own mama's death. Then, I wondered if he had anythin' to do with what happened to his granddaddy and grandma, Simon and Ruth Taylor. If I was a bettin' man, I'd say he sure 'nuf did. The words Esau, Matthew and Hannah was chantin' down by the devil's hole that night I snuck up on 'em was ringin' in my ears....

"DEATH TO THEM ALL!"

I wondered if Jeremiah knowed that Eve was with Annie in heaven now. Poor Jeremiah. Not only lost his wife but the one and only child they had belonged to the devil. On top of all that, Jeremiah was head of all the Taylors now. When Annie went to heaven, I 'least still had my children with me. Maybe they didn't stop me from goin' off and actin' all crazy at first but they sure 'nuf gave me the strength to toss that ol' demon outta me....with some help from Annie and Mae.

When Joshua and Daryl showed up, they said Jeremiah was gettin' ready to bury Eve. Well, that answered my question 'bout him knowin'. Joshua spoke up with his head hangin' down....

"First his mama and daddy and now his wife."

I reckon Esau just wore his mama out. They never had no more babies after he was born. Eve didn't have no problem gettin' pregnant 'fore Esau come 'long. It was carryin' the baby inside her for over two or three months was the problem. When Joshua, Jeremiah, and Daryl come by my cabin earlier tonight, Jeremiah said Eve didn't want no more children. She kept tryin' to tell him somethin' ain't right 'bout Esau but he didn't wanna listen. I guess cuz Esau was his first born *and* a son. That means 'lot to a man in these parts. After 'while though, he started believin' her the way she was wastin' 'way every day little by little. But by the time he did, it was too late. Eve was too far gone. We ain't got a lodge no more so our way of communicatin' with each other's been cut off. Usually when someone passed or somethin' important was happenin' like the birth of a new baby, the bell at the lodge is rung and everyone comes to hear the news or pitch in to help. Joshua and Daryl was both scared. I could see it in their faces. If they thought they was scared now just wait 'til I told 'em what I lay witness to. Didn't bring no joy to my heart to tell 'em the truth. Somethin' I knowed I had to do though. For everyone's good.

I started out tellin' 'em what I seen at the hole. Grace and Jacob went up to 'em and held their hands while I was describin' what I seen Matthew, Esau, and Hannah doin' and how their eyes looked and the different language they was talkin'. I didn't stop there though. I told 'em what the devil was tellin' 'em to do. They didn't know it but Joshua, Daryl, and Jeremiah's lives was in as much danger as their wives and their other children. Joshua asked me why my Annie died. They didn't understand if Grace and Jacob was from God why did Annie get to lookin' like the life was sucked outta her, too, just 'fore she died. I explained to 'em the best I knowed how. I told 'em what the twins told me....

"Annie and Mae was took by God to help Grace and Jacob when the time comes to keep the devil chained up for 'nother hundred years. Satan's gettin' stronger every day and gonna bust loose outta that hole with Matthew, Esau, and Hannah's help. That's why they was born....to kill Grace and Jacob and free Satan. We gotta stop 'em 'fore they kill anyone else. Mark my words, the way Martha and Rebekah's lookin' these days, they's next. It wasn't Eve's time to go to heaven. Esau killed her. It was the devil's doin'. Don't gotta worry none 'bout where she went though cuz I know she went to heaven. You's gonna say I's crazy but I seen my Annie and Mae after they went to heaven. And just 'fore we come up this hill to meet you, I seen Eve with Annie and Mae so I knowed she was in heaven 'fore you even said anythin'. They've been helpin' me out 'lot, too."

Just then, Jacob whispered somethin' in Grace's ear and she went to givin' my trousers a tug. After she told me what Jacob said, I said to the others....

"C'mon! Grace and Jacob's sayin' we gotta hurry!" When we took off runnin', we all hollered out at the same time....

"Hallelujah! Praise the Lord! Amen!"

Chapter 15

Proverbs 6:16-19 *These six things the Lord hates, Yes seven are an abomination to Him: A proud look, A lying tongue, Hands that shed innocent blood, A heart that devises wicked plans, Feet that are swift in running to evil, A false witness who speaks lies, And one who sows discord among brethren.*

Since Joshua Nelson's cabin was the closest to where we was, we went runnin' there first. His wife, Martha, was Annie and Eve's sister. She was born in the middle of 'em. Their son was Matthew. They had four children 'fore Matthew. Their oldest son, Steven, turned fourteen three years ago and married my daughter Emma. Rose was the next oldest. She's the one Samuel got his eye on these days. They got two other children, both girls. They's still too young to be settin' up house with anyone. They's eight and nine.

Joshua went to talkin' on the way to his cabin. I reckon he's got 'lot to get off his mind these days. I don't know. Sometimes when folk talk out loud or to someone else they get to figurin' everythin' out better. He started by tellin' us....

"My other kids was havin' 'lot of *accidents* since Matthew turned four so Martha sent 'em to live with Steven and Emma a few months back. I tried to stop her but her mind was made up. Now, I know why. I reckon if I'd of stopped her, they'd be dead now. I asked 'em why they was fallin' down and gettin hurt so much. They just went to puttin' their heads down and shruggin' their shoulders up and down. I's 'shamed to say I was thinkin' Martha was beatin' on 'em. They was just too scared to tell me anythin' is all. They's doin' real good since they went to livin' with Steven and Emma. None of 'em wantin' to come back home any time soon neither. When I go to askin' 'em, they start beggin' me to let 'em stay where they is. When it was just me and Matthew left, Martha started goin' downhill fast. She tried to tell me Matthew was evil. I didn't wanna believe her though. No man wants to think he's gotta son come from the devil. After 'while, she stopped talkin' 'bout it. When I'd come home from huntin', I'd see new bruises and cuts all over her like she was beat. One time she went to limpin' 'round the cabin. Couldn't hardly walk. Got to wheres when I'd ask her what was goin' on with her, she'd say she fell or bumped into a wall. It was all the time an accident. I reckon she figured tellin' me the truth didn't get her nowheres 'fore so she was better off just keepin' quiet. Matthew tricked me into believin' his mama was the crazy one. When she come to walkin' close to him, he'd throw his arms over his head to cover up his face like he was protectin' himself from her. She never smiled no more. I figured cuz a few of her teeth was missin' from her all the time fallin' down. When Grace and Jacob come to my cabin, Matthew, Esau, and Hannah picked on Jacob 'lot. I reckon cuz he was the weakest outta the two. I didn't see it then, but I sure 'nuf do now. Martha knowed. She tried to tell me but I refused to listen. Grace all the time jumped in and stopped 'em. She's a tough one. I don't know how she done it but she always come out the winner."

Then, he stopped, hung his head down, and started into sobbin'....

"Calvin, I's so sorry. I should've knowed."

Never took a likin' to watch a growed man cry but these was times causin' 'lot of that. Truth be told I done more than my share lately.

"Nothin' to be sorry 'bout," I told him puttin' my hand on his shoulder and givin' him a manly shake, "Time for us to get busy keepin' 'em from killin' anyone else."

I don't know why Emma never said nothin' to me 'bout her and Steven takin' in Joshua and Martha's kids. I reckon she had her reasons though. Probably thought I had 'lot on my plate already. She didn't wanna pile no more worries on me. 'Sides when someone asks one of us for a favor, we don't go braggin' 'bout it. We just do it and keep it to ourselves. Emma was always quiet that way. When Annie left us, Emma took over her chores and takin' care of the younger kids without ever complainin'. I know her mama's real proud of her. I sure 'nuf am.

When we reached Joshua's cabin, the front door was wide open. We walked in real slow on tiptoes. We didn't need to though. It was too late for any of that. Martha was layin' face up on the floor in a pool of blood. If I didn't recognize the dress she was wearin', I wouldn't of knowed it was her. She'd been beat with an iron fire poker stick. I knowed that cuz it was stickin' outta her right eye. Truth was it went clean through her eye and stuck into the floor on the other side. That there must've been Matthew's finishin' touch. Her whole face looked like a slab of beat up meat she was gettin' ready to fix for tonight's dinner. What

209

was left of her teeth was layin' scattered all 'round on the floor. Flies was swarmin' all 'round her. Joshua dropped to his knees and started pukin'. I went 'round tryin' to swat the flies back out the window but it wasn't doin' no good. Couldn't close the windows cuz the smell of clotted up blood and rottin' flesh in this warm weather would've been too much for any of us to take. I took Annie's handkerchief outta my pocket and put it over my nose. Didn't help much though. I put it right back in my pocket when I went to thinkin' this smell might take over my Annie's smell on it.

Matthew was nowheres to be found. It'd be my guess he'd be back soon 'nuf lookin' to kill Joshua next. I thanked God for givin' Martha the foresight to leave her kids with Emma and Steven. Givin' up her children like that most likely saved their lives but killed her more than that fire poker stick. It just finished the job I reckon. Everybody knowed Satan and his followers is sneaky. Never did nothin' out in the open. In my eyes, they's cowards. Over in the corner, I seen Annie, Mae, Eve, and Martha holdin' hands. A bright white light shined all 'round 'em. This time they was all smilin'. I don't know. Maybe cuz they was all together now. I had a feelin' Eve and Martha was smilin' though cuz they ain't gotta take no more beatin's from demons they was tricked into believin' was their babies. They found out the hard way what they really was. The devil just made 'em look sweet and innocent to get at their hearts.

"Wolves in sheep's clothing," I said outloud. "No disrespect to you, Caleb," I said lookin' down at our wolf friend and rustlin' the hair on top of his head.

When I turned to say somethin' to Daryl, he was gone. After takin' a few minutes to do some thinkin' 'bout what could've happened to him, I did a full turn 'round the room. That's when I seen Jacob, Grace, and Caleb was nowheres 'round neither. I sure 'nuf hoped Daryl went with the other three for his own sake but I had a real bad feelin' he was headed to his cabin to check on his wife, Rebekah. Off to the side of me, Samuel took to starin' down at Martha's lifeless bloody body. Grabbin' him by the shoulders, I jerked him 'round to face me.

"Son!" I hollered at him lookin' him straight on in the eyes, "Where'd Daryl, Jacob, Grace, and Caleb go?"

Takin' a big swallow and lookin' like I woke him from a trance, he said....

"Sorry daddy. I didn't know they's gone."

I knowed this was 'lot for a man my age to take let 'lone a soon to be fifteen year old boy like Samuel. I didn't know what I was gonna do now. I felt like that dog spinnin' 'round and 'round in a circle chasin' its tail I made fun of Jeremiah actin' like when Eve was givin' birth to Esau. Didn't bring no smile to my face now though. Just as I was 'bout to plop myself down on my knees and go to beggin' God to help me, to give me a hint what *He* wants me to do and where *He* wants me to go, Grace come in from the outside, took me by the hand, then said....

"Follow me, daddy."

The words *"savin' Grace,"* come to mind but all that come outta my mouth was....

"Hallelujah! Praise the Lord! Amen!"

In the meantime, Joshua went from pukin' to movin' himself over to where Martha laid on the floor now. He was rockin' back and forth on his knees with her dead body cradled tight in his arms. The harder he rocked her up and down and back and forth the more that fire poker dug itself into the floor with Martha's eye wrapped 'round it. 'Fore long, alls was left in Joshua's arms was her body. He done worked her head clean off and it was layin' 'lone in front of him on the floor. I don't think he even noticed bein' he was so filled up with sadness and grief. He kept tellin' her over and over 'gain how sorry he was for not listenin' to her. Takin' hold of the back of Joshua's shirt, I pulled him up to his feet. When I done that, Martha slipped outta his arms and hit the floor. Somehow her body lined up perfect with her head so you couldn't even tell they was separated. I told him,

"Grab hold of yourself now, Joshua. We got work to do to make sure Steven and your three girls still gotta daddy."

'Sides, I knowed in his weak condition, I couldn't leave him all 'lone for Matthew to have his way with him when he come back. He'd sure 'nuf have the upper hand and kill him. He ain't no child. He's a monster straight from hell. I knowed we had to find Daryl, too, 'fore he ran into Hannah and ended six foot under.

Grace went to pullin' me in the opposite direction I was wantin' to go but if she wanted to go up the mountain towards our land 'stead of down towards Jeremiah's then that's just how it'd be. I learned early on to do what Grace and Jacob wanted me to do. They's God's angels and I's just an ordinary sinnin' man chose by God to help 'em do what they was sent to do. If that meant goin' back up the mountain 'stead of goin' down, that's what we'd do. Followin' Grace, we passed through my family namesake's land and kept on goin' to where the lodge once stood. When Grace stopped, she said with a great big smile on her face....

"Look, daddy! Look what we did!"

Sittin' on the ground with Caleb at his side, Jacob had a half smile on his face.

"Well, I'll be!" I hollered out to anybody who'd listen.

Right in front of me the lodge sat lookin' just like it did 'fore the fire. It was put all back together. Not a burned piece of wood nowheres. If anybody needed proof there was a fire, there was four burned bodies covered up with blankets layin' on the ground outside the lodge. I reckon the families missin' 'em knowed who they was by now. Probably 'shamed to say cuz they knowed they didn't listen to God's warnin'.

"They ain't got nothin' to be 'shamed 'bout," is what I was thinkin' to myself. *"'Lot of people gettin' tricked these days, includin' me."*

I didn't recognize any of 'em. They's too burned up. By now, Joshua was done feelin' sorry for himself. He went right into bein' mad. Shakin' his fist in the air, he yelled....

"I'll hunt Matthew down and kill him myself!"

I believed him.

Ain't heard from Jeremiah since Eve went to heaven. Daryl must've run off to check on Rebekah and his other four children cuz he ain't nowheres 'round here. It was just Joshua, me, Samuel, the twins, and Caleb left. We had to find Jeremiah and Daryl 'fore the devil's helpers found 'em first. I knowed how I felt when my Annie was taken 'way from me. My heart was broke. It made me turn my back on God and I took to whuppin' my boys. If the devil would've sent someone to kill me, I would've stood up tall and stretched my arms out wide to give 'em a bigger target cuz I sure 'nuf didn't wanna live no more. I knowed we had to find Jeremiah and Daryl 'fore Esau and Hannah did.

When our great great great great granddaddies first come to this land in the mountains, they set everythin' up so the lodge is on the highest ground. After the lodge come the Sander's land, then the Nelson's, then the Taylor's, and last the Anderson's. I figured we should go to workin' our way down the mountain 'gain. Grace and Jacob must've been readin' my mind cuz they was lookin' at me noddin' their heads up and down. That meant we needed to go check on Jeremiah Taylor first since me and Joshua Nelson was here. He should've buried Eve by now. They didn't have no more children so without Eve, Jeremiah was 'lone. It come to me that none of us had no more children after Grace, Jacob, Matthew, Esau, and Hannah was born. I reckon it was a blessin'. No doubt in my mind it was how God wanted it to be. Like Grace said, everythin' happens for a reason. I reckon all that's happenin' is God's plan to get us to do what *He* wants us to do to reach the end *He* wants us to reach....we all knowed that's chainin' up the devil for 'nother hundred years so *It* don't go to takin' over the world and doin' what *It* wants with it. I knowed it ain't gonna be easy. Sure 'nuf 'lot more tears gonna be cried on the way. Most likely more folk gonna die. We had to do it though. It was our job to make sure Satan stayed chained up good and tight down in that pit for 'nother hundred years so all the sinners on Earth gonna get 'nother chance at redemption with the Lord. We gotta keep on goin' 'til the good Lord tells us to stop. I don't know how *He's* gonna do that but I know *He* knows.

'Fore we got to Jeremiah's cabin and since it was on the way, I wanted to stop real quick and check on Bobby and his family. When we got there, I told him all that was goin' on. I couldn't stop him from comin' with us. I caught 'Lizabeth outta the corner of my eye noddin' her head up and down at Bobby. Well, I thought to myself, I reckon we can use all the help we can get if we's gonna fight Satan. So Bobby grabbed up his firearm, hugged and kissed 'Lizabeth and his kids, and the seven of us, countin' Caleb, headed out the door. All the families owned 'lot of land up here in the mountains but we was determined to make it to Jeremiah's cabin 'fore anythin' or anyone come to harm him. The only way we was gonna do that was by pickin' up the pace. Joshua and me soon 'nuf found out we couldn't run as long or as fast as we did back when we was kids. We was huffin' and puffin' but we knowed we had to keep goin' if we was gonna reach Jeremiah and Daryl in time. So we did.

When we come up on Jeremiah's cabin, we was out of breath and pantin'. It was real quiet….and dark. Didn't see no candles burnin' inside. The moon was full and bright though so I reckon we'd have to count on God's light to show us the way. Soon as I was 'bout to call out to Jeremiah, Grace went to tuggin' on my trousers and puttin' her finger to her lips to shush me. Pointin' to the window in the front of the cabin, I took it she was wantin' me to peek inside. So I did. What I seen was the most awful thing I ever seen. Well, maybe not the worse of what I seen lately but close 'nuf. Jeremiah Taylor was standin' on a chair with a thick rope looped 'round his neck that'd been throwed over a ceilin' rafter. His eyes was closed and his head droopin' so I couldn't tell if he was knocked out or dead. Esau was standin' on the ground next to the chair gettin' ready to kick it out from 'neath him. His eyes was glowin' red as fire. He was lookin' right up at Jeremiah yellin' and cussin' at him. Just when I was thinkin' maybe Jeremiah was fakin' bein' dead cuz he didn't wanna look at Esau no more, the thought come to me that we ain't got 'lot of time for thinkin'. I motioned for everyone to back up and be quiet. They did. 'Long with God givin' me extra strength, *He* must've flashed a remembrance of what Simon and me was watchin' on that television when we went into the city cuz I went to runnin' fast as I could slammin' my body full force 'gainst that door and bustin' it down. Just when the wood from the door went to flyin' all over, I rushed into the room not knowin' where I was goin'. All I remember after that was right at the second my body went to slidin' sideways 'cross the room, I seen Esau kick

216

the chair out from 'neath Jeremiah. That's when I drawed my firearm from outta my pants, shot Esau in the middle of his two red eyes and grabbed Jeremiah by the legs holdin' him up in the air so the rope wouldn't go to tightenin' 'round his neck in case he was still breathin'. Hollerin' for the others to hurry in to help me, I felt like I was 'bout near ready to collapse. When they did, Samuel grabbed his knife outta his back pocket and cut Jeremiah down.

While Jeremiah was on his knees holdin' his neck, sputterin' and gaspin' for air, Esau laid on the floor of the cabin dead. Not far from his body laid Eve. Jeremiah never got 'round to buryin' her. When he finally got his breathin' slowed down, he told us....

"I reckon I was in shock when I seen Eve all cut up and layin' dead in her own blood on the floor. My heart was hurtin' so bad all's I could do was kneel down and grab her up in my arms and cry."

Well, thinkin' 'bout it must've hit him hard 'gain cuz in between sobbin', his voice choked all up when he tried to tell us....

"Esau went and cut her beautiful blue eyes out."

After sayin' that, he went to cryin' even harder. Reckon I never paid much attention 'fore but Eve had the same color blue eyes my Annie got. She was just a little bit of a woman like my Annie was on 'count of they's sisters I reckon.

Sittin' on the floor now and tryin' to catch his breath, he said....

"When Esau figured I was at my lowest and weakest, he must've come up behind me and hit me on the back of my head. I don't remember nothin' after that. Everythin' went black. All's I knowed was I started to wake up sometime between when Calvin come runnin' through the front door and Samuel went to cuttin' me down. The one thing I remember right 'fore everythin' went dark was I was prayin' for God to take me to heaven so I could be with my Eve."

Jeremiah and Eve didn't have no other children 'fore or after Esau. Eve lost three or four babies 'fore Esau come 'long. I remember how she come runnin' over to our cabin to tell Annie she was with child and was five months 'long. She said she didn't wanna say nothin' 'til she was sure it was in there good and solid bein' that she lost all the others 'fore this one. I don't remember ever seein' her happier than she was that day. Annie said the same back then. They grabbed hold of one 'nother and jumped up and down and 'round and 'round in a circle. They was laughin' and cryin' all at the same time. Big ol' smiles on their faces. Big ol' tears runnin' down their cheeks. Well, 'least we knowed now why this baby took. It belonged to Satan.

When Jeremiah went to sayin' the same thing over and over 'gain, "Ain't no other woman gonna ever take my Eve's place," I was thinkin' to myself, I sure 'nuf know what he's talkin' 'bout bein' I was feelin' the same way.

My Annie's been gone the longest and everythin' I's doin' now I pray God will take into consideration when decidin' my fate at the end of all this.

Eve was a bloody mess, just like Martha. Her arms and legs was all tied up 'fore she was stabbed to death. I don't know why Esau did that to her. She was so weak and skinny she couldn't of fought her way outta a paper bag. Her throat was cut from ear to ear. It looked like if you went and picked her up, her head would fall off....like Martha's done. The devil makes sure you got no will to live when *It* delivers that final blow. I gotta feelin' those three devil's helpers, now down to two, got the strength of full grown men and then some. It looked like Esau stabbed his own mama hundreds of times. Maybe more. Most likely worked himself up into a frenzy. He left the knife stickin' into where her heart was. Layin' on top of her chest was her two blue eyes. These demons come in the form of children was pure evil through and through. Esau Taylor was dead but Matthew Nelson and Hannah Anderson was still runnin' 'round loose. The twins kneeled down next to Jeremiah and laid their hands on him. 'Fore long, all the redness and bruisin' 'round his neck was gone. His heart slowed down and his pantin' stopped. Grace leaned over and whispered somethin' in his ear. When she was done sayin' what she had to say to him, he looked at her and said....

"Thanks, darlin'. That helps 'lot."

Knowin' my Grace, she told him she saw Eve and Annie together in heaven and they was smilin'.

Now, there was me, Joshua Nelson, Jeremiah Taylor, Bobby, Samuel, the twins, and Caleb. Time to go collect Daryl Anderson and his wife, Rebekah. If they's still 'round to collect. If Hannah ain't got to 'em first. I was hopin' they was still with the livin'. They had four other children 'sides Hannah. They was all boys. The oldest, Zachary, was thirteen. Daryl ain't only Annie, Martha, and

Eve's older brother, he's head of the whole Anderson family, too. So far, the Andersons ain't been fairin' too good in this battle 'gainst Satan. Somethin' had to change and I mean fast 'fore we was all gone.

The Anderson's land was last goin' down the mountain of all the families. On our way from Jeremiah's cabin to Daryl's cabin, the ground started into rumblin'. Nothin' like it done 'fore back at the cabin. Not bad 'nuf to kill no one or even so much as knock us to the ground. Just made walkin' a little harder was all. But we kept goin'. We knowed we had to get to Daryl fast. It stopped after a few minutes. Maybe it was the devil warnin' us to quit and go home. Maybe not. Maybe it was the devil lettin' us know *It* knowed we killed Esau. Maybe not. Maybe *It* was the devil tryin' to slow us down. Maybe not. I don't know why *It* done what *It* done but I knowed that was just a small sample of what *It* could do. *It* already robbed us of too much for us to stop though. We was comin'. All of us madder than hell and filled up with the Lord. I didn't know what we was gonna do but I knowed the twins knowed. Had to laugh inside myself when I went to thinkin' how if we wasn't goin' in the direction God wanted us to go, Grace would sure 'nuf go to tuggin' on my trousers to tell me 'bout it. We was eight strong now. Soon to be ten, I hoped. Just as we come up on Daryl and Rebekah's cabin, we heard kids screamin' and cryin'. I knowed sure as I was standin' there, Hannah had somethin' to do with what was goin' on inside. We stopped short of comin' too close to the cabin. Didn't want 'em spottin' us. We was thankful we seen the flickerin' of light inside from a candle burnin'.

Bobby said he was gonna see what he could see through the open window on the side of the cabin. We waited while he sneaked real careful like up to the house.

When he come back, he told us in a real low voice....

"Matthew and Hannah's both inside the cabin holdin' Daryl and his kids hostage."

Then, with his hands on his hips, he hanged his head down and went to shakin' it side to side all the time kickin' at the ground. I could tell he was madder than hell and thinkin' 'bout 'Lizabeth and his own kids.

"Rebekah's lookin' like she's dead." he said bitin' on his bottom lip to stop him from cryin', "Blood all 'round her on the floor just like Martha and Eve was. Daryl's standin' in front of his four kids tryin' to protect 'em. Hannah's holdin' a firearm wavin' it back and forth at all of 'em. Matthew's standin' next to her eggin' her on to *shoot 'em!* Hannah's screamin' back at him to *shut up!* I reckon she got sick of hearin' him naggin' her cuz ain't took but a second more and she raised her hand and whipped him 'cross the face with the firearm to shut him up. She must've got him real good cuz blood went to gushin' outta his nose and down over his lips. He didn't care none though. He just went to lickin' the blood off with his tongue and laughin' 'bout it. 'Fore long, sure as I's standin' here, it was all healed up 'gain like he never was hit. Their eyes was glowin' red. Matthew and Hannah's standin' in the middle of the room facin' the rear wall of the house. Their backs is to the front door. Daryl and his kids is up 'gainst the rear wall."

When Bobby finished fillin' us in, I knowed we had to act fast 'fore Hannah went to shootin' everybody. We couldn't go rushin' in and shootin' everywheres. If we did, we could hit Daryl and his children. When Samuel and Bobby huddled together for a few seconds, I knowed they was plannin' somethin'. When they was done whisperin' to each other, they turned to all of us and said they knowed what to do. Without no time to talk 'bout it, Bobby ordered the rest of us to stay put where we was just in case Matthew and Hannah come runnin' out. If they did, he told us to shoot 'em dead and aim for 'tween their eyes. The twins was noddin' their heads up and down, so the rest of us did, too.

Bobby and Samuel sneaked up to the front door and with one kick it flew open with splinters of wood flyin' everywheres just like what happened with me back at Jeremiah's cabin. I heard three shots and 'lot of screamin' and yellin' goin' on inside. All of a sudden, Matthew come runnin' outside holdin' onto his left arm with blood runnin' down it like he been shot. No sooner I thought that, Joshua runned out from where we was standin' and come face to face with Matthew. I reckon he thought it was his responsibility since it was him and Martha that brought him into the world. When Matthew seen his daddy, he went to beggin' him to help him. He fell to the ground holdin' his arm and cryin' like a baby. But we all knowed he ain't no baby. I just hoped Joshua remembered it, too.

"Daddy! Daddy!" he begged, "Help me, daddy. please!"

For a second, we saw Joshua lookin' at him like he was feelin' sorry for this boy he raised as his son. Joshua quick glanced back at us and that's when we knowed it wasn't pity we seen on his face. It was hate. Shakin' his head like he was disgusted, he grabbed Matthew up by the wounded arm he was holdin' onto and jerked him hard as he could to his feet. Lookin' him straight on in the eyes, he placed the nose of his firearm right between Matthew's eyes, and without thinkin' twice 'bout what he was 'bout to do, he pulled the trigger. *BAM!*

Right 'fore he shot Matthew, he yelled at him....

"This is for Martha, you s.o.b! And don't call me *daddy!"*

Later he'd say he was pretty sure God would forgive him for cussin' that one time. We all told him he sure 'nuf was right 'bout that.

Walkin' inside the cabin, we seen Hannah layin' on the floor face down with two bullets in the back of her head. That accounted for two of the three shots we heard bein' fired. Bobby said he told Samuel they was to take Hannah down first since she's the one holdin' the firearm and had her back to 'em. Soon as he seen Hannah was shot, Matthew went to runnin' outta the cabin. That's when Samuel shot at him hittin' him in the arm but they knowed we was waitin' outside to take care of him so they runned over to help Daryl and his kids. Sad to say, Rebekah suffered the same fate as Martha and Eve. Only difference was Hannah used the firearm she was wavin' 'round 'stead of a fire poker or a knife. Daryl and the kids was shook up but they was 'live and breathin'. It was a miracle none of 'em was hurt. Bobby and Samuel was spit shakin' hands off to the side.

Considerin' everythin' that went down, I'd say we come out with a win. I sure 'nuf was proud of my boys. I wondered if Annie was lookin' down from heaven at 'em. I hoped so. We was gonna find out soon 'nuf the war ain't even close to bein' over. After Daryl handed out shovels to all the men in our group, we went to buryin' Rebekah. We all knowed the mournin' part would have to come after this battle was over.

Standin' over Rebekah's grave we all shouted....

"Hallelujah. Praise the Lord. Amen!"

Chapter 16

Matthew 5:38-39 *You have heard that it was said, "An eye for an eye and a tooth for a tooth." But I say to you, Do not resist an evildoer. But if anyone strikes you on the right cheek, turn the other also.*

After we helped Daryl Anderson bury Rebekah, we went back up the mountain to Jeremiah Taylor's cabin to bury Eve and then Joshua Nelson's cabin to bury Martha. When we was done, we hung our heads in prayer. We burned Matthew, Esau, and Hannah's bodies. Fire somehow seemed fittin'. When we went to cleanin' the cabins of all the blood, Daryl took his four children and left 'em in the care of his younger brother, Thomas. Thomas and his wife got two children of their own. They gladly took 'em in. Folk up here never asked questions. Someone needed a favor they just done it. I reckon we all figured if they wanted us to know why, they'd tell us. Otherwise, it ain't none of our business. It was gonna be daylight soon. When we was all done diggin', buryin', burnin', cleanin' and prayin', I suggested we all go to the lodge to get some sleep. I had a feelin' there was 'nother round comin' up soon. Just cuz we did 'way with Satan's disciples didn't mean *It* ain't still a powerful force to reckon with. I knowed we might've slowed *It* down but we didn't stop *It*. There's strength in numbers I figured so best we stayed together, 'least for now. We could take turns bein' lookout that way, too. So we gathered ourselves up and headed to the lodge to sleep.

When we got to the lodge, Caleb right 'way settled himself by the front door. 'Sides the trapdoor leadin' to the tunnels, it was the only entrance and exit to the lodge. The trapdoor was sittin' in a corner by the back wall. After I locked it up good and tight, Jeremiah took first watch. Said he couldn't sleep no ways. I was real worried 'bout him. Lost his wife, mama, and daddy all in one swoop. Wondered if he felt he had anythin' to live for anymores. I don't think I would've. It was daylight now. We all said we'd take turns pullin' shifts. That way everyone could get 'least a couple good hours sleep 'fore nighttime come up on us 'gain. Whether any of us slept or not was 'nother question. We figured the devil most likely did most of *Its* evil at night when it's dark out so best to hunker down and grab what we could in the way of sleep now while the sun was out and shinin'. None of us knowed when we'd be able to sleep or even close our eyes 'gain. Couldn't even remember when any of us had anythin' to eat last. There was one mattress in the back of the room. Everyone gave it up for Grace and Jacob cuz they's kids. Since I took to sleepin' in the middle of 'em with my arms wrapped tight 'round 'em, I'd be layin' on it, too. I knowed the time was comin' soon when the twins was gonna be leavin' me. The way things was goin', I doubted they was even gonna make it to their seventh birthday like all the past Caulbearers done. I didn't like thinkin' 'bout that at all. Anyways, for right now, with Caleb at the front door lookin' out for all of us, I felt safe 'nuf to fall 'sleep. So did the twins.

I must've been sleepin' real good cuz when I woke, Grace and Jacob was sittin' over by the front door of the lodge with Caleb. Didn't even know they got up. Lookin' out the lodge window I could see night was sneakin' up on us 'gain. Nobody reported anythin' goin' on outside all day. Everyone decided to let me sleep the whole day 'way so I was well rested. I reckon they thought of me as their leader. Jeremiah didn't sleep a wink. Too much sadness in his heart I reckon. Sleep don't come easy when a man's got 'lot on his mind.

When I gathered everyone together, I was thinkin' we should 'least spend 'nother night at the lodge. If everythin' went good we could all go home the followin' mornin'. I got out voted though. Bobby, Joshua, and Daryl wanted to go check on their kids. Jeremiah just stood at the window starin' outside. I reckon it didn't matter much to him one way or 'nother. I invited him to come stay with us but he said he had to get used to stayin' by himself sooner or later so it might as well be sooner. Not my place to tell 'nother growed man how to do his grievin' so I left it 'lone for now. I told all the men to go 'bout their business as usual then. Someone said that was a poor choice of words since there ain't no such thing as *usual* in our lives no more....now that our wives was all gone....and Satan was out to kill all of us. Heck, if it wasn't for our children, we'd probably all jump into the fire and let *It* have us....long as we knowed God was gonna swoop us up to heaven 'fore we hit bottom. Our children already lost their mamas. Didn't want 'em to lose their daddies, too. We was heaven bent on stayin' strong together so we could fight the battle comin' up 'gainst the beast. We all knowed *It* might've been quiet and peaceful now but that could be *Its* way of trickin' us. Soon 'nuf there ain't gonna be no daylight left and if Satan was gonna raise his ugly head that'd be when he'd do it is what I was thinkin'.

Joshua thought it'd be a good idea for us to come up with some kind of signal in case one of us runned into trouble after we parted ways. Everybody thought that made 'lot of sense. He suggested we fire a shot in the air dependin' on where we was. That way we'd know which way to go. Workin' down the mountain, Sanders would be one shot, Nelson two, Taylor three, and Anderson four. We all agreed to that. Then we all packed up our gear and headed back to our cabins. It was almost dark out so it was too late to go huntin'. We all figured we'd just have to go hungry 'nother night. Nobody had much of an appetite no ways. Samuel or me would go huntin' in the mornin'. None of us minded eatin' vegetables we got stored in the root cellar. We had just 'nuf meat to feed the devil tonight. Didn't wanna go skippin' *Its* regular feedin's. *It* might go to wonderin' what we was all up to....if *It* didn't know already. Had to act as normal as we could. I was wonderin' if *It* knowed we killed Matthew, Esau, and Hannah. That sure 'nuf ain't gonna make *It* none too happy. Ain't no doubt they went to hell so I knowed sure 'nuf *It* knowed what we done to 'em. Reckon we'd find out more at midnight when we headed down into the tunnel to feed *It*.

On the way back to our cabin, Caleb darted off into the woods. I thought maybe he had some sorta wolf business to take care of. Grace and Jacob didn't say nothin' 'bout it so I didn't worry none. 'Sides, if it was somethin' bad, Grace and Jacob both would've stopped me from goin' even one step more. When we got home, I put a pot of water to boil on the hearth 'fore I went down into the root cellar to pick out some vegetables for all of us to eat. Without Annie, Emma, or Mae 'round to mind the garden, the pickin's was slim. By the time I come back up top, Caleb was back. There was three dead rabbits layin' on the floor in front of him. He was waggin' his tail and I swear he was smilin'. We all gave him a big hug and ruffled the hair on top of his head thankin' him. When I was done skinnin' those rabbits and cuttin' 'em up into bite sized pieces, I throwed 'em into the pot of boilin' water 'long with the vegetables. We was gonna be eatin' some rabbit stew tonight. I started thinkin' 'bout Jeremiah. I wish he'd of come to stay with us 'while. I'd take him a bowl of rabbit stew later on. He had to be hungry. I was hopin' Eve was lookin' after him from up in heaven. I don't know. Maybe she'd show herself to him like Annie and Mae did me. Maybe not. The only thing that was for sure these days was you couldn't be sure of nothin'.

Bobby went on back to his cabin to join up with 'Lizabeth and make sure his kids was okay. Joshua was headed to Steven and Emma's where his kids was stayin'. Daryl said he was goin' to his brother Thomas' to see his kids. Jeremiah, I reckon, was headed to his own cabin to be by himself. He mumbled somethin' 'bout makin' Eve a cross to put on top of her grave. After everyone left to go where they was goin', it was back to bein' me, Samuel, Grace, Jacob, and Caleb. When dinner was fixed, the four of us sat down, joined hands, and said a prayer thankin' God for the food in front of us, the strength *He* gave us to make it this far, and for fillin' our family with 'lot love for one 'nother. At the end of our prayer, everyone of us shouted loud as we could....

"Hallelujah! Praise the Lord! Amen!"

Caleb barked. I fixed an extra big bowl of rabbit stew for him. If it wasn't for him, we'd be goin' to bed with growlin' stomachs tonight. This used to be my favorite part of the day cuz we'd all sit 'round eatin', laughin', and talkin' together. My Annie had the most beautiful smile. She had a way of talkin' that made everyone take notice and listen. Sittin' here at the table now 'bout ready to eat this supper God, and Caleb, gave us, I caught myself lookin' over at Annie's empty chair at the table. For 'while I could swear I seen her face. I'd never forget what my Annie looked like. Red curly long hair, freckles, beautiful blue eyes, and a crooked smile when she was bein' sassy. She was just a little bit of a woman. Had to laugh inside myself. That Annie sure 'nuf was a wild one. No one could get me goin' like she could. Nobody gonna ever take her place in my heart or mind. Nope, sure 'nuf ain't. My heart had room 'nuf only for her. I looked forward to the day God's gonna be callin' me to heaven. I was thinkin' maybe I oughta stay 'round long 'nuf to get Samuel married off to a good woman though. Bobby, he's set up with a real good wife and children. Emma's got a strong man in Steven. She got her hands full with her own two boys and now Joshua's three children. Emma can handle it though. 'Sides, Joshua's daughter, Rose, was old 'nuf to help Emma 'round the house and with the younger kids. She's of marryin' age now. Maybe someday Samuel's gonna take her as his wife. Maybe not. Emma never was a complainer. 'Lot of times I thought she was stronger in her mind than Bobby and Samuel. She takes after her mama I'd say. I had to laugh 'bout that. Steven never stood a chance when Emma set her eyes on him. He probably never even knowed what hit him.

Mae was a mama's girl. She was all the time followin' Annie 'round. When Annie went to heaven, she went to followin' Emma 'round the cabin 'stead. If I was a bettin' man, I'd say she finally just up and decided to follow her mama right up to heaven. That's why she was climbin' that apple tree is my guess. The apple was probably somethin' she thought 'bout after she got up there. Maybe Annie gave her the idea from up in heaven. Grace always says everythin' happens for a reason. I reckon if one of the children had to go to Annie, it should've been Mae. God don't make mistakes. I knowed all the children missed their mama but not as much as Mae. She was the baby 'fore Grace and Jacob come 'long. After Annie went, 'lot of times I'd hear Mae cryin' herself to sleep. She tried to muffle it with her blanket, but I could still hear her. I remember when Annie was still 'live, durin' the night when everyone was sleepin', Mae would squeeze herself in between me and her mama layin' on a blanket on the floor. Annie just wrapped her arms 'round her tight and whispered....

"I love you, Mae. Always will."

They'd just fall back to sleep like Mae was where she was supposed to be. I reckon that's where she was now, too….right where she's supposed to be….wrapped up tight in her mama's arms.

Thankin' the Lord for the good food and good company, I tucked Grace and Jacob in 'fore I left to feed the beast. Samuel was still 'wake. He said he slept so much today at the lodge, he ain't tired now. I told him to stand by the window and keep watch then 'til I get back up top. Caleb laid down in front of the twins mattress. I reckon everythin' was at peace cuz if it wasn't, Caleb would be the first to let me know. Everythin' was quiet. The room was dark. I unlocked the trapdoor after tuckin' my firearm into the back of my trousers and headed down the steps to start my walk to the hole. I was carryin' a plate filled with moose parts. Didn't ever have to cook the meat cuz Satan liked it raw and bloody. Not that I cared how *It* liked it. Ain't gonna do no cookin' for *It* no ways nohows. This time, the walk seemed shorter somehow. Maybe cuz I had so much on my mind. Maybe not. Wasn't payin' much attention to where I was goin'. When I come up on the hole, I stopped real quick. When I looked up and seen Joshua and Daryl was there but not Jeremiah, I knowed right then there was trouble but didn't want *It* to know so I brought my eyebrows into touchin' my nose like Jacob always done and stared real hard at both of 'em. They looked worried. Each of 'em shrugged their shoulders like they was lettin' me know they didn't know where Jeremiah was. Broke my concentration when *It* spoke….

"What's wrong? Are you missing someone tonight? Don't worry. I know where he is. I doubt you can find him in time to save him. Never underestimate MY power! Do

you really think there is anything you say or do that I don't know about?"

I thought *It* was all done after *It* was quiet for a second or two, but *It* wasn't. *It* roared in the meanest most evil voice I ever done heard....

"YOU KILLED THREE OF MINE! AN EYE FOR AN EYE!"

We took to coverin' our ears and our noses when it yelled that out. The smell that come from *Its* mouth made me wanna puke. Smelled like dead rottin' flesh. When *It* changed *Its* roar to a calmer, softer tone, I uncovered my ears but doubled up on my nose.

"Isn't that what your God preaches!? Better hurry! Tick tock tick tock. Time is running out! An eye for an eye! Hahahahahaha!"

Its laughter echoed throughout the tunnel. After we throwed our plates into the pit, I motioned for the others to follow me. The three of us went runnin' fast as we could through the tunnel to the steps leadin' to the trapdoor in my cabin.

Throwin' the trap door open, I come up into the cabin huffin' and puffin'. Joshua and Daryl was right behind me. It was dark inside the cabin so after squintin' and focusin' my eyes some, I seen Samuel, Grace, Jacob, and Caleb was gone. I figured maybe they went to help Jeremiah. Maybe he was in trouble. I didn't hear no shots fired though. Jeremiah would've shot three times in the air if he was in trouble bein' the Taylors is third down the mountain. I wondered if we'd be able to hear the shootin' of a firearm when we was in the tunnel. I wasn't so sure.

Joshua and Daryl didn't think so. The devil ain't dumb. *It* knowed if *It* was gonna cause any of us harm, the time to do it would be when one of us was all 'lone and the rest of us was busy feedin' *It*. Gatherin' myself together, I told the others with as much calm in my voice as I could muster up....

"No time to panic."

I just wished I believed what I was tellin' 'em.

We headed off into the direction of Jeremiah's cabin. I couldn't think of nowheres else to go since the other two men was with me. When we got there, the rule *"not to panic"* was throwed outta the window when right smack dab in front of us we seen fire shootin' outta Jeremiah's cabin. Just a little bit closer to the cabin, I seen four figures standin' outside watchin' it burn. Next to one of the two little ones was a wolf. I took a deep breath in knowin' they was okay, then went to movin' down closer to where they was all standin'. When we reached 'em, I looked at Samuel and asked....

"What happened?"

He shook his head side to side and said....

"The twins told me they needed to go to Jeremiah's cabin. I told 'em we had to wait for you to come back from feedin' the devil but they'd have none of that. Well, you know how that goes. We all learned long time ago to listen to 'em when they's sayin' somethin'. 'Sides, Caleb took to jumpin' up on the cabin door and barkin' over and over 'gain so I gave in and opened the door. The twins and Caleb took off runnin' so I grabbed my firearm and followed after 'em. When we got here, we seen a fire burnin' in Jeremiah's cabin but Grace told me not to worry. Jacob went walkin' into the cabin and come out holdin' Jeremiah's hand. Ain't never seen nothin' like it. It was like a pathway was cleared through the fire just for Jacob. Anybody else would've walked in there like that, they'd of burned up on the spot. Even Jeremiah walked out in one piece."

When I looked over at Jeremiah, he was just standin' there with a look on his face like he wished he wouldn't have.

I knowed none of the others, 'cept Grace and Jacob, could see 'em but Annie, Mae, Eve, Martha, *and* Rebekah was floatin' in front of us. This was the first time I seen Rebekah with 'em. Eve winked one eye at me. I was glad to see God gave her eyes back to her. I nodded thankin' her for givin' the twins the message 'bout Jeremiah bein' in trouble. 'Least that's what I figured happened. Without no further discussion 'bout it, the five of 'em was gone quick as they come. Jacob and Caleb disappeared for a short time. I reckon he was doin' what he does to put a fire out. Sure 'nuf when he come back the flames was gone. The whole cabin wasn't burned to the ground but there was 'nuf damage to where we'd have to get to rebuildin' him 'nother one sometime 'fore winter come up on us. I told Jacob not to rebuild this cabin like he done the lodge cuz if nothin' else, it'd give everyone somethin' to do to occupy their minds when this was all over. Mostly cuz it forced Jeremiah into havin' to stay with us though. It was too dangerous for him to be stayin' 'lone. What happened here tonight was proof. I was thankful it didn't spread into the woods killin' no trees or forest animals. Everybody looked at one 'nother and shouted loud and clear....

"Hallelujah! Praise the Lord! Amen!"

Everyone 'cept Jeremiah.

We all decided maybe goin' our own ways wasn't what we should be doin' after all. So all of us headed back to my cabin to stay since it was the highest one up the mountain and closest to the lodge. The next day, we'd make our rounds to our families and tell 'em there'd be no more meetin's at the lodge 'til we said so. I didn't want to underestimate the power of Satan. I knowed *It* ain't as powerful as the Lord but I didn't know what else *It* could do to hurt us besides rumblin' and shakin' the ground, possessin' us, and settin' our cabins on fire. We didn't know it then but we was gonna find out soon 'nuf *It* could do 'lot more. Hallelujah. Praise the Lord. Amen.

Chapter 17

Luke 11:20 *But if I with the finger of God cast out devils, no doubt the kingdom of God is come upon you.*

One of the reasons I like sleepin' 'tween the twins is cuz it helps me forget the mornin' I woke up next to Annie when she went and died in her sleep. Makes me feel like I's not so 'lone I reckon. I just remember she was cold. Wanted to cover her up with a blanket but I knowed that ain't gonna do no good. Her freckles didn't go nowhere but her pale skin changed to 'nother color. Almost gray, I'd say. Her pretty pink lips turned purple. Her smile was gone so all that sassiness went with it. The sparkle that was always in her beautiful blue eyes turned dull and lifeless. I try to shake that memory outta my head when I go to thinkin' 'bout it. I don't like rememberin' her that way. I know enjoyin' sex is a sin but with Annie I just couldn't help it. I know she liked it, too. When we went to havin' sex, we'd cover up the pleasure part by sayin' we was makin' a baby. I reckon if we made a baby every time we had sex, we'd sure 'nuf have, I don't know, a whole cabin full of 'em. I don't know 'bout any of the other mated up folk here in the mountains. Sex ain't somethin' we sit 'round talkin' 'bout when we all get together for our monthly lodge meetin's bein' we ain't supposed to be doin' it to make us feel good. I don't know. Sometimes I go to wonderin' if it ain't God's way of givin' us somethin' to get rid of all the stress of daily livin'. I always felt real relaxed and calm after Annie and me got done doin' it.

My Annie was a real pretty lookin' woman but I loved her insides the most. She was smart, funny, sweet, and a little on the wild side. I reckon you could say she was beautiful all 'round. Inside and out. So many things I remember 'bout her. I don't mind thinkin' 'bout the good things but anythin' havin' to do with the day she went on up to heaven I try not to think 'bout. When I go to sittin' 'neath the maple tree where she's buried, I close my eyes and 'magine her sittin' between my legs like she used to do with her head and back leanin' up 'gainst my chest and my arms wrapped easy 'round her. She'd go to twirlin' a piece of her red curly hair 'round her finger when she was bein' flirty or thinkin' hard 'bout somethin'. When she'd smile and lift up one side of her mouth at me, I knowed she was bein' sassy. She was a real good mama to our children and a good wife to me. Sure 'nuf....*was*. None better nowhere is what I say. 'Least not for me.

'Fore Grace and Jacob was birthed, Annie went walkin' one day with Bobby, Emma, Samuel, and Mae. Every now and 'gain, she'd gather 'em up and tell 'em they was goin' on an adventure. They'd get all excited talkin' nonstop walkin' out the cabin. I reckon you could say they had a routine. The two girls was the ones who'd be holdin' real tight onto her hands on their way out and the two boys was holdin' onto 'em on the way back. This one time, they was gone 'while longer than usual. I remember thinkin' I needed to go off lookin' for 'em 'fore nighttime come 'round when all of a sudden all four younguns come tearin' into the cabin shoutin',

"Look what mama got daddy!"

Cupped real gentle like in her hands, Annie was carryin' a baby bird that fell outta it's nest. She took care of that bird for the longest time. Made it a nice little bed made up of twigs and leaves and set it down by the hearth to keep it nice and warm. Her and the kids went out every day diggin' up worms to feed it. I could tell she didn't like the feel of 'em squirmin' 'round in her hands by the twisted up look she got on her face. That didn't stop her though. I knowed better than to say anythin' to her. When Annie got somethin' in her mind to do, she done it. If I said a word to try to stop her, I'd get the *"look."* She was determined that bird was gonna live. When it got healthy 'nuf to fly, she cupped her hands real gentle like 'round it, walked outside, opened her palms face up in front of her, and watched it take off flyin' to the closest tree. Annie used to sing to that bird by whistlin' a tune she thought a mama bird would chirp. After Annie set it free, it come back every spring and chirped that same song Annie whistled to it when it was a baby. My Annie had a heart of gold. I cain't help but miss her. I wonder if that bird knows she's gone. Truth is, I ain't seen it in the spring not one time since Annie passed. Maybe it flew up to heaven to be with her. Maybe not. I know if I had wings, I sure 'nuf would.

We was goin' into 'nother summer soon. Grace and Jacob's gettin' ready to turn seven in the fall. I used to like it when one season passed into the next season. Not no more though. It just brings the time the twins is gonna be leavin' closer. I reckon Caleb's gonna go back to livin' with the other wolves then. I'd sure 'nuf like it though if he stayed with me. If he don't, all that'll be left is me. I ain't feelin' sorry for myself. I know God's got plans for all of us here on earth. I's not special. I's as much a sinner as everyone else. Gotta do my time on this earth like all the folk gotta do. We just need to be thankful to *Him* for givin' us life to begin with. 'Sides, if it wasn't for *Him* givin' me life, I'd of never met my Annie. Havin' even one day with her was better than havin' none. I keep tellin' myself someday my whole family's gonna be together 'gain in heaven. I reckon I can stand bein' 'lone for a time down here doin' what God wants me to do when it means some day me and Annie's gonna be together 'gain. I try not to look too far into the days comin' up no more. I learned from all this goin' on with the devil to take one day at a time. Every day we got here on earth, I reckon we gotta purpose to fill. By all that's been goin' on, I 'magine I ain't filled mine yet. Maybe Annie did. I was thinkin' her purpose is layin' 'head of her in heaven though since she was took so young. Like Grace told me, Annie's gonna help her and Jacob hold the devil down.

Ever since the fire at Jeremiah's cabin, the devil's been real quiet. I's sure *It's* up to somethin'. I know the Caulbearer holdin' *It* down is gettin' weaker by the day. Every day I go to thinkin' today's the day but 'fore you know it it's nighttime 'gain and 'nother day has come and gone. I don't know. Maybe the beast is waitin' to catch us when we's least expectin' anythin' to happen. Maybe not. Maybe God is waitin' for the twins to turn seven 'fore *He* does anythin'. Maybe not. Maybe *He's* waitin' for the devil to make the next move. Maybe not. All's I know is there's a whole lot more maybes and maybe nots than there's answers these days.

Jeremiah's been stayin' with Samuel, me, and the twins since his cabin burned down. We's glad to have him. When I lost my Annie, I went to drinkin'. That's when the devil grabbed 'hold of me for a time. I's sure glad God took me back into *His* fold. I noticed Jeremiah's been goin' to where he buried Eve on his land every day and puttin' flowers by the wood cross he made for her. It's a real pretty cross. I don't reckon he's thought 'bout takin' his rightful place in his daddy Simon's cabin since his burned down. Jeremiah's the head of the Taylor family now. I ain't gonna remind him cuz I can keep a better eye on him while he's stayin' with us. We was with him when he buried Eve. It was real sad when he placed Eve's pretty blue eyes in the two empty holes in her face where they used to sit 'fore coverin' her up with dirt. We was both wipin' the tears 'way 'fore we couldn't keep up with 'em no more and they went to rollin' down our faces. I wonder if she ever showed herself to him. I don't think he'd say if she did. He was always a quiet man. He helps Samuel and me out with the huntin' now he's stayin' with us. He more than earns his keep. He ain't never been a lazy man. The twins like him 'lot. He plays games like tag and hide 'n seek with 'em now and 'gain. I know that's makin' Annie and Eve real happy. He'd of made a great daddy. Too bad the first and only baby him and Eve had belonged to Satan. They didn't deserve that. No one does. Now we know why Eve carried this baby and none of the others. It's cuz Satan put Esau in her. I don't think Eve would've ever had a baby otherwise. I reckon she had female problems that made her lose 'em all 'fore they was born. Jeremiah's still young but we's not allowed to take 'nother mate if one of us dies. I reckon cuz it could get real confusin' when we passed if more than one wife, or husband, was waitin' for us in heaven. I know I wouldn't even if I could cuz far as I's concerned, I's still married to my Annie and nothin' never gonna change that. Ain't no one left to choose nohows when you's older than matin' age. At fourteen, there's plenty of girls to choose from. By the time you get to your twenties or so, the pickin's is slim. Only the spinsters left.

Last night when me, Daryl, Joshua, and Jeremiah left my cabin to feed the beast, *It* was actin' all crazy 'gain. The ground 'neath our feet was rumblin' and shakin' but we just kept walkin'. We all started singin' *Jesus Loves Me.* By the time we got to the hole, *It* stopped. Somethin' was different this time. The fire in the pit was burnin' higher and brighter. The devil's red eyes was glowin' up closer to the edge of the hole where we was all standin'. Not way down deep where they most of the time was 'fore. When I seen six more red eyes popped up next to *It,* I jumped back real quick so I couldn't see 'em no mores. Sure as I was standin' there, I knowed they was the eyes of Matthew, Esau, and Hannah. Lookin' over at the others, I seen Jeremiah starin' down at 'em all. He had a big ol' smile on his face. That's when he went to tippin' forward like he was 'bout to be pulled in. Soon as I jumped to grab him back, he dropped his plate of food and followed it into the pit. He was gone just like that. He didn't even scream. The way the other two men was actin' made me think they might've been put under *Its* spell for a time, too, so I quick grabbed Joshua and Daryl by the arms 'fore they went to joinin' Jeremiah in the fire cuz they was startin' to wobble 'round where they was standin'. When they snapped outta the devil's spell, we took to runnin' fast as we could back down the tunnel. All the way, we heard Satan's voice echoin' 'round us loud as can be,

"An eye for an eye! tick tock tick tock. Time is running out. Who will be next? Hahahahahahahahaha!"

When we got up top, I could tell the twins already knowed what happened. They was sittin' on their mattress real quiet like with Caleb layin' between 'em. Scared the crap right outta me when Caleb jumped up and went to lowerin' his head, barin' his fangs, and growlin' at Daryl, Joshua, and me. When he settled himself smack dab in front of Joshua though, I couldn't make no sense outta what he was doin' so I told him in kinda a rough voice,

"Caleb! Lay down and be quiet!"

I could tell he didn't want no part of what I was sayin' but he listened anyways. Once he laid back down with the twins, 'stead of growlin', he kept his eyes all squinted up and fixed on Joshua.

None of us said a word 'bout what happened to Jeremiah. It wasn't somethin' we felt like talkin' 'bout. Men in these parts ain't supposed to cry. If we went to tellin' the story 'bout what happened, we'd all be cryin'. I figured we could talk 'bout it when we woke in the mornin' so we just laid down on our mattresses and tried to sleep. Out of the corner of my eye, I saw Samuel shake his head back and forth real sad like 'fore he laid back down. He had to turn into a man 'fore his time is what I was thinkin'.

I was 'shamed of myself for lettin' such a thing happen to Jeremiah. Must've been somethin' I could've, would've, should've done to stop it. Maybe I been thinkin' too much of my own family's safety and not the others. I'd

243

be sure not to make that mistake 'gain. 'Specially since I was supposed to be the leader in all this. That way of thinkin' ain't gonna help Jeremiah none now though. No doubt *It* knowed Jeremiah was the weakest of the four of us bein' he lost his mama, daddy, and wife and had no survivin' children to look after. *It* said an *"eye for an eye"* so I got to wonderin' which one of us was gonna be next. To be even, *It* had to take two more of us. Jeremiah must've made up for us killin' Esau. I was hopin' God would make *His* move 'fore 'nother one of us dropped into the devil's hands. None of us minded goin' to heaven to be with our wives but fallin' into the devil's pit ain't somethin' none of us is wantin' to do. When I laid down between the twins and wrapped my arms 'round 'em, Grace whispered in my ear,

"It is not your fault, daddy. You could not have done anything to prevent it. Someday you will understand. Everything happens for a reason. Sometimes we have to be patient and wait to know why. God will let us know in due time."

My little girl sure was a smart one. I think she was a growed woman livin' inside a little girl's body. Jacob raised himself up, leaned over at me, and gave me a hug and a peck on the cheek. At the same time, he whispered in my ear,

"I love you, daddy."

I hugged him so hard back I think I 'bout broke him. 'Fore closin' my eyes, I told 'em both I loved 'em, too.

All night long into the early mornin' hours 'fore the sun come up, I couldn't stop thinkin' 'bout poor Jeremiah. I wondered what his fallin' into the devil's hole meant. Did it mean that he was gonna have to live in hell with the devil now? I's not one to question God but that there just plain out and out ain't right. Jeremiah was a good and righteous man. Anybody just lost all their loved ones standin' there starin' down into those evil red eyes would've tipped over and dropped down into that fire. When a man's broken, he needs some time to fill himself back up with God is all. Heck, the only reason I wasn't starin' down into that hole was cuz Grace warned me not to. I prayed God ain't gonna let that demon hold onto one of *His* children. I reckon it'd all come together at the end.

Just when I was layin' 'round doin' 'lot of thinkin', I heard a ruckus goin' on outside. When I seen Joshua already standin' at the window with his back to us and his firearm at the ready, I quick woke Samuel and Daryl. Grabbin' their firearms, they jumped up quick. Samuel went to joinin' Joshua at one window and me and Daryl run to the other one. When I looked out, I seen a pack of wolves standin' outside the front door howlin'. Maybe they was invitin' us outside so they could eat us. Maybe not. Maybe they was invitin' Caleb out so they could eat him. They sure 'nuf was gonna have a fight on their hands if that was the case.

They was growlin', howlin', and carryin' on like they wanted to eat us for breakfast. I figured this was some more of Satan's doin'. It was still mostly dark out. Caleb snarlin' and growlin' jumped up and was standin' strong in front of the twins. I turned 'round to tell the twins to get down low and stay behind Caleb when outta the corner of my eye I seen Joshua Nelson turn his gun to Samuel's head.

Just as he was 'bout to pull the trigger, Caleb come flyin' through the air 'cross the room. Knockin' Joshua off his feet, he landed on top of him and bit down on his gun hand. When the gun fell to the floor so did Joshua. That's when Joshua's eyes turned red and he started cursin' at everyone. His body was thrashin' and spinnin' all 'round the floor. I quick grabbed up some rope while Samuel and Daryl held him down to the ground. We wrestled him up to a chair, then tied his arms, hands, legs, and feet to it as good and tight as we could. Wasn't no easy job neither cuz he was foamin' from outta the mouth and jerkin' 'round like he was filled up with the devil. He was stronger than I ever knowed him to be. When his eyes went to rollin' back in his head, I knowed the devil was sure 'nuf inside him. Come to think of it, he was doin' just like we was told Simon Taylor done that night after he come back from feedin' the beast. No doubt this was the devil's doin'. I couldn't understand a word he was sayin' 'cept the cursin' words cuz everythin' else comin' outta his mouth sounded like he was talkin' in a language from 'nother country. It was 'lot like what I heard comin' outta Matthew, Esau, and Hannah's mouths when I seen 'em down by the hole worshippin' the devil. Poor Joshua was possessed by Satan. Now I knowed why Caleb was growlin' at him when we first come back from feedin' the beast last night. Animals got that sixth sense. They can tell those things 'fore we can. I heard 'bout the devil possessin' people 'fore. *It* even crawled up in me 'ways back and took me over for a time when I took to beatin' my boys. This was somethin' more though. Joshua looked like a demon. Other than seein' Matthew, Esau and Hannah by the devil's hole with glarin' red eyes, I ain't never in my life ever thought for a minute I'd lay witness to one of our own bein' possessed by *It* like that. I went to thinkin' how terrible it must've been for Jeremiah to walk in on his daddy, Simon, layin' on the floor dead with red foam runnin' outta his mouth and his tongue layin' on the ground next to him. If I didn't know it 'fore, I sure 'nuf knowed it now....Satan had to be stopped 'fore he went to takin' us all over. He was gettin' stronger every day.

When I looked back out the window, the wolves was gone. That was a blessin'. I told everyone to drop to their knees so we could thank God for gettin' us outta this one and to ask *Him* to have mercy on Joshua's soul so it could head on up to heaven 'stead of hell. Just as everyone dropped to their knees and was in a prayin' position, Joshua raised up off the floor still tied up in that chair and went flyin' straight up in the air towards the ceilin'. *WHAM!* All the time he was doin' that, he was laughin' like he done lost his mind. The top of his head took to bangin' into the ceilin' over and over 'gain. He just kept on laughin' and cursin' us. Up and down that chair went with Joshua tied up in it. *BANG! BANG! BANG! BANG!* Blood and brains was splatterin' all over the place. His face and clothes was covered in his own blood. His red face and red glarin' eyes made him look just like Matthew, Esau, and Hannah done that time I seen 'em praisin' Satan down by the hole. The devil sure 'nuf took Joshua over. There wasn't nothin' I could do to help him. *BANG! BANG! BANG! WHAM! SMASH! THUMP! BANG!* Over and over 'gain. Me, Daryl, and Samuel dropped to our knees and started sayin' the Lord's Prayer.

"Our Father which art in heaven,"

BANG! BANG! BANG!

"Hallowed be thy name,"

BANG! BANG! BANG!

While Jacob was bangin' his brains out and we was prayin', Jacob stood up and walked into the middle of the room. He was standin' right under the chair Joshua was flyin' 'round tied up in. Grace followed behind him. The rest of us got all quiet when he raised his hands up to heaven and took over sayin' The Lord's Prayer softly at first and then louder and louder. His eyes all the time stayed focused on Joshua. Grace joined him,

"Our Father which art in heaven, Hallowed be thy name."

BANG! BANG! BANG! BANG!

"Thy kingdom come, Thy will be done in earth, as it is in heaven."

BANG! WHAM! SMASH! BANG! THUMP! BANG!

"Forgive us our debts, as we will forgive our debtors...."

A couple more *BANGS* then Joshua and the chair he was tied up in fell back to the ground.... *THUD!*

Joshua was dead. Landed on his side. Most of the top of his head was gone. Brains and blood was all over the ceilin', walls, and floor. Jacob and Grace kneeled over him and prayed real quiet like for God to take him to heaven 'til his eyes turned from red back to their normal color. 'Cept for Grace and Jacob, we was all in shock after that. I don't know 'bout the others but I had a feelin' this was *an eye for an eye* number two. Matthew's killin' was paid for now. 'Least that's how I looked at it. I don't think the devil did though. There's me, Samuel, Daryl, Grace and Jacob left now. Our numbers was goin' down'.

While kneelin' over my ol' friend's dead body, I whispered,

"Hallelujah. Praise the Lord. Amen."

Chapter 18

Psalms 23:4 *Yea though I walk through the valley of the shadow of death, I'll fear no evil: for thou art with me; thy rod and thy staff, they comfort me.*

Samuel, Daryl, and me got done wipin' up the mess left from Joshua's head bein' used as a batterin' ram 'gainst the ceilin'. After we got done cleanin' up all the blood and brains left stickin' to the ceilin', walls, and floor, we all went outside and puked. When we got done doin' that, we thought it was only fittin' we bury our friend next to his wife, Martha, so we grabbed our shovels and hauled his body over to his cabin. After we buried him next to Martha good and proper and said a prayer over him, all of us went back to my cabin to take a nap 'fore the sun come up on us. The buryin' of our own was quick becomin' a habit none of us was takin' a likin' to.

When daylight come, I woke to hearin' the twins runnin' 'round the yard outside playin' with Caleb. He was a better babysitter than most folk I knowed. He loved Grace and Jacob. The twins had to grow up in 'lot of ways 'fore their time but they was still children. Annie was right 'bout that. They never did no cryin' over nobody we lost, not even their mama and little sister. I reckon they knowed better than any of us they was headed to a better place. 'Least that's what I always prayed when I was sayin' final words over 'em....that they was in heaven and not hell bein' the devil's the one who took 'em....'cept Annie and

Mae. That was a thought weighin' heavy on my mind. Now I knowed why Caleb was growlin' at Joshua when we got back from feedin' the beast. He was warnin' us. He knowed after Satan pulled Jeremiah down into his pit, he took hold of Joshua right then and there. That's why all those wolves was at our door. I reckon that was more than 'nuf proof animals sense things we don't. Joshua didn't deserve what happened to him no more than Jeremiah or Simon did. He's got three children left in the care of my Emma and his son, Steven. Joshua's oldest girl, Rose, she's ol' 'nuf to help Emma out with the chores 'round the cabin, watchin' over the younger children, and whatever else needs doin'. Heck, Emma had to take over for Annie when she passed. Emma was only eleven at the time. She done a darned good job, too. I gotta remember to tell her that one day when this is all over. I don't know. Maybe when Rose gets chose by some young man, she'll take her two younger sisters with her and raise 'em up for her mama and daddy. Maybe not. Maybe they'll stay put with their brother Steven and Emma. Maybe not.

Joshua, Simon, and Jeremiah all was good men. Martha, Ruth, Eve, and Rebekah was all good women. Grace keeps tellin' me it ain't my fault but I cain't help thinkin' there must've been somethin' I could've done. 'Stead, I helped tie Joshua up in his death chair. Well, one more to go. I wondered if it was gonna be me or Daryl. My guess was Daryl cuz we killed Hannah but the devil had 'lot of tricks up *Its* sleeve and *It* might get sneaky and take me 'stead.

"An eye for an eye number three comin' right up," I was thinkin' to myself, *"How'd you like him served? Raw, rare, medium, or well-done?"*

Well, I was madder than I's ever been. Five good women, one innocent child, and three honest men was gone. All of 'em doin' God's work from the day they was born. We don't know nothin' else up here in the mountains. It's what we been raised up to do from the time we's born. My daddy taught me, his daddy taught him and his daddy's daddy taught his daddy. We ain't got no dress up clothes or shiny automobiles to drive 'round in. Our women ain't walkin' 'round in them high heeled shoes, wearin' red colorin' on their mouths and faces, gettin' their hair all done up fancy schmancy, or wigglin' their bottoms from side to side when they's walkin' down the street. None of that high falutin' city stuff would last long up here. We's simple, hard workin' folks is all. Not one of us ever throwed in the towel and left the life we was born to live. We don't have no televisions for entertainment. Heck, ain't nobody got no time to sit down and relax long 'nuf to even watch such a thing no ways. Most folk up here ain't never even seen an automobile or a television. They only know what we tell 'em every five years or so when we get back from checkin' on the city folk.

We raise our children to take over when we go to heaven. We ain't leavin' 'em no fun and games. We's leavin' 'em nothin' but back breakin' hard as hell work. But it's righteous work given to us by God. Our families been doin' it for hundreds of years. Maybe longer. There's not one of us wouldn't give his life to help God save the world from Satan. Some of us already have. It's bad 'nuf *Its* followers is runnin' loose spreadin' evil everywheres. After I seen what *It* done to my good friends Joshua and Jeremiah, and what Jeremiah said *It* done to his daddy, Simon, I'm thinkin' it probably possessed the souls of 'lot of city folk. *It* gets inside you somehows and takes over your body. Annie and Mae, Eve and Jeremiah, Martha and Joshua, Ruth and Simon, and Daryl's wife, Rebekah, was all believers in God. They was all doin' their parts but they's dead now. I don't even know where Joshua, Jeremiah, and Simon ended up but it's lookin' like it was hell bein' that one of 'em fell into Satan's fire and the other two got took over by *It*. I worry 'bout Ruth, too. She decided to go with her husband, Simon, but where'd she follow him to? Far as I knowed, that ain't right at all. I gotta believe Grace when she said *"everything happens for a reason."* I know I gotta trust in the Lord. I reckon when the devil seen I gave up on God, *It* quick jumped inside me and made me go to drinkin' and beatin' on Bobby and Jacob. Don't wanna go doin' that ever 'gain. If I do, I'll just throw myself into the fire 'long with Satan cuz that's where I'd belong. I's gotta hang onto my faith no matter what. Gotta remember to fill myself up with the Lord every day so none of the devil can sneak back up in me. Satan's a tricky one. He's a liar to boot. I's not givin' up my faith for nothin'. No matter what. I just pray I don't gotta never bury 'nother of my children. Maybe Annie and Mae's gonna show themselves to me 'gain to remind me why I's doin' all this. Maybe not.

After we was all up and movin' 'round the cabin, Daryl went down the mountain to see his four children who'd been stayin' with his brother, Thomas, and his family. I knowed they's gonna be real happy to see him 'gain. He couldn't get over there fast 'nuf to see 'em, too. That Daryl sure 'nuf's a good man. He stood right in front of his children protectin' 'em from Hannah and Matthew. I knowed his wife, Rebekah, was proud of him. His sisters Annie, Martha, and Eve, too. I reckon if the devil goes to takin' Daryl next, his brother Thomas is gonna have to take over bein' head of the Andersons. 'Least til Daryl's oldest boy, Zachary, is old 'nuf to do it. He's only thirteen now so it'll be 'while. No sense thinkin' 'bout all that now anyways. Just play it by God I reckon. Daryl said he'd meet us back at my cabin come nightfall.

Samuel, me, the twins and Caleb went to visit Bobby and 'Lizabeth. My sister Sarah and her family come over, too. I had to laugh to myself when I went to thinkin' Sarah was just comin' to find out what was goin' on bein' she was the nosy one outta all the Sanders. None of us men told any of our families what we's goin' through these days with Satan. No reason to scare everybody. They all knowed somethin' was up anyways by the way we's actin'. Don't think any of 'em want to really know though. I reckon you could say they's turnin' the other cheek.

Emma and Steven stopped by with their two children and Joshua's three girls, includin' Rose. Seein' Rose put a smile on Samuel's face. They was standin' off to the side from everyone else flirtin' and talkin'. They was both matin' age now. When I seen the way Samuel looked at Rose and the way she looked at him, I knowed right then he was sure 'nuf gonna pick her for his wife when this was all over and done. If he was still livin'. It made me real sad to think he might not be. Bobby and Emma, too. I knowed Grace and Jacob was gonna be leavin' me soon 'nuf. Tried not to think too much 'bout that neither. When Karl and Tobias showed up with their families, and my brother Ray, his wife and six children come marchin' over from their cabin, it was like we was havin' an on purpose family reunion. The women all cooked up somethin' special and laid it out on a table outside. All the children runned and played with Caleb. None of 'em ever dreamed they'd be playin' with a real live wild wolf. Caleb loved the attention. He kept a watchful eye on all of 'em, 'specially Jacob and Grace. The littlest ones climbed on top of his back and he gave 'em a ride 'round the yard. All the adults sat 'round outside enjoyin' the sunshine and warm day. Bobby, Samuel, and me kept what was happenin' to ourselves but it was always in the back of our minds. We kept our firearms tucked into the back of our trousers and at the ready. The men folk up here in the mountains never had no need to carry their firearms nowheres 'fore. Just for huntin' is all. Everythin's different now. All the others suspected somethin' bad was brewin' but at the end of the day not one of 'em asked or brought it up....not even Sarah.

News travels fast in the mountains. Steven knowed his daddy, Joshua, was gone. I don't think he knowed the whole story but he knowed he ain't with the livin' no more. Steven was the new head of the Nelson family now but we wasn't askin' him to take over for his daddy yet. I told him when this was all over would be a good 'nuf time. He was grievin'. He lost his mama and his daddy. Satan robbed him of the honor of sendin' 'em to heaven so he had a personal vendetta, too. After Jeremiah went and fell into the devil's fire, his next oldest brother, Carl, would be takin' over as head of the Taylors. Esau was Jeremiah and Eve's only child but he didn't count bein' he belonged to the devil. Like Steven, we ain't askin' nothin' outta Carl yet neither. We wasn't thinkin' no farther 'head than that.

Everybody sat 'round eatin', talkin', and laughin'. Every now and 'gain I 'magined seein' my Annie runnin' 'round to everyone makin' sure they had somethin' to eat and was happy. She loved family get togethers. Little Mae, she'd be right behind her mama followin' her wherever she went. Annie would send her off to the other children to ask 'em if they wanted anythin' to eat. I think she always hoped she'd get caught up in runnin' and playin' with 'em. But she never did. As fast as she'd run off to ask 'em what her mama told her to ask 'em, she'd be back to followin' Annie 'round 'gain lickity split. I must've been smilin' real big cuz Emma come up to me and asked me what I was grinnin' so big 'bout.

"Ain't nothin' better or more important in the world than family," I told her jumpin' up from my chair, grabbin' 'hold of her, swingin' her 'round, and givin' her a big ol' kiss on the side of her face.

When sister Sarah seen that, she must've got all worked up cuz she went to beltin' out *To God Be The Glory*. Everybody joined in. I had to laugh to myself how much I enjoyed listenin' to her talk now. Always put cotton in my ears 'fore. Not when she went to singin' though. She had the voice of an angel.

God sure 'nuf gave us a beautiful warm day to do our visitin'. I knowed everythin' happened for a reason with God though so all's I could think of was the big battle must be comin' up on us fast. When the sun started goin' down, we passed out hugs and kisses 'fore headin' back home. None of us knowin' if we'd ever see each other 'gain. Ain't nobody said nothin' though. It was like a big secret everybody knowed but didn't talk 'bout.

When we got back to my cabin, Daryl was already there. We still had to go feed the beast tonight. Neither one of us was lookin' forward to that. We's the only two heads of the families of our generation left. We both knowed one of us was gonna be the devil's third victim. We just didn't know when, where, how, or who. We was all so wore out from a day of laughin', eatin', talkin', and singin', I tucked Grace under one arm and Jacob under the other, then we closed our eyes to take a nap. I hoped Annie would come to me in a dream while I was sleepin'. Caleb settled down by the front door. The trapdoor was locked. We was safe….'least for now.

I must've been real tired cuz when I woke it was near midnight. Daryl and the twins was just sittin' 'round bein' quiet. They said they didn't wanna wake me. I didn't dream of Annie. I don't know why she ain't comin' 'round no more. Maybe she was busy helpin' God with *His* final plans to keep the demon chained up down in the pit for 'nother hundred years. So like every other night at ten minutes to midnight, Daryl and me made our way through the trapdoor and down into the tunnel. Neither one of us done no talkin' on the way. We both dreaded goin'. When we got to the hole, we throwed our plates in and then turned 'round real quick like to start walkin' 'way fast. We didn't wanna give It no chance at possessin' us. I knowed It had to be up to no good though. It was bein' too quiet. Didn't see no fire shootin' out or red eyes peekin' up at the top of the pit. Daryl and me knowed one of our numbers was gonna be called soon 'nuf. All's I knowed was this was the quietest the beast ever was since I been feedin' It. It was up to no good....I knowed it. Just didn't know what It was plannin' is all.

While we was walkin' fast as we could without breakin' into a full blowed run back down the tunnel, Daryl asked me if it turned out to bein' his turn would I make sure his children was cared for. He said,

"Calvin, I don't like sayin' this cuz I ain't tryin' to make you sad but the truth is at the end of all this you's not gonna be left with no children 'cept those that's already growed and takin' care of themselves and their own families. I thought maybe you'd do me the honor of helpin' my brother, Thomas, and his wife watch over my four children. You know, just by checkin' in on 'em every now and 'gain. Maybe teachin' 'em a thing or two 'bout huntin', fishin' and stuff like that. Thomas got two girls and probably don't know too much 'bout the raisin' of boys. Ain't no hard feelin's if you don't wanna. Just say so. I just know you done a fine job raisin' your own and Thomas is gonna have his hands full with my four boys sure 'nuf."

Then with a real big smile on his face, he said laughin',

"They's sure 'nuf a wild bunch. Anyways, I'd just feel 'lot better 'bout dyin' if I knowed you was gonna be lookin' out for my kids is all."

"Well, Daryl," I answered him not knowin' if what I was sayin' was the truth, "I'd be honored to do that for you but you's gonna raise your own children when this is all done cuz you's not goin' nowheres no time soon. But you gotta promise me you'll do me the honor of lookin' in on my two growed boys, Bobby and Samuel, 'long with my daughter, Emma, every now and 'gain if I's the one to go. Caleb, too."

We both stopped long 'nuf to spit into our hands and do a handshake on it like we used to do when makin' a promise when we was boys. Truth be told, like me, Joshua, and Daryl done that time we snuck down into the tunnel by the hole when we was ten. In these parts, it was the next best thing to swearin' on the Bible.

When we got up top in the cabin, I pulled Daryl off to the side so I could have a talk with him while we was both still with the livin'. The twins, Samuel, and Caleb was all sound 'sleep. We both pulled up a chair and sat down at the table. When I leaned in towards him real close, I whispered,

"Listen now, Daryl. There's a trick to all this you know. Cuz we's related through your sister Annie I's gonna share it with you. I's gonna tell you exactly what you gotta do to keep the devil from gettin' inside you."

That's when Daryl went to leanin' in towards me tryin' to catch every word I was 'bout to say. I knowed after he seen Jeremiah fall into the devil's hole and Joshua bangin' his head into the ceilin', he was ready to say, do, and try anythin'.

"You gotta fill yourself up with God," I said, "from the top of your head to the tips of your toes. You gotta get on your knees and beg *His* forgiveness for any sin you done or any sin you thought 'bout doin'. You gotta be serious, too. Cain't be lyin' 'bout none of it. If you's honest with *Him*, you'll start feelin' yourself be filled up with the Lord the second *He* believes what you's sayin'. I know this is the truth cuz it happened to me. When my Annie died, I lost my way. I stopped believin'. I went to drinkin' and beatin' my boys. I ain't told no one 'bout that 'fore cuz I's 'shamed of myself for what I done. Annie's spirit come to me and slapped me outta what I was doin' wrong. That's when I got my faith back. I miss my Annie every day but God needs her more. I understand that now. I's so filled up with God now there ain't no room in me for Satan. Hallelujah! Praise the Lord! Amen!"

Daryl sat there starin' at me for 'bout a minute like he was tryin' to take it all in so when he went to doin' it he ain't gonna make no mistakes. All of a sudden right then and there, he fell to his knees and started into beggin' the Lord Jesus Christ to forgive him. He went on for the longest time 'til finally God must've believed him cuz he jumped up and went to shufflin' his feet 'round like he was dancin', wavin' his arms up in the air, and yellin',

"Hallelujah! Praise the Lord! Amen!"

Ain't long and I joined him. We was both sure 'nuf filled up with the joy and love of God!

All's I knowed was there's five of us filled up with the Lord in this room now. There's me, Samuel, Grace, Jacob, and Daryl. The pickin's was slim for Satan. I reckon he'd have to settle with two for three. Well, I knowed I spoke too soon when Caleb come runnin' outta nowheres with eyes glowin' red, snarlin', growlin' and teeth bared flyin' through the air goin' for my throat. The next thing I knowed I heard a firearm go off and Caleb was layin' dead at my feet. Firearm in hand, Samuel was standin' behind where Caleb hit the ground. He was cryin' harder than I ever seen him cry. The gunshot must've woke Grace and Jacob cuz they was sittin' up on their mattress, eyes wide open lookin' over at all of us starin' down at Caleb layin' on the ground dead. Jacob had his arm 'round Grace but neither one of 'em cried a tear. They both walked over to Caleb and laid their little hands on top of him. They probably thought they 'least should try to heal him. It was too late. He was gone. We all knowed it.

Samuel kept sayin', *"I's sorry"* over and over 'gain.

Nobody blamed him. Didn't matter though. He was blamin' himself. We all knowed he loved Caleb as much as the rest of us. It was Satan's doin'.

Grace and Jacob got up off their knees and went over to take hold of Samuel's hands. They both was smilin' up at him. Grace told him,

"Do not worry. It is not your fault. You had to save daddy. It is the way it had to be. You will understand someday. We all have to be strong and accept what happens."

Jacob stood at Samuel's side shakin' his little head up and down real fast. The twins led him over to Caleb and pulled him down to his knees with 'em. Daryl and me joined 'em. Surroundin' our wolf friend, we said a prayer askin' God to take him to heaven. We knowed it wasn't none of Caleb's doin'. It was Satan. Three for three. An eye for an eye.

"We's even," is what I was thinkin'.

I knowed this battle ain't gonna end in a tie though. Kneelin' over Caleb and holdin' hands, we all shouted loud and clear,

"Hallelujah. Praise the Lord. Amen."

Chapter 19

Revelation 20:10 *And the devil that deceived them was cast into the lake of fire and brimstone, where the beast and the false prophet are, and shall be tormented day and night for ever and ever.*

When the sun come out, we went to buryin' Caleb up on the hill under the maple tree where Annie and Mae was. He's a member of our family. He's as much a Sanders as any of us. Grace and Jacob both picked a bunch of pretty flowers and throwed 'em on top of him 'fore we covered him up. I said a nice prayer over him. Samuel was cryin' so hard his shoulders was shakin'. Just like I remember seein' little Mae do when Annie went to heaven. Jacob and Grace tried to make him feel better by holdin' his hands and smilin' up at him. They knowed Caleb was with God. We all loved him. He sure 'nuf loved Jacob and Grace. Samuel and me, too, I reckon. Jacob was his favorite though. I 'magine cuz he needed the most protectin'. I knowed Samuel was beatin' himself up inside. I tried talkin' to him. Nothin' I could say to him to make him feel better. This was somethin' he'd have to work out himself. I reckon it was part of becomin' a man.

When we was walkin' slow back down the hill and thinkin' hard, all of a sudden the sky got real dark, the clouds turned grey and the wind picked up. It looked like there was a real bad storm comin' our way. Grace and Jacob was 'head of us holdin' hands like they always done.

Without no warnin', Jacob stopped dead in his tracks. Turnin' to face us, he went to lookin' up into the sky all serious like. Heck, he looked madder than hell. I swear his forehead was so wrinkled up his eyebrows *was* touchin' his nose. When he leaned over and whispered somethin' in Grace's ear, I was thinkin' she was gonna be pullin' on my trousers shortly to tell me what he had to say. 'Stead, with her curly brown hair whippin' 'round in the wind and her blue eyes bluer than they ever been, she went to raisin' her hands 'bove her head reachin' high as she could up to heaven. In a voice loud 'nuf for all of us to hear, she said,

"It is time! The time has come for Satan to be stopped! God has spoken! Hallelujah! Praise the Lord! Amen!"

At the same time, Jacob was noddin' his head up and down faster than I ever seen him nod it. Me and Samuel dropped to our knees and hollered out,

"Hallelujah! Praise the Lord! Amen!"

When we raised ourselves back up off the ground, we finished our walk back to the cabin. Grace and Jacob hand in hand, not sayin' 'nother word. They wasn't smilin' no more neither.

By the time we made it back to the cabin, it was pourin' down rain. Never in all my time on earth did I ever see it rain as hard as it was rainin' today. I hoped there ain't gonna be 'nother flood like there was back in Noah's time. The skies was so dark, it looked like nighttime but without no stars or moon. I 'magine the sun went to hidin' real fast behind the grey clouds that took over the sky cuz it was nowheres to be seen. Annie used to call 'em *mad* clouds when they got that way. All four of us runned into the cabin soakin' wet from head to toe. Not sayin' a word, we dried ourselves off and changed into our one set of spare clothes.

Rememberin' what Annie used to do when the kids come in from the rain, I started a fire in the hearth and hung our wet clothes 'round it on the backs of chairs. When it started hailin' big balls of ice, I knowed sure 'nuf it was the wrath of God. They was comin' down so hard, Samuel, Daryl and me kept duckin' our heads down thinkin' they was gonna come crashin' through the roof of the cabin. They didn't bother the twins none though. It was thunderin' louder and lightnin' brighter than I ever seen it do 'fore. Wind was blowin'. Big balls of ice fallin'. Trees swayin' to where their roots was 'most bein' pulled outta the ground. Leaves swirlin' and twirlin' 'round and 'round, up and down. Darker than night out. Looked like I'd of pictured the end of the world to look like.

Daryl was watchin' the storm out the window. His hands was shakin'. I knowed he missed Rebekah but he had little kids to worry 'bout first. Bobby and Emma was growed with families of their own but I still worried 'bout 'em. Just cuz they's growed don't mean I's gonna stop worryin' 'bout 'em. Mae went to heaven with her mama so I knowed she's safe. Samuel's a man now and handles himself good as the next man. Maybe better. That don't make him no less my son. Grace and Jacob is God's children but they's still little. I cain't help but worry 'bout 'em. 'Sides, they's a part of me and Annie just like the others. I don't know how but I knowed this sky darkenin', wind blowin', rainin', hailin', thunderin' and lightnin' was

God's doin'. I figured it was *His* way of lettin' the devil know *It* went too far this time. I don't know 'bout nobody else but I was thinkin' God was awful mad 'bout somethin' and I had a pretty good idea what it was. It come to my mind when the devil went to possessin' an innocent animal, God done drawed the line. Animals got no sins. It'd be my guess, they get an automatic pass into heaven. Anyone gotta mind to send 'em off earlier, other than for eatin' to survive, sure 'nuf gonna deal with the Lord's wrath.

Ever since Jacob said what he had to say to Grace on the hill comin' back from buryin' Caleb, he got real quiet. They both did. Jacob never was one much with words no ways. Grace was always the talker. The twins sat huddled together on their mattress with their backs to us. They was whisperin' real quiet to each other in that language none of us could understand. I didn't even wanna know what they was sayin' cuz I knowed it had to do with the devil and the battle 'head of us. I was 'fraid the time was comin' real soon now when they was leavin' me. I didn't know how two children was gonna go up 'gainst Satan and win but if I was a bettin' man, I'd put everythin' I called mine on Grace and Jacob. They had God on their side. They had me, Samuel, Bobby, and Daryl, too. I'd put my own life out there if it meant it'd help 'em carry out what they was sent by God to do. No doubt in any of our minds that meant chainin' up that demon good and tight for 'nother hundred years.

I spent most of the day sittin' in Annie's rockin' chair waitin' for the storm to pass. Back and forth I rocked with my eyes closed and my head filled with remembrances back to the days when Bobby, Emma, Samuel, and Mae was little ones....'fore Grace and Jacob come 'long. I was thinkin' how much they loved the rain. Whenever it'd come pourin' down, they'd get all excited and beg Annie to let 'em go run 'round in it. Annie told 'em when it was rainin' and thunderin' the clouds was called *mad* clouds on 'count of they was all dark and hollerin'. 'Long as it was a hot summer day and there ain't no lightnin' shootin' down outta the sky, she'd strip 'em all down to their underwears and turn 'em loose to play outside. 'Fore I knowed it, she'd go to hikin' her dress up 'bove her knees and go runnin' 'round outside in her bare feet with 'em. I'd stand by the door laughin' and shoutin' out to 'em,

"You all done went crazy!"

Never joined 'em though. Sure 'nuf wish I would've now. One rainin' day, she taught 'em how to make mud pies and how to have a mud pie slingin' fight by throwin' the first one at Bobby. The fightin' was on after that. Mud pies was flyin' through the air. They even throwed one at me but I quick shut the door 'fore it hit me. When she taught 'em how to catch raindrops in their mouths, she told 'em whoever caught the most was the winner and was gonna get an extra big hug 'fore goin' to sleep that night. They'd run 'round with their little heads tilted back to heaven tryin' to count how many raindrops they done swallowed. Since we didn't raise no lyin' children and none of 'em was sure how many they caught, Annie declared 'em all winners givin' 'em all an extra big hug that night. When they was all done playin' outside, they'd come back into the cabin drippin' rain and mud all over the floor. Annie didn't care. She'd get down on her hands and knees and mop it all up after they went to sleep for the night. When they was done playin', she'd march 'em all over to the water pump up at the lodge and throw buckets of clean cold water all over 'em. I could hear 'em all squealin' and laughin' from way up where they was to where I was inside the cabin. Annie sure 'nuf loved all her babies no matter how big they got. Still does. They sure 'nuf loved her 'lot, too. Still do.

Grace and Jacob didn't say much the rest of the day. No one did. I knowed they was done makin' plans to take on the devil. Neither one of 'em cried 'bout Annie, Mae, or Caleb when they left us. No doubt they missed 'em. They wasn't sad though cuz they knowed they'd be seein' 'em all 'gain one day in heaven. That's what faith is I reckon. The twins knowed more than regular folks 'bout heaven and hell….and faith. They was walkin' talkin' examples of it. When it stopped rainin', the sun come out shinin' brighter than ever. I figured that meant God calmed down some and was happy 'gain. The plan to lock Satan up was 'bout to be put into action real soon. I could feel it in every bone in my body. Maybe Caleb passed some of his sixth sense on to me. Maybe not.

When the sun come out and was shinin' real bright 'gain, Grace come up to me sayin',

"Daddy, we want you, Samuel, and Daryl to follow us outside. We want to show you something."

Samuel and Daryl was 'sleep so I woke 'em. Everybody knowed sleepin' ain't never better than when it's done on a rainy day but if the twins wanted 'em to wake up and come outside, I wasn't gonna be the one to put up no argument with 'em. Grace and Jacob was holdin' hands when they stepped out the door into the sunlight. When the three of us followed 'em outside, they turned to point out a beautiful rainbow spread 'cross the sky from one end of the earth to the other. The twins turned to face us when they was standin' 'neath it somewheres in the middle. They motioned with their hands for us to stop where we was, so we did. Then, puttin' their fingers to their lips they both said,

"Shhhhhh."

Together they lowered their heads and folded their hands in prayer,

"Our Father, Who art in Heaven, hallowed be Thy name;Thy Kingdom come, Thy will be done on earth as it is in Heaven. Give us this day our daily bread and forgive us our trespasses as we forgive those who trespass against us; and lead us not into temptation but deliver us from evil. Amen."

Filled up with the Lord, Daryl, me and Samuel hollered out,

"Hallelujah! Praise the Lord! Amen!"

When the twins was done prayin' and we was done shoutin', they raised their heads back up to look at us. When they done that, mama and daddy, Annie and Mae, Simon and Ruth, Jeremiah and Eve, Joshua and Martha, and Rebekah appeared 'fore us as spirits. They was all surrounded by a white light. Between Jacob and Grace, stood Caleb. They was all smilin', even Caleb. Samuel dropped to his knees with his arms spread out and started cryin' out to his mama and little sister how much he missed 'em and loved 'em. Daryl kept rubbin' his eyes and shakin' his head like he didn't know if it was real or he was still 'sleep and dreamin'. He finally dropped to his knees like Samuel done. He told Rebekah he'd be comin' to join her when God's ready for him and Thomas was takin' real good care of their children. I sure 'nuf was happy to see Simon, Ruth, Jeremiah, and Joshua was in heaven. That was weighin' heavy on my mind and the twins must've knowed it. I reckon this was their way of showin' us all our loved ones who passed was with God and everythin' was gonna be alright no matter what else happened. All the spirits was holdin' hands and smilin' so we knowed they was happy. There was no doubt in my mind the day was gonna come when I'd be with Annie and Mae 'gain 'long with the rest of my family when it's their time. I don't know. Maybe this was a gift the twins was givin' Samuel, Daryl, and me cuz they was leavin' us soon. Maybe it was their way of givin' us hope and somethin' to smile 'bout when they ain't 'round no more. Somethin' to remember 'em by. A way of tellin' us there is life after death and they'd all be waitin' for us. All we gotta do is keep our faith in God. When they disappeared, we all wiped our eyes dry and headed back into the cabin.

That night at ten minutes 'til midnight when I opened the trapdoor, Daryl and me walked down the steps and headed out on our way to feed the beast. We was both filled up with the Lord. Daryl was still smilin' ear to ear from seein' Rebekah earlier. He couldn't stop talkin' 'bout it. Our moods was light and happy. Always done my heart good to see Annie and Mae. Our feet was hardly touchin' the ground. We both took to whistlin' a tune we learned as kids. I think tonight the two of us could've taken on an army of Satans. I was feelin' like I was floatin' on air. The way Daryl was actin', he was, too. We both had bigger than life smiles on our faces as we walked, skipped, and whistled our way to the pit. When we got up to the hole, we looked at each other and laughed after tossin' our plates over the edge. 'Stead of turnin' 'round right 'way to head back to the cabin like we all the time done 'fore, we started playin' 'round a little. We was bowin' to one 'nother and then hookin' our arms together to dosey doe, swingin' each other and skippin' 'round and 'round. Like we ain't got a worry in the world. Like we was kids 'gain. 'Round and 'round, faster and faster, laughin' harder and harder 'til next thing I knowed, my arm was empty. When I turned to see where Daryl went, I seen his feet disappearin' down into the hole followin' the rest of his body. I had to stop myself from jumpin' in after him. The tie's been broke I remember thinkin'.

When I dropped to the ground, I was screamin' so loud I was sure even the city folk could hear me. That's when I seen *It*. Not just *Its* eyes. I seen *"IT."* Satan come raisin' *Itself* outta that hole up to *Its* knees. *Its* eyes was red as fire and glowed in the dark. *Its* whole body, from head to feet, was covered in grey, peelin', snake like scales. *Its* long tongue was split in two at the end and was whippin' in and out like a serpent. Long, sharp fangs hung from *Its* open mouth drippin' venom. On top of *Its* head sat two big curved horns. *Its* long, powerful tail was slashin' all 'round from side to side, back and forth, over and under, up and down, threatenin' to knock me to the ground or maybe even into the fire. *It* thundered and roared the most evil, vile, ear shatterin', earth shakin' sound I ever heard. I covered my ears. When I breathed in the putrid stench comin' from *Its* mouth, I knowed it was the smell of the dead, rotten decayin' flesh of all the lost souls from the beginnin' of time who'd turned their backs on God. Flames of fire was blazin' and shootin' out all 'round *It* comin' from outta the bottom of the hole and shootin' up high as they could reachin' for the top of the tunnel. The ground went to rumblin' and shakin' worse than it ever done 'fore. I was thinkin' the tunnel walls and ceilin' was gonna cave in on top of me. The chains holdin' *Its* wrists was broke and they jangled 'bout in the air whenever *It* moved *Its* arms or hands. I hoped the chains 'round *Its* legs was still hangin' on and somethin' was holdin' *It* down there. When the demon reached out to grab me up with *Its* clawed hand, I jumped back and started into hollerin' *The Lord's Prayer* loud as I could. That's the first thing that come to my mind so I just yelled it over and over and over 'gain. I was huddled up in a ball down on my knees with my arms coverin' my head. I was shakin' so bad I heard my teeth clackin' together. I tried to crawl as far 'way from *It* as I could 'fore it went to possessin' my soul and I started jerkin' and foamin' at the mouth like Simon and Joshua done 'fore they went to heaven.

Then, it come to me. *It* maybe could break my bones but *It* could never 'gain break my faith in God! So takin' in a big gulp of God, I stood up tall, walked over to the edge of the pit, and opened up my arms wide like they was angel wings. I started in to yellin' the first thing that come to my head,

"STICKS AND STONES! STICKS AND STONES! STICKS AND STONES"

While I was hollerin' that loud as I could, the strangest thing happened. All of a sudden, the rumblin' and shakin' stopped. The fire went back down to the bottom of the hole. Satan was left standin' there real quiet. I figured it was me sayin' *The Lord's Prayer* over and over 'gain that made *It* stop or maybe when I went to yellin' *Sticks and Stones*. I remember askin' myself, why didn't I just do that 'fore when it went to possessin' the others. Maybe I could've saved 'em by just yellin' out a few words at *It*. I knowed deep inside me though, it ain't gonna be that simple. There was more to come. Maybe *It* was just takin' a break 'fore it unleashed all *Its* hell and fury on me is what I was thinkin'. That's when I decided to prepare myself to die and prayed God would swoop me up to heaven 'fore I hit the bottom of the pit. So with my head lifted to heaven, eyes closed, arms down and hands folded together, I dropped to my knees and started in prayin' for the Lord to take me. I was ready to die, to sacrifice myself so the rest of the folk in the world could have 'nother chance at gettin' right with God. So I could be with my Annie 'gain. I knowed now it ain't the city folk that's bad. It's just the devil jumped inside 'em 'fore God had a chance to teach 'em how to fill themselves up with *Him*. *He* was givin' 'em 'nother chance and it was up to me to make sure they got it. Finally! My purpose was revealed to me.

"Hallelujah! Praise the Lord! Amen!" I heard myself shout.

I kneeled on the edge of the pit prayin' for the longest time. Everythin' 'round me got quiet as night. I was waitin' for my body to be swooped up into heaven or plunged down into the devil's hole. When I figured 'nuf time passed for me to take a peek outta one eye to see what was goin' on 'round me, I was quick to find out *It* was still there but *It* forgot all 'bout me. Fact was, *It* wasn't payin' me no mind at all. 'Stead, *It* was squintin' *Its* eyes and bobbin' *Its* head up and down and back and forth like *It* was tryin' to see what was comin' straight towards *It*. *It* was lookin' full face forward now. Whatever was comin' had *Its* full attention. I went to openin' up both my eyes so maybe I could see better. When *It* went to crouchin' down and leanin' in towards whatever was headed *Its* way, *It* went to smellin' the air and whippin' *Its* long slimy tongue in and out of *Its* mouth like *It* might know what it was if *It* got a taste of it. A few seconds later, my mouth opened and my jaw hit the ground when suddenly out of nowheres and standin' smack dab in front of *It* was my daddy and mama and all the other patriarchs and their wives 'long with Annie and Mae, Simon and Ruth, Jeremiah and Eve, Joshua and Martha, and Daryl and Rebekah. They was all smilin' and holdin' hands in a line straight 'cross. The closer they marched toward *It,* the more *It* leaned in and sniffed at 'em. Just when *It* looked like *It* was gonna take a big bite of 'em, they all flew off to the side and up into the air. *POOF!* They was gone just like that and standin' 'lone in their place was....Grace!

Grace was standin' almost nose to nose with Satan holdin' her hand out like she was orderin' *It* to stop. I don't know if *It* was 'fraid or curious but *It* stopped short of reachin' out and eatin' her. All's I knowed was once *It* locked eyes with Grace, *It* frozed up for a time and wasn't makin' a move or a noise. Grace stood strong. After 'while, *It* threw curiosity out the window and reared *Its* mean, evil, ugly self up and went straight into bein' mad. That's when *It* took a deep breath in, held it, and then, lunged forward with *Its* mouth wide open blowin' all the fire and brimstone it could muster up right out at Grace. Annie and the others jumped back in front of her and held their hands out throwin' the flames right back at the devil 'fore they hit Grace. After throwin' *Its* arms in front of *Its* face and fallin' back a few steps, *It* leaned forward 'gain real slow like to give 'em all 'nother good look and sniff over. When *It* was practically all the way face to face with 'em, Grace and the others quick jumped outta the way and there stood.........*JACOB!* At his side stood snarlin', growlin', barin' his fangs, madder than hell..........Caleb! When the devil seen 'em, *It* raised up in the air high as *It* could, then fell back screamin',

"NOOOOOOOOOOOOOOOOOOOOOOO!"

Jacob stepped forward with his hands folded in prayer and his eyes starin' right into Satan's eyes. While *It* was screamin', Jacob was smilin' big as you please. I remember thinkin' he got a real nice smile. Loud as can be, he went to commandin' *It* to go back into the hole.

"BE GONE SATAN," his voice echoed over and over 'gain throughout the tunnel and out into the world,

"FOR IT IS WRITTEN YOU SHALL WORSHIP THE LORD YOUR GOD AND ONLY HIM SHALL YOU SERVE!"

While I was still standin' frozed up at the edge of the hole with my mouth wide open and jaw to the ground, I watched that little guy float up into the air 'til he was positioned right 'bove the demon's head. A bright white light shined all 'round him and down onto the beast. When Jacob started movin' down towards the devil, *It* went to slitherin' back down the hole fast as *It* could with *Its* tail tucked 'tween *Its* legs 'til all that was left was two red eyes way, way, way, way down at the bottom. Wasn't long and they was gone, too.

Grace come runnin' over to me and grabbed me by the hand. Jacob was floatin' 'bove the hole still smilin'. Satan was gone.

"Now it all come together," I thought to myself.

Seemed to me, Jacob was the true Caulbearer born to save the world all 'long. God must've sent Grace to protect him. "

"Grace was born to make sure Jacob made it here today to save mankind for 'nother hundred years" is what I was thinkin'.

I reckon *He* was givin' us 'nother chance at gettin' it right with *Him*. *He* wasn't givin' up on us as easy as we sometimes give up on *Him*. I knowed sure 'nuf I'd never turn my back on *Him* 'gain. I was glad *He* was a forgivin' God.

Jacob looked down at me and said,

"Daddy, take care of Grace."

Then, he looked at Grace and said,

"Grace, take care of daddy."

Grace kept holdin' onto my hand with a great big smile on her face. We both took to noddin' our heads up and down fast as we could while all the time lookin' up at Jacob. Big ol' tears was runnin' down my face. Part of 'em cuz I was sure 'nuf gonna miss the little guy. The rest of 'em cuz I was real proud of him. Lookin' at both of us with that bright white light still shinin' all 'round him and down into the pit, he said,

"I love you both. I will see you in heaven in a hundred years."

That's when he went to divin' head first down into the pit.

As we was walkin' 'way hand in hand, we heard Jacob yell,

"Hey! You forgot something!"

We both turned 'round and runnin' through the tunnel full steam 'head towards us was….Caleb!

Grace took to runnin' fast as she could with her arms wide open and a big smile on her face and I dropped to my knees with big ol' tears runnin' down my face shoutin' loud and clear

"Hallelujah! Praise the Lord! Amen!"

Chapter 20

Galatians 1:3-5 *Grace be to you and peace from God the Father, and from our Lord Jesus Christ, Who gave himself for our sins, that he might deliver us from this present evil world, according to the will of God and our Father: To whom be glory for ever and ever. Amen.*

Five years have come and gone since we had that run in with Satan. Samuel's twenty years old now. He married Rose Nelson four years ago. He wasn't no late bloomer. He just decided to stay with his daddy 'while longer in case I needed protectin' or company. After all, we was a team in the greatest battle ever fought on earth. Good 'gainst Evil. God 'gainst Satan. If that don't form no tight bond, I don't know what does.

Samuel and Rose moved into the cabin we built for 'em next to his brother, Bobby. They got three children, all of 'em boys, with one on the way. Rose's two younger sisters, who was livin' with Emma and their brother Steven for 'while, decided to move in with her and Samuel. I do believe the *rabbit* award my daddy gave to my brother Ray and his wife, and I was thinkin' 'bout givin' to Bobby and 'Lizabeth, might just end up goin' to Samuel and Rose. I gotta laugh 'bout that. I don't know. Maybe he's makin' up for lost time. I think they's like me and Annie was, coverin' up the pleasure part by sayin' they's makin' a baby. Only thing is, with all the babies they's havin', they just might be tellin' the truth. Samuel growed up into a fine man, husband, and daddy. He always was a good son. I knowed Annie was proud. Me, too.

Emma's been livin' on this earth twenty-two years. Her and Steven got four children, two boys and two girls. The littlest one is named Annie, after her gramma. She's the only one got red hair and freckles. I gotta say, outta all the grandbabies, she's a spitfire. Emma got her hands full with that one sure 'nuf. I always said Emma reminded me of my Annie. She don't got the red hair and freckles but she's got her mama's spirit. Steven and the kids sure do love her but what she says is the final word in that house. Just like her mama. When it's rainin', Emma runs outside with her babies like Annie used to do. Every once in 'while, Steven goes out to sling a few mud pies with 'em. I wish I'd of thought 'bout doin' that with Annie and the kids back in the day. Steven says he learned when he lost his mama and daddy, Martha and Joshua, that you never know when your last day on earth's gonna be so it's important to make the most outta every day the good Lord lets you wake up. He don't never say nothin' 'bout the time he almost died when his daddy shot him by accident and Grace and Jacob come 'long and saved him. I know that's somethin' he keeps in the back of his mind cuz he don't wanna worry Emma none. That Steven sure growed into a smart man. I know Joshua and Martha's both real proud of him. I's proud to have him as my daughter's husband and a part of our family. Sometimes, he slips and calls me daddy. It makes me feel real good inside when he does that. No disrespect to my dear friend Joshua who gave his life in the fight 'gainst Satan. Steven took his daddy's place feedin' the devil and headin' up the Nelson clan. We meet up every night at midnight down in the tunnel at the hole where the demon sits all chained up. One day his oldest son, Elijah, gonna be the one goin'.

Bobby's twenty-four. He's not only my first born but my first son. He turned out real good just like Samuel. Those two always had a special bond. They still go huntin' together. Sometimes they invite this ol' man to go with 'em. When I don't go 'long, they always make sure they catch 'nuf game for me, Grace, and Caleb to have for our supper. They's good boys and even better men. They don't like me to but every once in 'while I sneak out and catch a rabbit or two on my own. They think I'm gettin' too ol' for all that huntin' and stuff the men folk do up here in the mountains. I's thankful for their carin' but 'nother lesson God taught me is life is for livin' and I ain't dead yet.

I's all the time tellin' 'Lizabeth and Rose they sure was lucky to get my two boys cuz they was gettin' lots of the ladies eyes lookin' their way back in the day when they was of choosin' age. They know I's just jokin' with 'em though. I couldn't ask for two finer women to be takin' care of my sons and bein' my grandbabies mamas. Truth be told, Bobby and Samuel's the lucky ones. Bobby and 'Lizabeth stopped at five children. They got two girls and three boys. Bobby's all the time tellin' me I was right 'bout a man's first born son. He don't never let 'Lizabeth or the other children know but he says he cain't help it, Abraham's his favorite. I's gonna start takin' Bobby with me next year to feed the beast just like my daddy done with me. He's next in line in our family. After him, it'll be his oldest son, Abraham.

'Lizabeth, Emma, and Rose take turns on Sundays cookin' up dinner for us all. Grace, Caleb, and me ain't missed a Sunday dinner yet. God don't never give folk a more valuable gift than family. We learned that lesson the hard way sure 'nuf. Every Sunday, we gather at one of their cabins and talk, eat, and laugh 'til way past when the sun goes down. It does my heart good to see all the cousins playin' together. I got me lots of grandbabies now. Wish my Annie could've lived to share 'em with me. They would've loved her. She all the time talked 'bout bein' a gramma one day. Just cuz she passed, don't mean she ain't no mama or gramma though. Ain't no one gonna ever fill her shoes in those departments. After we get done eatin', all the grandbabies gather 'round and go to beggin' me to tell 'em a story 'bout their gramma Annie, Auntie Mae and Uncle Jacob. I got lots of 'em that's for sure. Even though Annie ain't here no more and they ain't never met her, she still brings lots of smiles to her grandbabies faces.

Bobby, Emma, Samuel, and Grace always pull up a chair to listen, too. They got 'lot of stories of their own 'bout me and their mama. None of 'em ever tell the story 'bout how I whupped Bobby and Jacob. I thank God for that. I's sure not proud of what I done. Grace keeps her brothers and sister up on how Annie and Mae is doin' in heaven. She always adds somethin' 'bout Jacob, too. Truth is, there's not a day or night goes by I don't think 'bout all three of 'em. I sure miss 'em. We all do.

I cain't tell you how many wolf rides Caleb done gave the little ones. They all love him. He's real gentle with 'em, too. I know he loves Grace and me but Jacob was always his favorite. I reckon Jacob just wanted Grace to have someone to talk to and hang 'round with after he was gone so he sent Caleb back. Maybe that's his way of sayin' thanks to his sister for protectin' him all that time. Sometimes Grace and Caleb go off for a walk together and I can hear her jabberin' on and on. Caleb goes to lickin' her face all over like he used to Jacob. Grace just laughs and laughs and laughs when he does that. She's all the time rufflin' Caleb's hair on top of his head. My one arm got empty at night where Jacob used to lay so Caleb took his place. Funniest thing, me layin' there with Grace tucked 'neath one arm and a wolf 'neath the other.

Well, I guess that takes us to Grace, Caleb, and me. We's three peas in a pod. We's still a team. Cain't talk 'bout one without mentionin' the others. Grace stopped agein' in earth years at seven years old. She sure 'nuf gotta ol' soul though. I know her and Jacob was sittin' at God's side long time 'fore *He* gave 'em to me and Annie. She's as beautiful now as she was the day she was born to us. Long dark brown bouncy curls all over her head. And those eyes, those deep blue put you in a trance eyes. My Annie's eyes. My big dimple on the right side of her cheek don't hurt none neither. I was thinkin' if she aged like we do, she'd be twelve now and all the boys would be lookin' to choose her. When I go to teasin' her 'bout that, she turns to me with that turned up mouth all sassy-like and those big blue beautiful eyes, puts her hand on her hip, and says….

"Daddy, I am God's child and your daughter. I was not put here on this earth to marry and have babies."

I believe her. She ain't one to tell lies.

One night, 'while back, when we was sittin' up on the hill under the maple tree where my Annie and Mae is laid to rest, Grace started tellin' me a story. She laid her sweet head on my shoulder like she always done since she was a baby and I'd go to wrappin' my arms 'round her. I loved the times we sat under the maple tree the best, just the three of us....countin' Caleb. Everythin's always quieter at night. In the springtime, there'd be a breeze goin' through our hair, 'least what I got left of mine. Doin' battle with the devil ages a man. 'Least it did me. Grace said....

"When Jacob and I were born, daddy, God sent us to you and mama for a reason. I know it always seemed as though Jacob was the weakest of us two, but he really was not. The best way I can think of to describe it is by saying God hid Jacob's strength so he would not be revealed to the devil ahead of time. He was God's secret weapon. It was my job to protect him so all the others would think he was weak. You have to admit, daddy, he even had you fooled."

I surely had to laugh and nod my head up and down on that one. Then she went on sayin'....

"God gave us both the same powers. I still have those powers but I cannot use them unless *He* tells me I can. The original plan was I would go with Jacob down into the devil's pit to help hold Satan down for another hundred years because there is more evil in the world now than there ever was before. God decided in the end though that I would stay with you because you were going to be left all alone. I think mama had something to do with that. Besides, it was always *His* intention that you be left on earth to tell the story to the others. Since you experienced it first hand, *He* figured you were the best man for the job. *That* is your purpose in life."

That brought a big smile to my face when she said that. Finally, I knowed for sure what my purpose is. Continuin', she said....

"Sending Caleb back to us was Jacob's idea and God agreed. He is here to protect us, love us, and remind us of Jacob and God's love for us. If ever Jacob weakens and the devil becomes stronger again, I will join him to help him hold *It* down. If it has been one hundred years though, a new Caulbearer will be born to take Jacob's place and he will come to heaven to be with us and God. You do not have to worry daddy, Jacob is very strong and doing just fine. He is happy and proud to be doing God's work. It is the reason he was born. It is his purpose. We will be with him again. One hundred years on earth is like one day in heaven when you have forever in front of you. There will come a day when a Caulbearer will not be born to save humankind though. That will be the day God will unleash Satan upon the earth. We are safe for now. Also, I need to tell you when you go to heaven, Caleb and I will go with you. Until then, Caleb will stay as he is now. I, too, will remain as I am now and I will always be healthy. I am sorry, daddy, but you do not have the privilege the other heads of the families have always had. You cannot ask Bobby to send you to heaven. I think that is because mama talked *Him* into letting me stay with you. I think it was a compromise. God will determine when *we* go. That time will be when you have fulfilled your purpose of passing on the story. *He* will know when that is. *He* promises not to let you suffer with sickness or the ailments of ageing. I will know ahead of time."

I sat there under that tree with my eyes closed, holdin' my little Grace, and listenin' to her sweet voice. I felt at peace and filled up with the Lord knowin' her and Caleb was gonna be stayin' with me now and goin' to heaven with me some day.

"Oh yes, daddy," she said, "I almost forgot. The most important thing of all for you to know is God said I could let you see mama and Mae one time each year. You can pick when. I think mama had something to do with that, too."

I had to laugh at her sayin' that cuz I know it's hard to say no to my Annie when she goes to puttin' her mind to somethin'. Well, you know I jumped up and told Grace....

"Right now would be just fine with me for seein' my Annie and little Mae."

Grace laughed and then there right 'fore my eyes stood Annie and little Mae. They was still holdin' hands and smilin'. Annie told me not to worry none 'bout 'em. They was happy in heaven. Both of 'em said I'd be real happy like they is one day when God brought me home to *Him* and them. Annie come up to me real close, looked me straight in the eyes and with her mouth turned up on one side all sassy-like she said....

"Now Calvin, you take good care of our little girl, Grace."

I nodded my head up and down and said,

"Yes, maam, I sure 'nuf will."

She always called me *Calvin* when she was tryin' to get her point 'cross. Then, in that sweeter than sweet voice she said….

"I love you, Cal."

My eyes filled up with tears and my voice went to quiverin' when I told her back….

"I love you too, Annie."

Every year on that same day, me and Grace go up to sit under the maple tree and I ask her to bring my Annie and Mae to me. I sure 'nuf am one blessed man. I ain't never lost my faith in God 'gain. I sure 'nuf never will. I's just glad the good Lord found it in *His* heart to forgive me.

We all still go to the monthly meetin's at the lodge. The heads of the families still take turns tellin' the story we been passin' down from generation to generation for hundreds of years. We've added some to it now though. The part 'bout Jacob and Grace and how it come 'bout we helped God defeat Satan. That story is always left for me to tell towards the end of the meetin' so it'll be fresh in everyone's mind when they head for home. I ask all the folk not to treat Grace any different cuz of the part she played in the savin' of the world. She don't like 'lot of attention. I reckon you could say she's humble.

Caleb goes to the meetin's with us now. All the families say he's a Sanders and got as much right bein' there as anybody else. They's sure 'nuf right 'bout that. Sister Sarah belts out a few songs every month like she's always done. I gotta laugh, she's still the loudest one there.

She starts with *Climbing Jacob's Ladder* and finishes with *Amazing Grace.* I don't got the nerve to tell her she's got 'em backwards bein' that Grace come out first. Then, I go to thinkin' maybe she don't. I don't stick cotton in my ears no more when she's talkin' cuz God taught me to be thankful for every second I got with good friends and family.

All the folk up here is good folk. We all just lost our way for a time. We come through for the good Lord in the end though. I reckon that's all that matters to *Him. He* sure 'nuf gotta big job keepin' all *His* flock in the fold safe and protected from the devil. I know *He* gives us every chance at gettin' it right. The good Lord don't give up on us as quick as we 'lot of times give up on *Him.* We's blessed to have a forgivin' God cuz ain't no one perfect. We's all sinners.

Just like generations 'fore and generations 'fore that, every night at ten minutes to midnight I pull out my daddy's timepiece, grab a plate, throw a couple rabbits, racoons or whatever I got layin' 'round on it and me, Grace, and Caleb open the trapdoor in the floor of our cabin, go down the steps, and head into the tunnel that leads to the hole where the devil lays prisoner. I's the last of the heads of my generation left to feed the beast now. Joshua, Jeremiah, and Daryl's all gone to heaven. Grace and Caleb's been goin' with me since Jacob took over down there. We all wanna make sure he's okay. I sure 'nuf miss that little guy. Now I know why God made him so hard to love at first. I's still real sorry and 'shamed 'bout that. Everythin' happens for a reason though. Sometimes we just gotta wait 'til God decides to tell us why.

Every night, at the stroke of midnight, there we all stand 'round the devil's hole. All the families represented. Calvin Sanders, Steven Nelson, Carl Taylor, and Zachary Anderson. Zachary took the reins over from Daryl's brother, Thomas, two years ago when he turned sixteen. Grace and Caleb stand off to the side and wait for me to throw my plate in with the others. After all us men throw our plates down into the hole, and the other three men leave, a bright white light come to shinin' up outta that hole. Grace says that light is Jacob's spirit. I reckon when the devil is busy feedin', he can let up on *It* a little. Ain't never seen no glowin' red eyes or fire nowheres near the edge of the hole since Jacob took over. Grace and Caleb always go off 'ways by themselves. I can hear Grace talkin' in that strange language her and Jacob always talked. She goes to laughin' and Caleb goes to lickin' at the air. I know he's kissin' Jacob's face. His tail just goes to waggin' back and forth faster than I ever seen it go. After 'while and right 'fore the light disappears, I hear a little voice whisper in my ear....

"I love you, daddy."

I always get all choked up when I tell him back,

"I love you too, son."

I wish I could wrap my arms 'round him and give him a hug and a peck on the cheek. But I cain't.

Then, Grace, Caleb and me turn 'round and head back down the tunnel. Grace and me holdin' hands with Caleb walkin' 'tween us. I swear that wolf gotta big ol' smile on his face. Our steps sure 'nuf a little lighter knowin' one of our own is protectin' the world and all the folks on it from total annihilation. Filled up with the Lord from my head to my toes, I cain't help but holler out loud and clear 'nuf for mountain and city folk 'like to hear....

"HALLELUJAH! PRAISE THE LORD! AMEN!"